Michael A. Riegler

A Dragon

Outside the Church

Copyright 2023

by

Michael A. Riegler

All Rights Reserved

ISBN—978-1-312-13761-5

Printed in the United States of America

Published by Lulu.com

Raleigh, North Carolina

I dedicate this book to:
Amber, Cyerra, Savanna (Hazel and River),
Ashley, Sydney, Spencer, Amanda and Audrey.

Preface

The characters and events portrayed in this book are fictional. The people are largely based on composites of several different parishioners in the churches I have served, or from stories I have read or heard. After that, the imagination takes over and embellishes for dramatic effect. *A Dragon Outside the Church* is not an autobiography. Pastor Nathan Martin is not me. His wife is not my wife.

That is not to say the book does not contain truth. It does. I love God's Church, the gathering of all Christian believers. I love the people I have served as pastor, and the people I am serving right now. And, most of all, I love God—the Father, the Son and the Holy Spirit. So, if in the reading of *A Dragon Outside the Church*, we are led to question our own attitudes and practices—if we are at any moment uncomfortable—then good. In the spirit of a challenging sermon and a good *call to action*, let us seek to better be God's Church.

Note: While this novel was completed in 2023, it is purposely set in 2018. Neither the Covid pandemic nor the disaffiliation of thousands of United Methodist Churches from the UMC are germane to the story, yet it seemed unrealistic to write about 2023 without mention of those events.

Part 1

Who are We?

Chapter 1

Nathan

Jennifer and I walked into the sanctuary of our newly created church for the very first worship service. We hesitated at the bottom step to the platform and giggled. We didn't even know where to stand. I motioned her to an old, massive Pastor's Chair on the left of the platform, while I entered the pulpit on the right.

"Good morning!" I said. When one is not sure what to say, it always helps to start with a greeting.

"Good morning!" responded most of the 43 people sitting in the pews.

I had a sermon written and a program to follow. One way or another we were about to have a worship service, but it didn't feel right to ignore the context of the moment.

"Welcome to the inaugural worship service of the *WWW.God Christian Church*. While the name might sound like some sort of internet thing, the three Ws actually represent God's Word, God's Way and God's Will. I am Nathan Martin. Should you choose this place as your church home, I will be your pastor."

"Morning, Pastor!" came from a pew in the front and two in the back.

"Good morning, people of God," I responded. "I will not be the only pastor. Right over there," I said, motioning to my left, "is the Reverend Jennifer Martin, who is also my wife."

There was a mixed murmur of recognition, approval and uncertainty.

"Honey, would you like to say a few words?"

She moved gracefully to the pulpit and said, "I think we have *good-morninged* enough, so I will just say hello. I am Reverend Honey."

That got a good chuckle.

"We are new at this," I interjected. "Perhaps I will need to work on what terms to use."

"I move we stick with *Reverend Honey*," shouted a man sitting in the third pew.

It was a wonderful guy named Frank, who had followed us from my previous position as pastor of the East Fork First United Methodist Church. His soon-to-be wife, Sylvie, punched him in the shoulder for being loud in church. He responded by continuing.

"We like how obviously you love your wife," he nearly shouted, "so Reverend Honey fits fine!"

"Second!" shouted a man I had never met.

"All in favor?" Frank asked with glee, "say *Amen!*"

Nearly everyone in the room, including Sylvie, shouted *Amen!*

A moment of silence followed, then I turned to Jennifer and said, "Sorry . . . Honey."

Nearly everyone laughed, including Jennifer. Nearly everyone. As the laughter died down, a couple stood up. I had met them only minutes before. All I knew about them was their names were Bill and Clara.

Bill said, "Could you please clarify for us the roles the two of you will fill, if this church goes anywhere?"

The mood in the room immediately became wary and quiet.

I gulped and said, "Certainly, Bill—it is Bill, right?" He nodded. "Good. Bill. As it appears now, I will be what might be called the Senior Pastor. I will be doing most of the teaching and preaching. As you will soon learn, if you are around her very long, Pastor Jennifer (this seemed like no time for Reverend Honey) is highly gifted with discernment, a close relationship with Jesus, and an unusual openness to the Holy Spirit. She will be the Minister of Spiritual Growth and Formation."

"Will she preach?" Bill asked, with a definite negative connotation on the word *she*.

I felt a wave of panic mixed with anger. It was obvious where this was going. I resisted the temptation to try to salvage or avoid the situation.

"Yes, whenever she has something important to say, she will preach."

"Why do we need two pastors in such a small church?" Bill pressed on.

"For one reason only," I replied. "God set it up that way, which to be honest, was a surprise to us, as well."

"*If* you are being honest, then you are just as surely wrong. God would not call a woman to the pulpit, when God's own word expressly prohibits women from preaching."

"That is not nearly so clear as you believe . . . Bill," I said as calmly as I could muster. "In any case, God has called us both to minister to this place, and so it shall be."

"I am sure you would like to get on with your so-called worship service," Bill snarled. "I would appreciate a minute to get out of range. Come on, Clara, we're leaving."

Without a sound, the entire congregation—heads turning gradually to the door—watched Bill and Clara walk out.

"Well," I said after they were gone, "I knew not everyone who checked us out would necessarily stay, but that has to be some kind of a record."

The few laughs were forced and nervous.

"Bill was right about one thing," I continued. "I do want to get on with worship. It is, after all, our reason for being here. I will add only this before we begin. A few days ago, God went to extraordinary measures to bring us through difficult times in my previous church, and bring us here. I know it to be true, because a man far greater than I discerned it to be God's will. For those of you who wish it, we will have plenty of time to get to know each other's stories and create some new ones, together. Let us worship our God."

Pastors often have nightmares of worship services gone wrong. This one, so excitedly anticipated, was decidedly off on the wrong foot. Tension remained in the air. Even though I was speaking smoothly enough, the opening prayer felt halting and uncertain. I peeked at my little, fledgling congregation, gauging their reaction. They seemed unsettled, but perhaps the unsettled one was me. A responsive reading designed to inspire unity and togetherness instead inspired only half-hearted murmurs.

I glanced back at Jennifer, wanting to share my panic and fear. I felt my forehead wrinkle, my teeth clench and my eyes bug out, trying to convey my dismay without words. But my Jennifer's face was anything but a mirror image of mine. Her forehead was smooth and relaxed, her eyes half closed. Her smile was soft and sincere. She was pleasantly immersed in what was going on around her. Seeing my tortured countenance, she responded with a brighter smile and a slight nod.

I turned back to the people and paused for a long moment. They sat expectantly, waiting for something to happen—trusting something was about to happen.

"You might as well find out right away," I began, "that the Sunday morning program, or bulletin, represents only the order in which things may or may not happen. Despite whatever is listed next, I feel the need for a word from God. If you have a Bible with you, please turn to Psalm one hundred."

Several people started leafing their way toward the right spot. Jeremy, a promising teen who had followed me from East Fork UMC, found it first with a few taps on his ever-ready tablet. As the rustling of pages died down, I read:

> **Make a joyful noise to the LORD, all the earth!**
> **Serve the LORD with gladness!**
> **Come into His presence with singing!**
> **Know that the LORD, He is God!**
> **It is He who made us, and we are His;**
> **we are His people, and the sheep of His pasture.**

> Enter His gates with thanksgiving,
> and His courts with praise!
> Give thanks to Him; bless His name!
> For the LORD is good;
> His steadfast love endures forever,
> and His faithfulness to all generations.

"It is He who made us, and we are His; we are His people," I repeated. I felt better. "I think we should sing now," I announced. "Another bit of proof of our humble beginnings here at Triple-W (where'd that come from?) is we have music sheets for only two songs. It seems *How Great Thou Art* is in order. Let me introduce our . . . keyboardist. Yes, we will call her the keyboardist—Condi Cloverton. Condi has come with us from our last church and there is something special you should know about her."

I stopped talking and looked over at one of the finest classically trained musicians our part of Michigan had ever seen, poised over a hastily borrowed electronic keyboard that suddenly looked like a toy. If Jennifer and I had gone through a time of great change at East Fork UMC, so had Condi.

"She is," I continued, "an especially devoted disciple of Jesus Christ. Condi, please lead us in our praise and worship of God."

It took her a minute to collect herself and get started. I am sure she expected me to praise her great talent, as that is what she had long been used to hearing. But, today was a new day for all of us. I sneaked a peek at her husband Kevin, alone in a pew as he would always be. He was rapidly tearing up, but still managed to flash me a quick thumbs-up. Condi began to play, somehow wringing beautiful music from a cheap, inadequate instrument. *How Great Thou Art* has certainly been better sung than we did it that day, but rarely with more enthusiasm. Come what may, we were underway.

Chapter 2

Jennifer

"Pastor, I am Leta Walsh and this is my husband Art. We are so excited to be here. The service was just wonderful."

I realized I was staring back at this lovely woman, without saying anything.

"I'm sorry," I finally said, stumbling over my words. "For many years any time I heard someone say *pastor* they were talking to my husband. It's going to take some getting used to."

"Oh, it will be natural soon enough," Leta continued. "You obviously have the gift. That prayer you offered was as personal and heartfelt as any I've ever heard, and I've been in church for a lot of years."

"Well thank you," I replied. "It just came out. It felt as if I was simply having a conversation with God, but in front of a crowd. These are new experiences for me."

"I think we are all going to experience new things here. Wonderful things. I have hoped for a place like this, and it is finally happening."

I was beginning to like this Leta Walsh very much.

"We had better let Reverend Honey go," Art chimed in. "She has other people who want to talk with her. Plus, I hear there are cookies in the back room."

"Art!" Leta chided. "Don't you think it is a little forward to call her that?"

"What?" he responded. "There was a vote."

I laughed. "He's right," I said. "There was a vote, moved and seconded."

"See," he said through a big grin. "Can't blame me!" As he steered his wife toward the cookies, he paused to look me directly in the eyes. "We'll be back next week, Pastor," he said sincerely. "Don't you spend a minute fretting about that character who dragged his wife out of here. Some of us can tell when there is a God-thing going on. It's his loss that he can't."

"Thank you," was all I could think to say as they moved along, but Art and Leta already seemed God-sent to me.

Alone for a moment, I scanned the room. After the acrimonious exit of the couple who could not stand to be in a building where I would be called *pastor* there remained forty-one congregants. *How many others are upset by me?* I couldn't help but wonder. I was feeling for the first time the sting of being clergy—respected, even revered, but an easily criticizable target at the same time. I was going to have to get used to what I had seen my husband live with for years. Still, I felt comfortable and confident I was in the right place doing the right thing. God had called me to this place and to this task.

I watched several people clustered around Nathan, enthusiastically asking questions, laughing and sharing the moment. Chief among them was Frank, bellowing on about his excitement for our new church, while his fiancée Sylvie watched him adoringly. I was startled a bit when someone touched my elbow.

"Reverend Martin," young Jeremy began, "this is my new friend Edwina Fine. She spent many years in this place, back when it was a Congregational church."

"Yes," I replied, "I have heard so much about you. We owe you a huge debt of gratitude for keeping this church alive until God decided to use it again. It is wonderful to meet you."

"I need no thanks," she said, a strong, clear voice emanating oddly from her frail, elderly body. "I prayed many years for God to bring this building back into His use. What joy it is to finally see it happen."

"Well," I said, taking Edwina's hand in mine, "you can be sure you have served God well."

"She is not finished, either," Jeremy interrupted. "Mrs. Fine said this would be her only visit to our new church, because her work was done. I told her that wasn't okay, because God has more for her to do and we are going to need her wisdom around here. So, I am going to pick her up on Sundays so we can sit in our spot together. My dad is a contractor. I texted him and told him I was going to start taking drugs and getting arrested and stuff if he didn't build a ramp on Triple-W—I really like that name—so Mrs. Fine could get in easier. Don't worry, we kid around like that. But he said he would have it done by next Sunday. Is that okay?"

Jeremy finally stopped and took a breath. He appeared so excited he was having trouble standing still.

I looked at Edwina. "Can't argue with youth," she said, her face beaming.

"Pastor Nathan!" I yelled. "Pastor Nathan!"

The room quieted as Nathan stopped whatever he was saying and turned toward us.

"Jeremy has arranged for his father to build an access ramp on the church so our new friend Edwina can come to church regularly. He wants to know if that's okay."

As my husband smiled and prepared to say something eloquent, Frank hollered, "So moved!"

Three others chimed in, "Seconded!"

The others called out, "Aye!"

After a long pause (I know my husband well enough to know when he is creating drama) Nathan shrugged his shoulders and declared, "Motion carried."

The people cheered and laughed and moved toward the cookies. Nathan stayed back with me.

"Well, Reverend Honey," he said, while sneaking a quick kiss, "it has been quite a day so far."

"It really has," I replied. "There are a few who aren't too sure what is going on, but mostly that is an inspired group back there snacking. Can you hear them?"

I paused while he quieted and listened carefully. Our new congregation was boisterously getting to know each other.

"Yes," he eventually replied, "they are definitely excited."

"It's more than that," I said. "They are doing something we rarely heard in our other churches."

"What? I don't hear anything unusual."

"Dear husband, work on listening deeper. They are talking about church . . . faith. They have taken your message to heart. You told them to *Keep First Things First,* and God is the first thing. Most of them get it, and they want to start right away."

Chapter 3

Nathan

We were finally alone. The first service at the new *WWW.God Christian Church*—rapidly taking on *Triple-W* as its conversational name—had been wonderful and scary and intense and draining. As Jenn and I were now closer than ever, both personally and professionally, we were anxious to process what just happened, and to decompress from it. We settled in, twisted open a couple bottles of some miracle spring water (Jenn was trying to get us off the Diet Coke) and prepared to talk.

"So, what do you think?" Jenn asked in an obvious attempt to get the conversation rolling.

I finished off a big swallow and said, "No bubbles, no taste, no pleasing properties whatsoever."

"Not the water, wise guy. You know what I'm talking about."

"Oh, you mean that little worship thing we just did?" I replied with a grin.

She just glared. "Right," I continued. "My over-riding feeling is it was one of the best events ever. Just to know God willed it and then it happened. How great is that!"

"I'm right there with you," she said. "It all happened so fast and then there we were, in a whole new church with a whole new bunch of people, worshipping and praising away. I admit I was a bit awestruck."

"Okay," I said, "so we agree it was a pretty big deal. How do you think it went?"

"For the first time," Jenn said, "I really understand the desire you have always had to analyze each service right away. It is different to be doing the presenting, isn't it."

"I'm glad you noticed. After preparing all week to do a service and preach a sermon and all the other parts, I think it is completely natural to want to measure how it went, even though it can't actually be measured."

"But that isn't going to stop us from trying," Jenn said.

"Of course not," I replied. "Now that we have said all the politically correct stuff, what did you think?"

"All right," Jenn began, "not in order of importance, here are some observations. I was pleased to have over forty people show up. It felt like a good start."

"Me, too," I said, trying to agree without interrupting her train of thought.

"I was immensely relieved to see Condi and Kevin walk in, both because it got me out of trying to play and because it promises good music in the future."

"You would have done fine," I lied, "but it will make for an attractive music program."

"How about we don't call everything a *program?*" Jenn asked. "Can't we just have a talented, inspired musician who will please God and motivate God's people to worship more deeply."

"Good point," I replied with a big smile, to hide my annoyance at being corrected.

"And while we're still on the music," Jenn said, "I think you have two more things to say, one where you lied and one where you left out something that ought to be out in the open."

"I don't know what you are talking about," I said a little defensively.

"Yes, you do," she said softly. "When did you lie?"

I knew, but I said, "I didn't lie, exactly."

"Come on."

"All right. I might not have been completely honest when I said you would have done fine with the music. Actually, your rehearsals were . . . less than stellar."

"No joke," she laughed. "But I was going on with it if I had to."

"*That* is the stellar part," I said.

I stood, moved to Jenn and kissed her, then sat back down.

"I love you, too," she said. "Now, tell me the thing you felt or thought when Condi walked in, that you don't want to say out loud."

Knowing I couldn't hide, I just said it. "I was thrilled to see she left East Fork UMC and had come to be with us. Most of me was excited to have her here, but some of it was totally inappropriate satisfaction that East Fork would not have her."

"How do you suppose I knew that?" Jenn asked.

"You, too?"

"Of course. I felt the same way about Kevin and Jeremy, Janice, and Frank and Sylvie."

"You forgot Jane," I added. "I was kind of gloating, even."

"Me, too," she said. "Let's just admit it, pray for forgiveness, and move on. With all that is going on, we are going to experience all kinds of feelings."

"Agreed," I said, "and, seriously, this will be excellent for the church. Kevin is a human resources guy. Janice is the best secretary I ever had."

"Isn't that supposed to be, *Administrative Assistant?*" Jenn asked.

"Not according to her. And, Frank and Sylvie are just filled with joy and encouragement."

"What about Jeremy?" she asked.

"I don't know for sure," I said. "He just turned seventeen. But that kid is amazing. One day he'll be running things, whether it is a church, a business, or maybe the country."

"How about the way he handled Edwina Fine?" Jenn asked.

"That was a favorite moment for me."

"Me, too. We don't often see the young and the old mix so well, and I just love Edwina's story."

Jenn continued, "It seems clear God has had this whole thing in the works for a long time. She kept the church legally open for over twenty years after people stopped attending. She told me she never knew why she had to, only that she must."

"Remind you of anyone?" I asked.

"You mean Pastor Carl?"

"Yeah," I said, feeling a rush of emotion at the mention of his name. "The way he worked for months refurbishing the church building . . . not knowing what was coming next . . . and . . . you know . . . everything."

Jenn smiled and spoke softly, "You mean how he worked just as hard refurbishing you?"

Pastor Carl had brought the old building that now housed the Triple-W church back to life, mostly with his own two hands. I say mostly, because once God put us together, I helped out some, too. While we worked on the church, Carl worked on me. I had been discouraged and confused, unsure of my call to be a pastor, even unsure of my faith. I was mired in the politics, bureaucracy and pettiness of church culture. In fact, I was drowning in it. Carl helped me to identify the conglomeration of secular forces, consumerism, turf wars and power struggles, church hierarchy and a culture of personal preferences as a kind of modern-day dragon, that could be identified and fought. I named my dragon *Agendor* and with Carl's help I got back on track and recommitted to be the bold, prophetic voice God had called me to be, willing to battle Agendor when and wherever necessary.

Before Carl, I had been failing in my marriage as well. I didn't do anything overtly awful, but I did put Jenn's needs behind the never-ending, often petty, demands of the people of the East Fork First United Methodist Church. Pastor Carl helped me set that straight, too, and now Jenn and I were closer and stronger than ever.

"Well?" Jenn asked gently. Evidently, I had been silent for quite a while.

I let out a little teary-eyed chuckle. "Yeah, I really miss him. With all this unfolding so fast, it sure would be nice to be able to lean on him a bit."

"I miss him, too," she said, "even though I barely knew him. But I think for right now, we are supposed to lean on God."

"Yes," I replied, gathering myself, "and so we are doing just that. What else did you notice today?" I added, kicking the ball back into Jenn's court.

"Well," Jenn said, "I noticed wherever we go Agendor manages to follow."

"Which way are you talking about?" I asked.

"Was there more than one?" she asked.

"Oh, yes."

Jenn continued, "I am talking about the whole 'the Bible says women can't preach' episode."

"I'm sorry, Jenn," I replied. "That had to hurt."

"Yes it did, at least for a while. I felt like I was under a microscope and on trial all at the same time. Eventually, positive things washed most of the hurt away. But, what are we going to do about stuff like that?"

"This one was actually easy," I said. "Just let them walk away and be glad to be rid of them. But other things won't be as simple. Virtually everyone in the sanctuary today came in with their own set of beliefs and doctrines they picked up somewhere else. Some of those beliefs they will be willing to change or modify as part of our new venture, but others they will not give up. And, with each one of them it will be something different."

"How can we possibly handle all that?" Jenn asked.

"I have no idea. And, we haven't even determined what the Triple-W core beliefs or guiding principles are!"

Jenn closed her eyes and pinched the bridge of her nose.

"This is going to be a lot to think about," she said. "Can't just listening to God and saying *yes* to Him be enough?"

"I don't know, Jenn. I really don't. Church bodies are used to lists of beliefs and doctrines and ready-made answers to big questions. We have a long, long ways to go to figure out what we're doing here."

"Great," she replied, "but not today. What else? You said there was more than one Agendor incident."

"I don't know yet how big any of this is, Reverend Honey."

Jenn leaned over and punched me in the arm. "Yeah, thanks for the new nickname!"

"Sorry about that," I said. "I didn't plan it, but my point is in there. How did we decide to call you Reverend Honey?"

"We voted," she answered.

I explained, "We voted by shouting out a motion in the middle of a worship service, which was seconded by another shout. A person who has no particular authority called for the vote, and everyone who happened to be sitting in the room voted by more yelling. Bim Bam Boom, a new policy."

"Sounds kind of scary when you put it that way," Jenn commented.

"Yes, but I am not exactly sure in what way," I said. "We did it after the service, too. A couple of shouts and a bunch of yells and we are evidently getting a new access ramp."

"But that's good, isn't it?" Jenn asked. "We should have a ramp."

"Of course a ramp is good, but we have already set a precedent at Triple-W church. Business is done by mob rule."

"Wow."

"Yeah, wow," I replied, "and the kicker is, I don't even know if that is bad or good."

"What do you mean?"

"Well, it might mean we are on the verge of a chaotic mess, or maybe this is what a complete lack of Agendor looks like! I am not sure whether to worry or celebrate."

Jenn looked at me long and hard. Then she moved over and enveloped me in her arms, and kissed my neck. I liked where this was heading.

"You know what?" she asked, her voice low and sort of gravelly.

"What's that?" I asked, my voice full of hope.

"My head hurts from all this serious talk, and I only want to do one other thing today."

"Anything you say, Sweetheart."

"After we get something to eat, let's . . ."

"Yes . . ."

She finished, "go look at a couple of open houses. We are still living in the East Fork UMC parsonage, and it is creepin' me out!"

Chapter 4

Nathan

Things happened fast following the first Sunday at Triple-W. Elderly sisters Berta Lou Gallagher and Virgy Lou Dekker, who had alternately been supporters and thorns in my side during my years at East Fork First UMC, had gifted us with fifty thousand dollars to help buy a house. They sincerely wanted to help us, I think, but they also wanted us to vacate East Fork's parsonage as quickly as possible, so a newly-appointed pastor could move in. Thinking about what awaited the next pastor there made me shudder. Jenn and I felt guilty taking the money, but evidently they were secretly very wealthy, so we got over the guilt in short order and bought a nice little ranch-style home roughly halfway between downtown East Fork and our new church. We would not be living so close to the church building that we would suffer the constant scrutiny of staring eyes, but we would be able to be at the church conveniently and often, from only five miles away.

The development of the church was a blur. In the first three months attendance doubled. Fueled by word-of-mouth and the workings of the Holy Spirit, new faces appeared each Sunday. Most had long and involved experiences in the Church. They had one thing in common; they were looking for something beyond what they had found in their previous churches and denominations. As our numbers grew the momentum of newness carried us through. At Sunday worship we prayed much more than is common. Jennifer continued to develop as a prayer-leader. Her Spirit-filled words often left the congregation in awestruck silence. We sang, mostly from a collection of donated United Methodist Hymnals. The United Methodists produce a dandy hymnal.

At the third week of our existence as a church, a fine baby grand piano showed up in the worship space. Condi Cloverton worked magic on that piano, accompanying the congregational singing with spirit and flair, and offering her praise to God with inspired *special music* pieces usually heard only in top-of-the-line concert halls. We read more scripture aloud than most congregations would tolerate. I preached for twenty or forty-five minutes and no one seemed to care which. The services ran for anything between an hour and two hours, without a single complaint. The people listened, some took notes, and many had questions after the service. It all seemed too easy to be true.

As much as I loved the little church building, I was soon wishing for more space. We could only seat about a hundred, and we were already approaching that. Sunday morning newcomers were beginning to stand in the small space behind the back pew, searching, with panicked faces, for an open place to sit. Not four months into our existence, the congregation would have to separate into two services. We also had a handful of children showing up with their enthused parents. What would we do with them? Would we follow the normal progression and start a Sunday School? Nursery? Vacation Bible School? How? Where? Or, might we simply fold the children into the adult worship services? As we pondered and prayed over next moves, another concern became obvious. As I had once predicted, the newness wore off.

"After services today," I announced one Sunday, "we will stay for a brief discussion. While it is a great problem to have, I think we can all see we need to do something about the increasing attendance and the growing number of children in our midst. God is blessing us richly and, with God's guidance, we have some decisions to make about what happens next here at Triple-W."

As I moved on to the beginning of the service, there was an odd murmur in the room. There was a vibe I hadn't expected and couldn't quite get a read on. Still, we had an excellent time of worship.

Afterward, I said, "We have concluded the formal worship service and will now move to an informal discussion of church business. The most obvious place to start regards the challenge of crowding in the sanctuary. We are simply growing too big for our britches! Isn't God good!"

There were several shouts of affirmation and the nodding of many heads. However, the atmosphere of agreement was soon shattered.

"When we are going to address the lack of programs for our children," Jim Walters nearly shouted. "There are at least a dozen kids here every week," he went on, "including our three."

Jim, his wife Amy and their three children, ranging from seven-years-old to twelve, had shown up about six weeks into our new adventure together and had been weekly fixtures ever since. The children were well-behaved in the worship services and seemed engaged in whatever was going on.

Jim continued, "I think it is high time we put together a Sunday School class, and a youth group."

"And what about Vacation Bible School this summer," added Amy, "and what are we going to do about church camp?"

"That's fine," Cora Shenfeld broke in. "We do need things for the young people, but what about us older folk. Now, I only mean to point out what's true when I say it is the older people who pay for most of what goes on in any church, including this one."

The hair stood up on the back of my neck. Memories of church governance by self-centered preference flooded my mind. For years I had wrestled with, managed and done battle with such attitudes. There was always going to be some of that—there almost had to be. People are filled with their own experiences, their own knowledge and their own opinions. They often honestly believe whatever it is they prefer automatically becomes what is right. I have been guilty of the same many times myself, although I have learned to catch myself in the act a lot more quickly than I used to. I had hoped in coming to this small, new, radically different church start-up I had largely left Agendor behind. And, to this point, I had. Sure, there were instances of people pushing for what they wanted. After all, people are people wherever you go. But on this particular Sunday, at an almost impromptu meeting to make a few plans, I first felt that perhaps Agendor had been just hiding in the bushes.

Still, I had to admit to myself what Cora had just said was largely true. The finances at the *WWW.God Christian Church* were healthy, with Jennifer's and my modest salaries easily covered, all the bills paid in full and a bit left over each week. Most of the money was indeed given by the older members.

"Why," Cora said, gathering steam, "our kitchen still has no appliances, not a stove or an oven or even a refrigerator. How are we going to start having the spaghetti suppers, pancake breakfasts, luncheons and all the proper social functions of a church if we don't outfit our kitchen? What are we waiting for?"

"Well," I said, "I see we have much to . . ."

"How about some senior citizen outings, like bus trips and such?" shouted a mature voice from the back pews, so abruptly I didn't even catch who said it.

"I think we need to concentrate on getting some mission work started," chimed in Alan Grimard, another of the new and active members of the congregation. "I have been waiting for a chance to speak up in favor of getting a good, old-fashioned mission trip organized, maybe to Haiti or somewhere in Africa. God has given us plenty, and we need to share with those who have almost nothing."

"We need to take care of our own, first!" Cora yelled as loudly as she could get her little voice to go. "Then if some of you want to go help somewhere else, fine, but not until!"

"All right! All right!" I said firmly, holding up both hands as a stop sign. "Clearly this is going to take more time and more organization than I had assumed. Let's . . ."

"No. Please stop," came the serene yet powerful voice of my wife.

Chapter 5

Jennifer

After a few months of serving as the Minister of Spiritual Growth and Formation, I was beginning to realize what often seemed like a sudden and jarring movement of the Holy Spirit was really the culmination of a longer period of discernment. I will not pretend my husband Nathan and I had not been caught up in the whirlwind that was the *WWW.God Christian Church*. We certainly were. It was so exciting to come to worship service every Sunday and see more people in the pews—new faces just about every week. It seemed like an instant measure of success. Our church was growing and it seemed good. Much of it was good. New people. Good people, engaged and excited about what was going on at the new church—their new church. Nathan's preaching was steadily developing in depth and inspiration. I had never heard him preach so effectively. Condi's music was inspired and often took my breath away. During my own time leading prayer, I often lost myself in intimacy with God. I would *come back* to the reality of the sanctuary filled with people and not be sure if I had prayed for two minutes or twenty.

Still, something was not quite right. I felt it. For weeks I said nothing, not even to Nathan, but a couple of weeks before what we now call Blow-up Sunday, I had expressed my discomfort. He listened—bless his heart—but I am not sure he shared my dissonance.

So, I prayed and meditated and prayed and listened. I had not felt a strong message or prodding, until just then.

"I don't think we want to go down this road," I said. "I do not believe our answers lie in programs or plans or busyness."

The whole congregation hushed and seemed to be looking at me with great expectancy. I thought there would be immediate rebuttal, but it did not come.

"This church," I continued, "is here only because God willed it. By the rules and assumptions of human beings, it was dead a long time ago. Furthermore, God used mostly one man to bring it back to life. None of you had the blessing of knowing Pastor Carl, but many of you have heard about him. He was the most devout and obedient Christian person I have ever met. I'll even admit I sometimes wondered if he were human at all. Anyway, he renovated this sacred building with his own two hands—with some help from my husband, once they teamed up. Pastor Carl had no idea what would happen with all his work, nor did it occur to him to ask. He would simply do as God commanded, step by step, until God gave him further direction. It was a thing to behold. We, Nathan and I, and, I hope, you, have tried to emulate that devotion, obedience and patience. We have failed."

I pulled out my Bible and opened to John 3:16, where I kept a few precious pieces of paper. No one spoke.

"Let me read to you from a couple of communications from Pastor Carl. I cherish these things so much I keep them in my favorite Bible. The first is from the newspaper article and advertisement Pastor Carl used to announce the opening of what we now affectionately refer to as Triple-W. Please be aware that God—through Carl—did this without first checking with Nathan or me. Quoting the article:

> We are pleased to announce that the former *Grant Center Township Congregational Church*—closed for over 20 years—will be reopened as an independent church. Worship services begin this coming Sunday morning, at 10:30. Pastor Carl Rider, who has completely renovated the building, explained, this will not be a typical church.

"There won't be much for social events or pot-lucks or clubs or committees or any of that. It will be for truly dedicated Christian people, who find themselves unable to resist God's call to a deeper, more active, more obedient and more dedicated faith. Those newly seeking Christ would be better off to try a different church." The name of the church reflects Reverend Rider's description, albeit in a way that has to be studied a bit. The church will be called *WWWGod Christian Church*. "It sounds like an internet thing," Rider admitted. "But what it stands for is: God's Word ... God's Way ... God's Will. It will be a church of high expectations, not a church for dabblers or the faint of heart. It will never be a large church, but I expect it will be a powerful place." Reverend Rider went on to explain more about the mission of the church. For details, please see the attached paid advertisement.

The people of the congregation still did not say anything, but they began to get restless. As I turned to the page that contained the paid ad that was part of the Big Announcement, I noticed several people giving each other sideways glances, shrugs and even a couple of shakes of the heads.

"The ad says," I continued:

Sincere, practicing Christians of any background are invited to the inaugural worship service at the new, nondenominational *WWWGod Christian Church*. The church will seek to live out God's Word ... God's Way ... and God's Will. The service time will be 10:30 Sunday morning, beginning immediately. The newly renovated church is located at the crossing of Compton and Williams roads, ten miles west of East Fork. If you are ready to turn your entire life over to God, please attend.

"There's more," I said. "I have never shared this with anyone but my husband, and I hope he will forgive me for sharing part of it now. This is from a personal letter Pastor Carl left for us, before he went away to wherever it was God sent him."

I read:

> God has been clear. Your next assignment, your next calling, is right here. This place has been prepared as sacred space. A home base. A launching pad for whatever God wills next . . .

"I am skipping some personal stuff here," I said, then continued,

> The gifts that both of you bring to this place are not to stay imprisoned here. This shall be a center of a great outward expansion of God's Kingdom. Rightfully, you will have practical questions. Thanks to a very old woman named Edwina Fine, this building has never ceased to be a legal church (she said she always knew God would bring revival). The incorporation papers have been regularly updated, meetings held, contributions given, all that is required. The file box includes the incorporation papers (you will need to form a new board very quickly; Edwina is running out of living members to keep things going) and the still-valid 501c3. The deed is included. Paperwork to change the name, as well. You'll work out the rest. The point is, this is a church in every sense of the word, except for not yet having a congregation. That is now in the hands of the Holy Spirit.

"I said we failed," I continued. "I did not mean we have failed at all things, or even very many. But we—Pastor Nathan, me, and most of you—have failed to practice the unquestioning obedience to, and patience with, God that Pastor Carl so ably demonstrated. We have been caught up in success and growth and our own thrill of the new. The problem is, God wants something else from us. God wants this church to be small. We want it to be big. God wants us to avoid the distraction of social events or potlucks or clubs or committees or any of that. We want to form committees and programs and social groups and fellowship meals.

God wants this church to be for truly dedicated Christian people, who find themselves unable to resist His call to a deeper, more active, more obedient and more dedicated faith.

"In short, God does not want this to be a typical church. God already has hundreds of thousands of typical churches. God wants this church to be something very different, and yet here we are, about to run headlong toward typical. I am stating with great confidence, we need to slow down—back up even. We need to stop planning. We need to worship and pray and study and meditate and listen. God will give us what is next. To do anything else is to lose sight of why God is working something special here in the first place."

I stopped talking, suddenly aware I had been going on and on, speaking with an authority I did not actually possess. My words—if listened to—did not allow for discussion or the open airing of opinions. I had just shut down the entire congregation, nor had I thought to consult the lead pastor—my husband—before I did it. I noticed I was barely breathing.

"Well," the voice of Alan Grimard spoke from the pews, "Pastor Nathan, what say you?"

I watched my husband gather himself. I became intensely aware I had painted him into a corner. Would he try to find a diplomatic way to reign me back in, and start over? Would he agree with me? Would he punt?

Chapter 6

Nathan

As I watched and listened to my wife, I felt the need to make sure my mouth wasn't hanging open. Once again, she had astounded me with her certainty, her clarity and her boldness. Since our relationship had changed—it was very different to have your long-supportive spouse become an equal in professional ministry—I had by necessity learned to think and respond very rapidly. During her pronouncement, and in the twenty seconds I could afford to take since she finally stopped talking, a myriad of things ran through my head. *What is she doing? Stop! How am I going to fix this? Wait a minute—maybe she is right. What would Pastor Carl say about this? Who is the "lead" pastor around here, anyway? Maybe it's not really me!*

What I actually said out loud was, "This is hard for me. For a lot of years, I have built my career and my thinking and my strategizing on common measures of success. I have always cared about church growth, greater attendance, bigger offerings, new and better programs, excellent performance reviews and even the praise of people whose opinions I value. I tried to include pleasing God in there, but I'm not sure I always succeeded. Pastor Carl tried to train most of that out of me. I'd like to think he was successful, but in reality it is so easy—so enticing—to fall back on the excitement of numbers and growth and energy.

"Alan, you asked me what I say. As hard as it is . . . as scary as it is to contemplate the ramifications, I can only say

Jennifer is absolutely correct. I cringe at the thought of losing any of you. I cringe at the thought of slowing down what has seemed to be a very good thing. But everything Jennifer said about how this church came to be, and how it is to be unique instead of common, is spot on. Pastor Carl was the master at waiting for God's instructions. I'm afraid I am still only the apprentice. So, thank you, Jennifer.

"We will not start anything new at this time, except to redouble our efforts to worship, study the scriptures, pray, listen and wait to discern the will of God. Then, we will do however much or however little God calls us to do. Period. I hope all of you can stay on and see where God takes us. However, if you find God wants you elsewhere, or you believe your family has other needs, please let me know and I will personally help you find another church. God bless you all. Let's close in prayer."

I prayed a long prayer. It was half a sincere prayer, repenting that we had strayed from God's will and rededicating ourselves to better listening. The other half was to make it clear the discussion time was over. Our beloved Triple-W church would be as close as possible to what God told Pastor Carl it would be. Let the chips fall where they may.

The chips did, indeed, fall. Not a single person took me up on my offer to help them find some other suitable church, but evidently many of them did it on their own. By the very next Sunday our over-crowding problem had been solved. Jim and Amy Walters and their three kids? Gone. Cora Shenfeld? Gone. About forty others? Gone. The worship service went fine, at least on the surface. But the atmosphere was stilted, the give and take was awkward and the singing lackluster.

By the next Sunday, the group had diminished to the point that I announced, "Let's not do the regular-type service today. We can't pretend things are not very different from just a couple of weeks ago. Let's begin with a good, long session of private prayer and contemplation."

I confess, while the others were praying, I was taking stock. My darling Jennifer, in her manner of devotion and connectedness that brought me to envy, was deep in closed-eyes prayer. Devoted musician Condi Cloverton had moved from her seat at the keyboard and was in a pew holding hands and praying with her stalwart husband, Kevin. Janice Pohl, my trusted secretary who had followed me from the comfort and stability of East Fork UMC to our uncertain venture here, sat with Jane Petra, another former member of the East Fork UMC. Then there was the best second-time-around couple ever, Frank and Sylvie. They were my most dependable supporters back at the old church and now here at the new. Other than Jennifer, there was no one I could count on more. Not only that, but a few weeks before we had done the first and, so far, only wedding in our new congregation. They were now Frank and Sylvie Osborn. Jeremy Clark, just turned seventeen, was the last of the United Methodist carry-overs. He now sat with his new friend—the only connection back to when the refurbished Triple-W building was a longtime Congregational church—and over five times older than Jeremy, the sainted Edwina Fine.

Thankfully there were still a few left who had joined us only after Triple-W opened. They did not all jump ship. Art and Leta Walsh were on a true journey with God. Francine Cook was still with us from the first Sunday. John and Shelley Drobena, Michelle Garner and Jeff Conway were hanging in with us. There were a few others, a total count of thirty-six—seven fewer than we had on the day we opened. This was now the congregation of Triple-W, thirty-six dedicated souls, mostly confused and anxious about what the future would bring.

"Let's bring our prayer time to an end," I announced. "I think it is time we had a talk."

I left the sanctuary for a moment and returned with a couple of folding chairs. I set them up on the floor, facing the congregation. For this discussion, I didn't want Jennifer and I to be sitting *on high* above the people. They had a great deal invested in the uncertain experiment that was our new church, and I wanted them to feel free to speak up. I was anticipating a long and perhaps painful process of trying to figure things out.

"Before Pastor Jennifer and I say anything," I began, "does anyone have any thoughts on what to do next?"

I wasn't expecting much, but I thought I could at least make it look like I was listening.

Chapter 7

Jennifer

As I watched my husband struggle to find a way to fix things—I had finally come to realize his need to fix whatever went wrong was an authentic desire to serve God and others—my heart broke for him. I knew full well what he had put into our new church, and what he had to give up to do it. My husband is a good, devout, powerful Christian and a true prophet—yet he is still just a man. He was willing to trust and follow God's direction—my goodness, look how much he had changed already! But, now, he was a bit shaken, even though he would never show it so others would notice. But I saw it. I saw it in that moment, sitting in sixty-year-old folding chairs, in front of our tiny congregation.

After he asked for input from the people, he sat silently as an entire minute went past . . . then another. I knew he was practicing his newfound waiting skills. Just as I was about to butt in and rescue him, Condi Cloverton spoke up.

"Seems to me," she said, "if we are going to follow the description of the church that came from Pastor Carl, we should do just that. Shouldn't we take a close look at those ideas and requirements and traits and try to follow them?"

"Makes sense to me," Art Walsh chimed in. "But I can't remember all of what it was."

"I have the gist of it right here," said Janice Pohl, ever the efficient secretary. She flipped the pages of her notes and read:

- Not a typical church
- Not much for social events, etc.
- Unable to resist God's call to deeper faith
- Newbies should go somewhere else
- High expectations—not for the faint of heart
- Won't be big
- Will be powerful
- Give your entire life to God
- The church is a sacred space
- Launching pad for the expansion of God's Kingdom
- Congregation up to the Holy Spirit

"Then let's do that!" Edwina exclaimed. "All of it!"

My heart warmed. Just listening to the enthusiasm and the trust coming from these good people lifted me. I looked at my husband. He was grinning and sitting taller.

"Well, I think that is an excellent start," he said. "I . . ."

"It's more than a start," interrupted Kevin Cloverton, "it's a mission statement or a creed or whatever you want to call it. It should be our operating instructions."

I was amazed and gratified to see new wisdom, new strength and new certainty coming from people who rarely spoke out on weighty issues. I glanced at my husband, hoping he wasn't feeling shut down by the bold statements of the others. He was anything but. He was on his feet, bordering on laughter.

"All right, then," he all-but-shouted. "What would this new thing look like?"

The was a bit of a pause, but it was in all ways the very epitome of a pregnant pause.

"How about this?" Jane Petra asked. "I think maybe this makes sense."

I was frankly shocked. Hardly ever did we hear more than a *good morning* or a *goodbye* come out of Jane's mouth.

"Then let's hear it," my husband replied. "I am all ears."

"Okay, here's what I'm thinking. How about we take a cue from Nike, and just do it? We don't even try to be what people think is a complete church. We have wonderful worship with great music and powerful prayers and—what is the right word? Prophetic? Yeah, prophetic sermons. So, we keep doing that. No worries one way or another about who shows up. We already don't lock the doors, so the people who can't resist God's call to be here, can be here. Everyone else can get what they need at a typical church... I mean that with all love and sincerity. There are lots of perfectly fine churches around. But here's what I think is important. We—each of us together and separately—do more here. If this sanctuary is a sacred space, then we should fill it with glorious music and prayers and scripture-reading and preaching and just being here with God. I mean lots of times, both planned events and randomly. If Condi feels like playing, she should come here and play her heart out. If Pastor Jennifer—Pastor Honey, I guess—has the urge to pray, why not do it here? Pastor Nathan, is there a rule that you need a big audience to read holy scripture or preach God's word? I've always wondered about that. Maybe you just walk in and start preaching. Maybe we say, 'Hey, Condi's playing. Let's go sing!' I feel like I'm not making any sense at the moment, but I am trying to say if this is supposed to be a powerful place—God's power, not ours—shouldn't it be just crammed full of God stuff?"

Abruptly, Jane stopped talking. Her face was red, her breathing rapid and her eyes wet. She was shaking a bit and appeared to be having trouble reorienting herself. I moved to her and took her hand.

"I'm so happy for you," I said.

"For what?" she murmured.

"Holy Spirit moments are to be cherished, and you just had one."

"Wow," she said. "So that's what it's like."

The whole group—even my always-in-action husband—sat quietly and let what had just been said sink in. Just as it looked as if Nathan was going to say something, probably to proclaim some sort of organizing summation, tiny, aged Mrs. Fine spoke.

"Jeremy, Honey, do you know how to set up one of those computer things where there is a live camera shot of what's going on, and anybody can use a computer to look at it?"

"Sure," he replied, "all you need to do is set up a camera and livestream it—that's what you call it when it is going out live—and people can log into it and watch."

"From where?" she asked.

"Well, anywhere in the world. All you need is an internet connection."

"Can they hear, as well as see?"

"Of course . . . I mean, yes, ma'am."

Edwina lovingly patted Jeremy on the wrist as she asked, "All the time? Can it be on all the time?"

"Yes. That can be done."

"Excellent!" she concluded, her face lit up with glee, "Then that's what we do. We do all the stuff Jane said, and any other ways we can think up to love God, and we put it out there for the whole world to see, twenty-four seven!"

Chapter 8

Nathan

We were both pretty quiet on the ride home from the church. Things had gone in directions I had not even considered, and I admit to being a little stunned at the rapidity of the whole thing. It seemed one minute we were wallowing in confusion, and the next we were ramping up to a whole new approach. After agreeing to pray over the entire arrangement and listen for God's approval, or to be given completely new instructions, we scattered each in our own direction. I don't think I had said two words to Jenn since we left the parking lot. Once we plopped into our usual his and her recliners, the silence begged to be filled.

"So, what is it?" my wife started the process.

"What do you mean? What is what?" I asked, something I only say when something is actually bothering me.

"Please don't make me beg," she replied. "There's something going on and I want to know what it is."

I remained quiet for another minute or two, before I caved. "I'm honestly not sure. I guess it just feels weird, the way everything just came pouring out like that, and the next thing you know we're on a brand-new tack. Back in our United Methodist days it would have taken three conversations, a meeting to set up a feasibility study, a task force to bring the study to the Trustees, Finance and Worship committees and, finally, a proposal to the Church Council, who would probably table it for further discussion. We would have had months to think it through."

Jenn smiled sweetly—too sweetly, I thought—and asked, "Are you missing Agendor?"

"Not funny!" I snapped.

"And you didn't answer the question."

"No, I certainly don't miss Agendor! It's just that when people start spewing things without thinking about it..."

"What?" she interrupted. "What happens when people don't form committees and have meetings?"

"Are you trying to piss me off? What are you doing?"

"No, I am not trying to . . . irk you, dear. You were surly all the way home. I feel like there is an inconvenient truth hiding under this discussion, and I want you to acknowledge it."

"Oh, yeah? If you know something I don't, why don't you just go ahead and tell me what's wrong."

I had gone a bridge too far. Jenn's face froze up. Her jaw clenched and her neck started to redden. She tilted her head back and lowered her eyelids to half-mast, regarding me with controlled disdain as she contemplated my fate. It had been months since we sniped at each other like this—actually, I became increasingly aware I was the only one doing the sniping—and it felt awkward and uncomfortable. She waited.

"Fine!" I said. "All of these things got decided, and no one even bothered to check with me. When did I lose control?"

"Oh, Honey," she said. "I'll go get you a bowl of ice cream, while you take a minute and try to think about what you are saying."

By the time Jenn returned with two modest bowls of Cookies N' Cream, I was feeling calmer and extra stupid. Half way through my bowl of comfort, I finally spoke up.

"Well, I kind of got rolling down a wrong trail on that one, didn't I."

"Yep," she replied, "but you'll get over it. Things are happening crazy fast. Emotions are going to crop up here and there."

"We spend all this time trying to let God be in charge and get away from all the Agendor stuff, and I get all bent out of shape because God-things start happening. What's up with that?"

"Just admit you're human and let it go. God already has."

"You sure?"

"No," she said with a laugh.

After we finished our ice cream, I asked, "So, Reverend Honey, what do you think about our plans for a new way to do church at Triple-W?"

"You first."

"Okay. As much as I hate to admit it, I think this may be a true inspiration."

"Oh, it is," Jenn replied. "Straight from the Holy Spirit."

I started to feel annoyed again, but I pressed on, "It does create a way to live out Pastor Carl's instructions. I'm not going to know how to act with all that freedom, but we'll figure it out as we go. Pretty scary stuff, though."

"Scary how?"

"Uncertainty. No direction. A small, stagnant congregation. No idea where enough money will come from. You and I may need to get real-people jobs. Lack of coordination. Everyone doing their own thing might get crowded. No vision statement. No measurable goals. We'll be breaking just about every rule of successful church growth."

"Well," Jenn chimed in, "that works out because we're supposed to stay small."

"I know, I know. I'm just not entirely sure how that is going to work, and, before you have to tell me, I realize that is exactly as Carl taught me—don't worry about what is next. That is up to God. I'll get there."

"You will," she said. "You are His choice for the job."

I contemplated for a long bit, before I finally added, "Now you. I went first, what do you think?"

"What I think doesn't matter, because this played out in a right way. What is next will follow. But I must say, I am excited about it. It seems like an authentic, organic, natural way of serving God and being His church. We do what we are called to do, and no more. And, it will affect the world however God sees fit."

"Yeah," I added, "it was something how Edwina came up with the idea of livestreaming continuously. I hope she isn't disappointed to learn there are millions and millions of choices on the internet. Thinking the world is watching is like thinking you're famous because your name is in the phonebook."

"True. True. But . . ."

"But what?"

"If your name is in the phonebook, people can find you if they really want to."

Chapter 9

Jennifer

A highly motivated, extremely intelligent teenager can work marvels. Thanks to Jeremy and his contractor father, it took less than a week for the Triple-W sanctuary to be fully outfitted for 24/7/365 livestreaming. By the very next Sunday worship service we were, technically at least, on display to the whole world. Of course, it was not very likely anyone was actually watching. But, still . . .

As I knew he would, my darling husband had gotten past his snit about not being in charge and was quite excited. There were only thirty-four in attendance—Frank and Sylvie were on a belated honeymoon to Niagara Falls. It was so cute when they asked to visit Nathan and I *for a talk.* We were worried there was some sort of problem. Instead, they asked our permission to miss a Sunday service for their big trip! Bless their hearts. Anyway, with thirty-four of us in the church building, Nathan opened the service with his typical *Good morning people of God*! line, then looked straight into the new camera and added, "And welcome to all God's children, everywhere." A new day had dawned.

It was a lovely service, but at the same time kind of strained. Nathan preached a fine sermon based solely on Matthew 16:24, which reads, *Then Jesus said to his disciples, 'Whoever wants to be my disciple must deny themselves and take up their cross and follow me.'* It was a powerful message on what it takes to be a true disciple of Jesus Christ, especially the willingness to be ready to do whatever God asks of you. However, Nathan's usually polished style was halting and clumsy in spots. Several times I saw him glance at the new camera and too late try to add a flourish or gesture to his delivery. His rhythm was off and he didn't seem able to get it back.

I was mildly amused until I discovered myself in the same predicament. It had become our habit for me to pray extemporaneously shortly after the sermon. It was meant to be a Holy Spirit led time of deep connection with God. All of the sudden I found myself self-consciously dropping in the occasional *Thee* and *Thou* and *Thine*—something I never do. Twice I caught myself opening one eye and sneaking a peek at the camera. It must have looked like something out of a comedy routine.

Even Condi, a seasoned on-stage performer, started throwing looks and head bobs and superfluous hand motions toward the never-blinking camera. Evidently, being on display for all the world to see was more than we could handle.

Later, over cookies, we laughed and admitted to our discomfort. After listening for quite a while, Jeremy chimed in, failing to suppress a giggle.

"Would you like to know how many people were tuned in world-wide?" he asked.

"Sure," Nathan answered, "I guess I hadn't thought about it."

"Well," Jeremy said, "I checked. There was one. And I'm pretty sure that was my dad, making sure it worked."

Edwina Fine laughed uproariously. She was turning out to be quite a hoot.

"We're fine in front of a sanctuary filled with people," she said between laughs, "not to mention God Himself. But throw in one guy on a computer and we stumble all over ourselves!"

"It was your idea," I retorted, "so it's your fault!"

We all had a good chuckle, but then things got quiet as we each retreated to our own thoughts. Finally, Nathan spoke quietly. "We'll get used to it," he said.

In the days that followed, we discussed additional uses of social media. We considered developing a website to offer continual news and information about the doings of the church. We talked about setting up accounts on Facebook and Instagram and Twitter, so we could connect with others and promote our ministries. In the end we agreed our new-found identity as the church that seeks to join God in His work—instead of creating our own agenda—was not compatible with a lot of self-promotion. So, we set up a website at www.godchristianchurch.org. It would start and remain a single homepage, featuring our name, location, contact information and a picture of our little church building with thirty-six (we waited for Frank and Sylvie to return from their honeymoon) devout people waving from the new ramp.

The rest would be up to God.

Chapter 10

Nathan

After an embarrassing first performance, we got our act together. It is amazing how easy it is to get thrown off your game. I have done at least a thousand worship services, including those I knew were being recorded, without discomfort. But as soon as we turned on that twenty-four-hour never-tiring camera-eye, things got weird. We adjusted quickly. I preached like an experienced preacher. Jennifer prayed from the heart, without distraction, and Condi played beautifully and sincerely. A new normal formed.

That's not to say we didn't keep working on the new system. Having chosen this path as the best way for the Triple-W church to honor God, we wanted to figure out how to do it well. The first thing was to smooth out the regular Sunday worship service. Check. The next step was to increase worshipful events during the rest of the week. Since the guiding principle was to allow a sort of organic spontaneity in our offerings, we decided the rule would be, no rules. I would go to the church and practice my preaching or give a speech or muse about whatever came to mind, whenever the urge struck me. Jennifer would do the same. She would drop in at the church as she felt inclined, and speak or read aloud or preach or, especially, pray. She was rapidly becoming a master of prayer. And Condi would use the church as a place to practice or play concerts for God, or anything else.

As Jenn and Condi and I were usually the most visible members of the congregation, it seemed obvious we would develop our new system in this way. However, there would be no limits. If anyone in the group felt moved to go into the church and offer something they were welcome to do so. The only requirement was a loosely-held idea that it would be somehow good for God, the Kingdom, and His people. And, so it began.

"I'm heading over to the church," I said one Tuesday afternoon.

"Good, I've been hoping for some time alone," quipped my ever-supportive wife.

"Funny. I'm not sure how long I'll be. I am working out a few things on my sermon."

"Okay, Honey. Supper's at six. You're taking me out, so don't be late."

"I'll be back," I replied. "Never want to miss a good home-cooked restaurant meal."

On the short drive over, I prepared myself for my first time rehearsing a message alone—but maybe not alone—in the church building. My longtime habits actually did not include much out-loud practicing. I typically thought about messages almost continuously, juggling various ideas for meaningful topics or scripture passages. I would pray from time to time, asking God to let me know what I needed to preach. Once I felt moved in a particular direction, I would read the passage in at least six different versions of the Bible. I found it really helpful in discerning what the translators were trying to say as they attempted to wrestle ancient Hebrew or Greek into modern English. Then I normally did additional free-form reading. I might go through a commentary or two. Maybe google it and read what some smart person had to say. Once I determined a purpose or a goal for the sermon—*What did God want said about this?*—I would begin to write. First I selected a beginning, a middle and an end (there are several endings any sermon might have, and most preachers fail to grasp the first/best ending!). Then I would flesh out the rest by imagining myself preaching the message. I would write the topic sentence of each still-in-my-head paragraph, until I had a complete list. That would constitute my only notes. It did not matter if my notes were worded perfectly or free of misspellings and typos. I would *complete* the sermon as I preached it, so it would come out sounding and feeling natural—almost spontaneous.

As I approached the crossroads of Compton and Williams Roads—the home of the Triple-W church—I had just such a list on the seat next to me. It read:

From 2 Tim 4:1-5—English Standard Version

Preach It Plain, Pastor!

1) Good morning!
2) The cornerstone of the worship service varies a bit from one Christian denomination to another.
3) All facets of a worship service are important, of course.
4) The:
    a. Call to Worship
    b. The music
    c. The singing
    d. The offering
    e. The announcements
    f. The preaching
    g. The sacraments
    h. The Liturgy (The work of the people—order of service and memorized or repeated rituals)
    i. And, of course, the praying.
5) About the only thing you just can't do a worship service without is prayer.
6) In some, like the Roman Catholic Church or the Episcopal church, the liturgy and the sacraments are the most emphasized part of the worship service.
7) The preaching—the sermon or homily or message—is somewhat secondary. In most Protestant churches, ours

included, we tend to emphasize the preaching . . . the sermon.
8) What does the Bible tell us about the role of preaching in the church...the church universal... the Church Jesus established here on earth?
9) Let's look again at our scripture for today.
10) Reading from the English standard version, 2 Timothy 4: 1-5 reads:
11) **(Verse 1) I charge you in the presence of God and of Christ Jesus, who is to judge the living and the dead, and by his appearing and his kingdom:**
   a. Timothy (and all future preachers)
   b. I tell you in the presence of God the Father and God the Son
      i. God the Son who I remind you will be the final judge of us all...those who have already died and those who are still alive...and by the power of who Jesus Christ is and what he has done
   c. It is your duty to:
12) **(verse 2) preach the word; be ready in season and out of season; reprove, rebuke, and exhort, with complete patience and teaching.**
   a. Preach the Word
      i. Solid, biblically sound preaching and teaching that is of God's word...not something of our own making.
   b. Be ready in season and out of season
      i. In season means to preach in the easy, convenient times in front of friendly, supportive believers, when preaching is expected.
      ii. Out of season means to preach in difficult places in front of resistant and hostile

people at times when preaching is not expected or welcomed.
- c. Reprove
  - i. Convince…make the case…clarify
- d. Rebuke
  - i. Correct…point out mistakes…get back on the right track.
- e. Exhort
  - i. Encourage…cheer on…motivate to keep on trying and keep on doing.
- f. With complete patience and teaching
  - i. In ways that are effective and work well to lovingly help each individual to understand and live out God's word.

13) **(Verse 3) For the time is coming when people will not endure sound teaching, but having itching ears they will accumulate for themselves teachers to suit their own passions,**
   a. For the time is coming when people will not endure sound teaching
      i. The people will not want to hear teaching that is:
         1. difficult
         2. hard to understand
         3. requires change
         4. requires sacrifice
         5. at odds with the ways of the world
         6. not what they want to hear

14) but having itching ears they will accumulate for themselves teachers to suit their own passions,
   a. But wanting to hear what they prefer to hear or what they already agree with or will give them permission to believe and do as they see fit,

A Dragon Outside the Church 47

they will seek out such preachers as will preach what makes the people happy, whether it is truly God's word or not.
15) **(Verse 4) and will turn away from listening to the truth and wander off into myths.**
   a. In operating this way, the people and their churches will turn away from God's word, and begin to believe things that are not of God's truth.
      i. By the way…this infraction…this mistake…this heresy is practiced equally by overly conservative, fundamental Christians and overly liberal, change-what-we-don't-like Christians.
16) **(Verse 5) As for you, always be sober-minded, endure suffering, do the work of an evangelist, fulfill your ministry.**
   a. As for you (Timothy and all future preachers)
      i. Be real, real serious about what you are doing.
      ii. Understand the sacred burden placed on those who are called to preach.
      iii. Be prepared to suffer along the way.
      iv. Do the work you have been called to…the spreading of the Gospel of Jesus Christ, God's word…to all who will listen…and keep at it with those who won't.
      v. This is what you have been called to do.
17) There are many ways to preach.
18) Many styles and techniques.
19) There is no need for all preachers to do it the same way, as long the message belongs to God.
20) I strive to be for you the kind of Preacher that is called for in this scripture.

21) I won't always get it just right, but I will always return to God's word and do it again.
22) It also matters that what is preached assists you in your Christian Walk, as you seek to love God and to love each other.
23) That means we need to know how to apply God's word to the lives we lead.
24) So, I am announcing today, that I am about to do something dangerous.
25) Something we Pastors are advised not to do until we have been in a church for at least five years…if we are to do it at all.
26) **Explain Why!**
27) **Announce:**
   a. Over the next weeks and months, I will invite you—no matter who you are or where you are from—to communicate to me what subject, topic or scripture you would like to hear preached.
   b. I don't guarantee to preach an entire sermon on every suggestion individually—some may need to be combined—but I will address your topics.
   c. I ask—and I say this in all sincerity—that you pray for me and for each other…that we may grow in understanding of how God would have us live out even the most difficult parts of these lives he has provided for us.

    I still had some details to work out, but I had chosen this particular topic and the line of reasoning because I had become profoundly aware my role as preacher and prophet had just changed dramatically. I would no longer be preaching to build a congregation. The remaining remnant of the *WWW.God Christian Church* had agreed we were going to do only what God wanted us to do. For the first time in my career, I would be one hundred percent free to preach whatever God desired. This first sermon of a new season was designed to get that started.

I entered the church and took my customary spot at the pulpit. I arranged my notes and looked them over one last time. It is my habit to begin preaching behind the pulpit and, at times that felt right and natural, I would walk about on the stage and speak without notes, until it seemed appropriate to return to the outline. This process might happen anywhere from once to a dozen times in one sermon. Now, here only to practice, I felt strangely nervous about getting started. I realized the never-blinking eye of the camera was still on my mind.

I closed my eyes and prayed aloud, "Dear Heavenly Father, I come to you as your servant, anxious to say the words you want said, no more and no less. Help me to know what that is. Be clear with me. I am really trying to listen. Amen."

I forced myself to begin. At first, I just read the words and tried to complete each paragraph with more words. It sounded okay, but was clearly more of an intellectual exercise than anything filled with meaning or inspiration. I paused a couple of times to scribble a note or reminder about something useful. I also crossed out the whole beginning about different denominations who emphasized the role of the sermon more or less than one another—interesting to me, but likely boring to everyone else.

Once I got into the part about the kind of preaching God wants, I actually got kind of fired up. My volume picked up, my monotone was replaced by more dramatic pitch and timbre. Words began to flow—better words than I had written down. I wanted to stop and make some notes but couldn't. The very thought of truly dedicating myself and my voice to God's purposes, without caring about whether people would compliment me or not, was exhilarating.

When I finished, I realized I had just preached one of my best sermons ever, and I did it in an empty church. For almost all of my pastoral career I would have been disappointed for having *wasted* a good performance. But now, I finally understood. It was not a performance of mine. It was a delivery of what God wanted said. It was not wasted. It was not missed. The One for whom I preach and to whom I preach, was with me.

I sat for twenty minutes. Strangely, I was quite worn out. I stood up, drank from my water bottle and headed toward the door. At the last moment, just out of curiosity, I detoured over to the computer setup. The counter showed that the viewing audience in cyber world was three.

Chapter 11

Jennifer

It was strange watching my husband preach all by himself in the little church I loved so much. It seemed almost voyeuristic, tuning in on a computer screen. I was not there, but kind of there, seeing and hearing in real time everything going on. I do so love that man. I also love to watch him work. I know better than any other human how flawed he is, and how fragile, and how sincere and devout and prone to worry. Nathan has his ups and downs, but when he is *in the zone*, he is something else. He and I doing ministry together was an incredible blessing.

I was surprised by how much Nathan's sermon moved me. I have never been big on watching church on TV. The few times I ever started, I always quickly grew bored and changed the channel. But watching and listening to Nathan was mesmerizing. Even the stops and starts and pauses to make notes seemed to make the experience more real, more genuine. When he returned home, we went out to dinner and talked long into the evening about our growing spiritual connections.

"Something unusual is happening," Nathan concluded. "In all my years as a pastor and a preacher, I have never felt anything quite like this."

Later, even after my husband was long asleep, I pondered what the *something unusual* really was. While I was already fully confident God was moving in magnificent ways, I also came to understand we were barely on the cutting edge of what was to come. I talk to God all the time, and I know He often communicates with me. But that night, as I tried to pray myself to sleep, I heard for the first time in my life an audible word from God. It felt good and safe and warm and wonderful, and immediately after hearing it I fell fast asleep.

"Hold fast," was all I heard.

Chapter 12

Nathan

We started leaving our home computer on all the time, tuned to our own Triple-W webcam.

"Jenn!" I shouted. "Come here, you're going to want to see this."

She scurried in from the kitchen, drying her hands with a paper towel.

"What's so exciting?" she asked.

"Condi's at the church, and she's playing up a storm."

She was. At 3:45 in the afternoon, on a random Friday, Condi Cloverton was offering up nothing short of a concert.

"Wow," Jenn said, "I don't know exactly what that is, but it is beautiful." We watched and listened a bit longer before she added, "Look at her go."

We pulled up chairs and sat down. We just couldn't look away. She finished what was obviously a performance piece, and then switched gears and moved to a more familiar melody.

After a few bars I said, "Those are the hymns for this Sunday's service. She's practicing."

It didn't seem like practicing. She played beautifully, but that wasn't the most amazing thing. It was her demeanor, her countenance, that drew me in.

"Look how immersed in the music she is," I said.

With her eyes closed, her face relaxed, her forehead smooth, her mouth a gentle smile, she seemed to lift herself toward the heavens.

"She is not immersed in the music," Jenn whispered. "She's immersed in God."

We sat there for over an hour. When she finally finished, Condi gathered her things with quiet dignity. We could tell she was still experiencing the ecstasy of the music. Her arms filled with books and folders, she started for the door, but hesitated, then turned around. She stepped up on the stage and moved to the old rugged cross. She shifted her load to one side and brought her free hand to her lips. After kissing her fingertips, she reached up and touched the cross. As she turned and walked out of the camera shot, her eyes glistened with tears.

"I have an idea," I said. "Let's get in the car."

This time Jenn didn't question why. We got in the car and headed toward the church.

"I don't think we're going to catch her," Jenn said. "She goes another route."

"I know," I replied, "that's not what I'm after."

We finished the trip in expectant silence. Once we arrived and parked, I took my wife's hand and marched her into the sanctuary. I paused for a moment, a little afraid to look, but then moved to the computer table.

"Seventeen," I said.

"Seventeen," Jennifer repeated. "Who would be watching? Who would even know to watch on a Friday afternoon?"

"I don't know," I answered. "Could be our own people. Hard to say. Let's go get a hamburger."

After a quick trip to one of our favorite joints, a couple of excellent burgers, with fries, and a lot of conversation about not much, we drove back to Triple-W and went in for another look.

"Still seventeen," I said. "How about that?"

"Why does that matter?" Jennifer asked.

"It means sixteen other computers, besides ours, are being kept turned on to our site."

"Really," Jennifer said softly.

I waited while she seemed to ponder the meaning behind this knowledge.

"Who are they?" she asked. "Do we have any way of finding out who they are?"

"I don't know," I replied, "but I know how to find out."

I pulled out my cellphone and pushed on the name *Jeremy Clark*. After a couple rings he answered, which surprised me a bit. Usually, I had to text to get his attention.

"Hello, Jeremy. Your old pastor needs some help. We have a few people tuning in to our livestream—seventeen to be exact. Is there a way to tell any more about who they are?"

Carefully following instructions, I let Jeremy guide me through a few keystrokes on the computer. Soon the list I was searching for popped up.

"Thanks Jeremy, looks like we've got it. Sure," I said. "East Fork, East Fork, East Fork, Montague, Edmore, East Fork, West Fork, Lansing, Mears, East Fork, Phoenix, wow, Phoenix, Redford, Wichita, East Fork, Beulah, Cedar Springs. Yeah, I don't know what to make of this, either. We'll have to do a little more research, I guess. Thanks again, Jeremy. You are a blessing. Bye."

"We can't get names, but we can see where the computers are," I started to explain to Jennifer, but it was quickly obvious she had heard everything. She had that *deep in thought, I'm not even here right now* look she gets when she is on to something big. I settled in for a long, patient wait, but in only a few seconds she spoke.

"No more than seven of those can be from our congregation, including us."

"I know," I whispered.

"Two of those aren't even in Michigan."

"I know," I repeated.

"But how? Why? Who? What is going on?"

"God only knows," I replied, "and I mean that literally. Obviously, somebody is watching and listening, but I can't begin to fathom how that could be."

"We need to do something!" Jennifer let out, her eyes bugging a bit with excitement.

"And what shall we do?" I asked, probably a little condescendingly.

"I don't know what is second," she said, "but first we pray!" She took my hands in hers, looked up and gazed to the heavens through closed eyelids. "Oh, good and holy God," she started, "we are so blessed . . ."

I stopped her. I shook my hands free and took her gently by the shoulders. "Hon . . ." I said.

"Wha . . ?"

It took her a moment to refocus, then I whispered, "I think you need to do this up there."

I pointed to the chancel with its pulpit and chairs and the magnificent old cross, all of which happened to be in view of the always-seeing camera lens.

She contemplated quickly, then leaned forward and whispered, her breath warm and pleasant on my ear, "This is our ministry now, isn't it."

I only nodded, my mind whirring with feelings and thoughts. Jennifer moved to the platform. She grabbed both arms of one of the massive chairs and dragged it directly under the cross. She picked up a Bible and sat down. Clutching the still-closed sacred book to her chest, she closed her eyes, took three or four slow, deep breaths, and began to pray.

I stayed just out of camera range and listened and took her heartfelt prayer into my own heart. My Jennifer was developing more each day, into a powerful Christian woman—part pastor, part teacher, part mystic and one hundred percent disciple of Jesus Christ.

I marveled at my wife. To be honest, I envied her a bit as well. She was way beyond my ability to connect with God—to actually experience Him in the here and now. I had always been an intellectual Christian. I had studied and learned a great deal about God and His word and way. I could—and still can—answer almost any question one might have about God, the Bible or the Church. But I could never be *with* God like Jennifer did so naturally, readily and deeply. But now, *maybe I'm getting better at letting God in*," I thought, as I realized she was saying her amens and I couldn't tell if the prayer had lasted for ten minutes or fifty.

As she recomposed herself, I snuck a quick look at the computer screen.

Thirty-one.

A new wonder started soon thereafter.

"Honey, come here a minute," I called out. I didn't even know where she was, but I was pretty sure she was in the house somewhere. She was.

"Coming, Nathan." She quick-shuffled in, doing her best imitation of Edith Bunker dutifully answering Archie's call. "What can I get for you, Mighty Nathan?"

She tried not to laugh, but failed miserably. I often wondered what people might think if they could see how their pastor-couple acted in private.

"Very funny. Maybe we should vote to change Pastor Honey to Pastor Funny Pants."

"Up to you," she replied.

"Okay," I said, "I just wanted to show you this."

I moved aside and turned the computer screen toward her.

"Take a look at the last two emails."

She read out loud, "Hello, Pastor Nathan, this is Mark Wilder."

"He was on the Staff Parish Relations Committee back at East Fork UMC," I interrupted.

Jenn continued, "I am happy to see your ministry is thriving. I always wanted to get a straight answer on what the Bible says about slavery. Might you do a sermon on that? Thanks, Mark."

"Sure, start out with an easy one," I mumbled.

Jenn moved on to the final entry. "Greetings, Reverend Nathan Martin. I am Melanie Cooper, from Wichita, Kansas. I have recently discovered your church online. I must say it is an unusual setup, but still I am drawn to return again and again. Condi Cloverton is a revelation. May I record her to listen to later? Anyway, I and my family have been affected in multiple ways by abortion. If you really mean to preach by request, I would like some insight into the faith implications of abortion. Thank you so much and may God bless your ministry. In Christ's love, Melanie Cooper."

"Now we know who is watching in Wichita," I said.

"I hope you're still happy you asked for requests."

"At the time, there wasn't supposed to be anybody listening."

"Surprise!" Jenn said with a giggle. "Oh wait," she went on, here's another one. She opened up the latest message and read, "'I don't know who you think you are, you royal . . .' Okay! Let's just delete that one," Jenn shouted.

"Well, one thing for sure," I said, taking Jenn into a big bear hug, "the game is on."

Chapter 14

Jennifer

Our ministry continued to baffle. Our Sunday morning worship took on a depth of meaning and connection I had never experienced before. It is hard to explain what I mean. Nathan had always preached technically excellent sermons. He is an accomplished teacher. But, now, his messages took on a level of connection—there's that word again—I felt so strongly I could almost see it. He had become a conduit—a direct link from God to each person in the sanctuary. Sitting on the platform, I could observe each face and no matter who I was looking at, he or she seemed to be hearing something uniquely powerful and moving. Something meant just for them.

Perhaps it was Nathan's new way of sermon preparation, or his own budding relationship with God. At some random time during each week, he would disappear from home and reappear at the church, on screen. He would invite the Holy Spirit into his *process* and commence to work out his next sermon. I kept expecting him to resort to completing and polishing a manuscript before going to the church to *practice*. After all, it only took three weeks from the time we started counting for the number of online followers to surpass four hundred in constant contact and spiked to a total of over seven hundred for Sunday services. And yet, during the week, my wise and thoughtful husband did not give into the temptation to play to the weekday audience. He chose not to publish a rehearsal time or follow a predictable schedule. Nathan did not attempt to appear prepared. Once the week's scripture was chosen and the core message he intended to give had been sketched out, he would feel moved to head over to the church and *work it out with God.*

Once he got rolling Nathan would start and stop and make notes and continue building his sermon, adding things in and scratching others out. At times the process was slow and uncomfortable. He would struggle over and over again with a section of the message until he got it right or scribbled it out in frustration. Then, he might get on a roll and preach for several uninterrupted minutes, the pace and pitch and timbre of his voice rising and lowering, emphasis created by delivery and timing. His laughter and his tears coming without effort, he sometimes appeared to be as surprised as anyone else at what had uttered from his own mouth. And he would stop abruptly, make a note and mumble, "Okay, so that's what you want."

I found the process fascinating and every bit as meaningful as the finished product. I never failed to watch and listen, sitting at home in our living room, as my husband worked. I was clearly not alone. As the tally of people routinely tuned in to our livestream grew, so did the geography spread. We now had viewers from nineteen states plus Canada, Mexico and, of all places, Australia. At the same time, Sunday attendance had changed very little. We still could not comprehend what exactly was going on, nor did we try too hard to find out. As Nathan put it, we just had to *Pastor Carl* this one, and let whatever God was doing proceed without too much interference from us.

Then, without trying, we got a clue. Another couple of weeks had passed and our *numbers* kept ticking up. At times we were approaching a thousand.

On a Thursday morning, Nathan was on the computer doing who knows what. He started hollering, "Honey, come here a minute! Jenn, come here!"

I figured I would finish what I was doing. Nathan is always getting excited about something.

"Come on! Hurry up!"

As I walked in, he said, "Look at this."

He was on Facebook, probably keeping up with stuff some of our parishioners put on there.

"What do you make of this?" he asked, pointing to a particular post.

I read, "This is Carla from Colorado. She's playing! Please share."

"It's from Shirly Ogden," Nathan said. "She is a member back at First UMC."

"Yeah, she shared it," I replied, "but it started, evidently, in Colorado."

Nathan said nothing, but quickly punched the keys necessary to get the screen back on the Triple-W feed. Sure enough, there was Condi in full praise mode, sending spectacular music up to God and out over the internet.

"Look at that," he said.

"Look at that," I said.

We didn't speak for a while. We were already getting caught up in the music.

"People are telling each other," Nathan whispered. "People all over the place are telling each other when to look in."

"Yes," I whispered back. "It's not like being lost in the phonebook anymore, is it. God has put us on the map."

Chapter 15

Nathan

A few days later Jenn was away, having a spa and shopping day with her daughter, Lisa, who lives in Lansing. I was home alone, working hard on sermon-prep to the point where my brain wasn't thinking very clearly anymore. I took a break and was running through emails and such, just to stay caught up and rest my mind for a while. I came across a Facebook thread that seems to have started with, *There's somebody new at WWW.God! Check it out and share!* The thread continued with variations of: *Who are they? I don't know. What are they doing? I'm not sure. I think the farmer-guy is just reading scripture? What's the woman doing? Nothing. No, she's not doing nothing—she's adoring. Adoring? Who's she adoring? God, I think. But she seems to be adoring the farmer-guy, too. He's not really a very good reader. No, he's all over the place . . . keeps stopping. Yeah, he's not very smooth . . . but . . . But what? I can't stop watching him!*

The comments went on and on. I turned to shout out to Jenn to come and check it out, but she wasn't there. Felt weird. I've gotten where I share everything with her. So, of course, I quickly switched over and tuned in to the Triple-W live feed.

There they were in all their glory. Frank and Sylvie. Best people I've ever met, and as down home and rough around the edges as they are good. With Frank in his jeans and flannel shirt—although it was clear it was his best flannel shirt—and Sylvie in a simple housedress and dated hairstyle, they looked to be fifty years late to the party. Frank's gnarled and slightly bent body stood at a lectern arranged in front of the cross. It was the smaller lectern, not the actual pulpit. Although I certainly wouldn't mind, Frank would never feel proper about speaking from the pulpit. *Only a God-picked Reverend should use the pulpit,* Frank had declared more than once. He was reading from the Bible. It only took me a moment to recognize he was in Genesis, Chapter 1, near the end.

"*Then God said,*" Frank read, loudly and clearly and haltingly, "*Let us make man in our image . . .* Hey Sylvie," he interrupted himself. "What do you suppose that means, 'our image?' If it's God talkin' shouldn't it be "my image" or somethin' like that?"

"Seems like," she answered. "I'll put it on the list." Sylvie sat off to the side—just on camera—and wrote frantically on a note pad. "I'm thinkin' maybe it means Jesus and the Spirit was there with God," she continued.

"Wow, wouldn't that be amazing!" Frank exclaimed. "I can't wait to ask Pastor Nathan about that one. Boy, this Bible stuff just gets better and better, don't it!"

"Yes, husband," she said, "it sure does."

He went on, *in our likeness, and let them rule over the fish of the sea and the birds of the air, over the livestock, over all the earth, and all the creatures that move along the ground.* "See there, Sylvie, God put us in charge of the whole earth and everything in it. That's why we have to quit messin' everything up and start takin' better care of the planet."

"Yes, sir," she beamed. "We sure do."

So God created man in his own image, in the image of God he created him; male and female he created them. See there Sylvie! Men and women he made, right there together. Equals. I knew that had to be true, cause you're a better person than I'll ever be. Better'n most you're ever gonna meet, too."

"Quit yer gushin' and get back to readin' God's word, husband." She tried to scold him a bit, but her tears got in the way.

I admit it. At first, I panicked about Frank and Sylvie broadcasting at the church. They are not who I would pick to do the public speaking. But once again God had better plans, using the least likely of people to do his work. Frank and Sylvie were mesmerizing. The simple reading and the heartfelt, emotional reactions to discovering what God wants us to know made for a totally uplifting experience. I watched for another half an hour, until Frank suddenly stopped and walked off without one word of closing, other than, "That's all for today. Come on, Sylvie, let's go home." And Sylvie walked out, as well, just a couple of steps ahead of Frank.

Eventually, Jenn got home and—after I inquired about Lisa and remembered to compliment her new hairdo and pretend I was interested in her various purchases—I told her all about Frank and Sylvie at the church. I pulled up the Facebook thread. It had now reached over a hundred comments! I waited as patiently as I could for Jenn to finish reading through every last one of them.

"Wow," she finally said. "This is getting more amazing all the time. What exactly did Frank and Sylvie do?"

"Well, mostly, Frank read scripture and Sylvie listened."

"There had to be more to it than that."

"Kind of. Frank would stop once in a while and marvel at something. Sylvie would marvel some, too, and then write down questions on a pad of paper. It appears they will be hitting me up with a list of things they want answers to."

"Can I see it, yet?" Jenn asked.

"It won't be archived yet, but if we go to the church, I think I know how to do it."

Minutes later we were in the car.

"Why has attendance at the church not gone up?" Jenn asked. "I mean, I know we agreed not to care about that—and I don't—but it seems weird we are getting so much online attention, and every Sunday it is pretty much the same people. Even the few visitors we've had have all been one-timers."

"Oh, I understand the question," I replied. "I've wondered the same thing. But I do think I know the answer."

"Pastor Carl," Jenn said before I got the chance. "He said *WWW.God Christian Church* would be small but powerful. Do you think the Holy Spirit is keeping it that way?"

"Bingo," I said as we pulled into the still-gravel parking lot, "bingo, bango and bongo."

Once inside, I stood staring at the computer system. I had hoped I would remember what Jeremy taught me about saving a segment of the recording and moving it into our *Archived Activity* file, but, faced with all the buttons and slides I lost my confidence.

"I think we had better wait," I started.

Jennifer interrupted with, "Nathan, I think you better find a way to look . . ."

I pushed ahead, "No, really, I'm afraid we might lose it all together. Maybe . . ."

"That's okay . . . forget it," she added, "but still . . ."

"Still what?" I asked, trying to keep the edginess out of my voice.

"Look at the number."

I looked. The day's audience had peaked right about the time Frank and Sylvie would have been wrapping up.

Twenty-seven thousand, six hundred and three.

Chapter 16

Jennifer

Another Sunday service came around and it was time for my now-traditional prayer. Typically, I would take anywhere from five to twenty minutes for Spirit-led extemporaneous words of praise and gratitude, worry and confession, celebration and mourning or whatever else came to mind and heart. This day, the Holy Spirit took me away from the typical and gave me a speech to deliver instead. I opened my mouth and out came:

"I am all-in with God today. Father, Son and Holy Spirit. All-in. Sold-out. Holding nothing back. For a while everyone in this room has understood—at least in our heads—that this little church is God-ordained to be something unlike other churches. Pastor Carl knew it first. Then Pastor Nathan and I knew it . . . except for the times when we forgot. Along the way each and every one of you has known and felt it, too. That's why you are still here. But we are—all of us, myself included—a stiff-necked and stubborn people. We do not learn easily. Jeremy, would you please check right now and see how many people are with us and with God, even though they are not in this place?"

Always on the ball, Jeremy jumped up and was soon reporting, "Michigan, Wyoming, Delaware . . ." he paused for a long moment before continuing, "forty-three states, Mexico, Canada, Australia, Ireland, Liberia, France, Italy . . . do you want me to do all of them? There must be fifty."

"No, that's fine Jeremy. Thank you. And how many are there?"

"A hundred and nine thousand and a few more. The number keeps changing."

"One hundred and nine thousand plus. Four days ago, I was astounded when the number hit twenty-seven thousand. And, I am ashamed to say, I wondered and I doubted. I searched for explanations other than the only obvious answer. How can we be surprised? We have been told repeatedly and in many ways that God wants this to be a small and powerful church. How can that happen? How can that promise come to fruition? The first answer is simple—any way He desires! It is now abundantly clear that God's will is that we become a Kingdom-force on social media, while our physical numbers remain small. It does not make human sense. The more well-known we become the more people should show up. Right? But God has brought people to us online. The internet is filled with all kinds of things. Some good and some bad and some intensely evil. God has decided to increase the presence of the Kingdom in cyber space. And, for reasons that matter not at all, he has chosen us. This little group of people in this little building in this out-of-the-way place. So, celebrate. Give thanks. Pray. Listen. Grow closer to God and hang on tight. Life in the future will be a whole new thing. Jeremy, if you wouldn't mind, check the number again. I know it's only been a couple of minutes, but humor me."

"Sure, Pastor Jennifer. No problem."

When Jeremy got over to the computer, he pulled up short and looked back at me with bug-eyes.

"It's okay, Jeremy," I said, "just tell us what it says."

"If you hadn't said everything you just said, I would think this was broken. But, I'm all-in, too! Three hundred and eighty-two thousand and climbing!"

Chapter 17

Nathan

"Hello, Pastor Nathan," said the voice on my phone. "You may not remember me, but this is Alicia Skiba. I met you a while back when . . ."

"Hi, Alicia!" I interrupted. "I remember you well and pray for you from time to time."

When I first met Alicia, she was a young and green freelance reporter—not so long ago, really—who got involved in a story when I was still the pastor of the East Fork UMC, just a few miles from Triple-W. I was in a *battle royale* with Bob Williams, a powerful church member who was trying to wrest control of the church from me and the United Methodist way of doing things. It was a chaotic, volatile mess that soon caught the attention of the local, state and even national press. At first, Miss Skiba jumped on all of the innuendo, half-truths and speculation to write some sensationalistic gossip that had little to do with the truth. However, as we got to know each other a bit, she started to recognize what she had been doing was cheap and unfair. She proved to be a thoughtful and serious-minded person, who eventually recused herself from the story in order to explore more carefully what was actually going on.

"Really?" she asked quietly. "You pray for me?"

"Yes," I said, "Sometimes. We pastors try not to forget anyone, but we definitely do not forget a thinking person like you."

"Like me?"

"Sure. Thinking, pondering, wondering—maybe even searching."

"Wow," she said. "I didn't realize you thought of me that way—or at all."

"I do. What can I do for you, Alicia?"

"Okay. A few weeks ago, I got a job with the *Muskegon Chronicle*, reporting, writing features—kind of a catch-all position. As you know, the Muskegon area is tied quite closely with the whole West Michigan scene, including Grand Rapids and East Fork."

"Sure," I said, just trying to let her continue talking.

"Well, anyway, I have expressed an interest in writing some faith-based stuff, and so, when we were in a story meeting the other day and everybody was talking about your new church, I let them know I actually know you, sort of, and asked if I could be assigned the story."

"Wait a second," I said. "What do you mean everyone was talking about our church? Why?"

"Oh, I'm sure you know why. I thought maybe, with the avalanche of requests you must be getting, maybe you would remember me and throw me a bone."

"No, I really don't know," I said. "Please enlighten me."

"Your church—WWW.Com, right?—is all the rage. Trending ahead of everything else on *Facebook*. I hear you are getting millions of hits on your livestream."

"We are, but I didn't think anyone else knew."

"Oh, yeah. People are loving you guys, at least most of them are. That sermon you just did on abortion, where you said safe, legal abortions should be available in a free society, but the church should be more willing to preach it is rarely, if ever, the best Christian response to an unwanted pregnancy, really kicked up a whole new kind of debate out there. And your call for a loving, caring response to women, and men, who are suffering in the aftermath of earlier abortion—and the grace and forgiveness of Jesus Christ that is always available to them? Wow, people everywhere are talking about that. Most in agreement, but now the pushback is heating up. Surely you know that."

"Actually, no. I have received a few responses to that and some other things, but nothing like you are describing."

Alicia went on, "Its more than that, of course. A lot of people are loving the teaching and praying and the music—oh my, I love the music!"

"You have been watching, yourself?" I asked.

"Yes, for weeks now. I watch my Facebook account to find out when something is happening, and once I find something it is almost impossible to quit watching until it is over, because I am afraid I'll miss something. And, I always watch the Sunday service. I guess it is my way of going to church."

"Alicia, I have to admit you are blowing my mind. I mean, the counts on the livestream are growing so fast we can hardly keep track, but this is the first time I have come face to face with what that means to the people who are tuning in."

"What about all the other reporters and newscasters?" Alicia asked. "Surely you have been getting snowed under, just like the last time you were in the news."

"No. No." I hesitated to say what I was about to say. "You are the only one so far."

"How can that be?" she asked. "You are the talk of the internet, and now everywhere else, too. Some are calling you a modern-day prophet; some say you're dangerous. Your wife is being hailed as a spiritual guru and your pianist could fill an arena right now. No one knows what to make of the Bible-reading guy, but they love him. Your address and email and even your phone number is on your website. Don't get me wrong, Pastor Nathan, I believe you because you don't lie, but it seems impossible you aren't deluged with reporters trying to get in on the buzz."

I sat quietly for several moments, a little stunned I must admit. Then my thoughts cleared up a bit. I felt myself smiling. I chuckled a bit into the phone.

"Are you alright?" Alicia asked.

I broke into laughter—open, full-throated, cleansing laughter.

"Pastor Nathan?"

"Well, Alicia, the way you describe the situation it does seem impossible we haven't heard from the sensationalistic press. But sometimes I still forget nothing is impossible with God. There are a lot of things playing out in unexpected ways, but once we take the time to listen and think and ponder and even discern, each mystery starts to make sense."

"Okay," she responded, "what is the sense behind this mystery?"

"This one's easy," I explained. "God has been keeping things quiet until now."

"Until what?"

"He has been waiting on you."

"Me!? How can that be. What would God want with me?"

"I am not sure of all the details, but I think it is clear He has a job for you, probably to communicate our story to the world."

Now it was Alicia's turn to go silent. I practiced my finely honed waiting skills and said nothing. Eventually she spoke.

"How can this be? I am not the right person for such a task. Surely there is someone more educated, more experienced, more famous that would be a better choice. I am not equipped for this!"

I laughed some more.

"Alicia, this is getting easier to understand by the minute. This is God's way, picking not the most qualified or obvious person for a sacred task, but someone unexpected. The Bible is full of such stories. And, don't worry. There is an old saying that 'God does not call the equipped, but rather equips the called.' You are called. How soon can we meet?"

Chapter 18

Jennifer

"Okay, dear husband," I said, "what exactly are we doing here and why are we waiting for a reporter?"

"I told you, she is not just any reporter. I know you remember her from the fiasco back at East Fork First. She gave us some heartburn at first, but then she turned out to be all right."

"Of course, I remember her, silly. I'm just messing with you. But why are we meeting her and why here at the church?"

Nathan looked me a moment and seemed to be gathering his thoughts. Then he said, "I believe she has been called to join us in our worldwide ministry, and probably to specific purposes."

"Called?" I said, "as in called by God?"

"Yes, exactly," he replied.

"All right," I said. "I am not easily shocked anymore. Tell me why you think that."

Nathan gave me a quick rundown of his conversation with Miss Skiba.

Afterward, I said, "I have to admit, I have often wondered about how it can be we now have followers in the millions, but everything else seems to stay the same. Attendance is steady, giving seems to come in just as we have needs, and we have surprisingly little email traffic, except a few sermon topic requests."

"Strangely so, don't you think?" Nathan added.

"Yes," I replied, "and now that you bring it up, I guess it is weird we haven't had people coming around trying to get the story. I don't think this amount of social media traffic happens every day."

"Not in churches, for sure," Nathan said.

He walked over to the computer and took a look.

"A new high," he said. "We're over six million right this minute, and there isn't even anything going on. Imagine what this Sunday will bring."

"Are we going to broadcast this meeting?" I asked.

"I don't think so, at least not until we see where this goes. There's a car door slamming. It's probably Alicia."

It was, indeed, Alicia. After the re-introductions and a few minutes of small talk, we got down to the discussion at hand.

"As I told your husband," Alicia began, "I did a little maneuvering at my new job and got permission to come out on this story. I honestly assumed you would have a media madhouse going on, because you and the WWW.God Church are the hot topic of the day. I admit, I am not used to crediting God with unusual events, but I don't have any other explanation for why I am the only one here."

"We have gotten more and more used to seeing God at work," I replied. "For the moment, it seems clear that He is in control, here. Alicia, what do you think is going on?"

"That's a lot to figure out," she said, "but I know a couple of things. Firstly, this is bigger than you seem to realize. The buzz is growing by the hour. And, it is not just gossip or passing interest. People are talking about faith and religion in new or at least reinvigorated ways."

"It's called *revival* or *awakening*," Nathan chipped in.

"Yeah," Alicia continued, "and it is happening on Facebook threads, with new groups forming up all over the place, in different countries and languages. Podcasts are jumping on board. Twitter exchanges by the millions. And the activity spikes every time something happens here—the prayers and the music and that odd scripture reading . . . sorry, I shouldn't have said odd."

"Oh, it's odd," both Nathan and I said at once.

"Anyway, it gets really serious after each Sunday sermon, or even the weekday rehearsals. I still can't believe those people aren't swamping you."

"Go on," Nathan said quietly.

"Well, I hesitate to say this, but the more the revival type stuff ramps up, the more pockets of opposition are coming on the scene. Your explanations about the Bible and matters of faith are being met with churches and denominations and preachers of different persuasions who are arguing that what you are preaching is off base and they know what God really wants. And then there are the atheists and atheist groups—the *Free Us from Religion Coalition* and the like. They seem to be getting real wound up."

"Alicia," I said, "what is your gut feeling about all this? What do you think is coming?"

"I can't be at all specific," she answered, "both because I don't know and I don't even have a command of religious terminology. But, what I feel is out there, not too far off, is some sort of bloodless, religious cyberwar or some similar event. I am not sure, exactly."

Alicia's voice trailed off and stopped.

"And?" Nathan asked.

"And, you two are going to be in charge of God's side."

Chapter 19

Nathan

After the meeting with Jennifer and Alicia, it seemed necessary to take some action. I was confident that the unexplainable way Alicia came back into our lives—as a lone representative of the media and with insight that seemed possible only through divine inspiration—was meant as a sign for us to get prepared. Prepared for what I was not at all sure.

We got the congregation together and shared what knowledge we had—which wasn't much—and clued them in to what we thought was going on. We introduced Alicia to the group and talked about how she was going to fit in. She was, after all, a reporter sent out to get a story and bring it back to her newspaper employer. She was also confused by her sudden initiation into a church full of ardent believers. Alicia was at best a seeker, trying to figure out if all this God stuff was even real, and yet divine power was running through her and helping her to know things she could not possibly know.

After a great deal of talk and prayer, we arrived at a place of accepting that Alicia was moving in God-directed ways, and we would have to trust that her role would become clear. We all agreed she should write a story on what had already happened at Triple-W, without getting into what might happen next. That seemed reasonable, being we were already letting anyone watch who felt like it, anyway.

We made a plan. It seems silly now, as we had no idea what we were planning for, but we made a plan. Everyone in the congregation was assigned a job. Some were to scan social media for signs that the cyberwar had begun. Others were to pray extra vigilantly to keep us strong and ready. Jennifer and I prepared some talking points and responses to probable arguments and controversial topics. Alicia agreed to act as a sort of double-agent, writing her story but at the same time interpreting the *buzz* going on in the news world. We also agreed we should not tip our hand by visibly changing our ministry too much, so we agreed to continue doing the things that by now had become part of an online routine. I continued preparing my sermons in front of the camera, Jennifer prayed, Condi played and Frank and Sylvie plowed their way through scripture.

We got all geared up and lived on high alert for weeks, and not much happened. Other than the counts of our livestream visitors continuing to grow—by this time we had hit eleven million—nothing new of note occurred.

One evening at home, after this had gone on just about as long as I could stand, I said to Jenn, "I don't get it. Were we just mistaken? Are we moving down the wrong path?"

"I don't think so," she answered. "The things that came to us through Alicia seem quite clear."

"Then what?" I persisted. "Is there something else we're supposed to do?"

"Yes," she said. "I think this is one of those times to ask ourselves 'What would Pastor Carl do?'"

I felt a wave of annoyance. Momentarily it felt as if Jenn was invoking the name of my absent mentor to manipulate me into calming down. Basically, it worked. It took me a couple of minutes, but I let my defensiveness down and felt my shoulders relax.

"Yeah, you're right," I said. "Carl wouldn't have expected anything to happen next. He would just say, 'If God wants anything else from me, He'll let me know,' and go about his business. Nothing seemed to bother him."

"What if it did?" Jenn asked. "Bother him, I mean. What if it did?"

"He never seemed bothered."

"But that doesn't prove anything," Jenn continued. "Don't you think maybe Carl had simply learned to gracefully do the thing that was hard? Maybe it wasn't not caring, maybe it was caring more about what God wanted out of him. You think?"

I had to think about that for a bit. Jenn waited.

"Yeah, could be," I said. "But if that's true, he sure was good at it."

"For sure," Jenn agreed, "and maybe that's our answer to the what would Carl do question."

I said, "So, you think what you and I need to do—mostly me—is to do the hard thing, and wait on God until something comes?"

"Yes, and by the way, I'm having a hard time of it, too."

"Okay. Together, we wait like champion waiters!"

Jenn smiled and said, "We wait!"

Chapter 20

Jennifer

We didn't have to wait long. Maybe God just wanted us to get our heads straight first, or maybe His timing simply arrived, but three days later things blew up. On Friday, May 3rd of the year of our Lord 2018, at 7:21 a.m. I was in the bathroom in our home. I had only been awake a few minutes and was in the first moments of pulling myself together for the upcoming day. Nathan was still in the bed, but he was awake and was hollering something about how he was going to get up and take on the world, in just a few more minutes. He never stops with the funny. Then, I heard a noise. I am forever grateful I decided to pull on my old, over-sized terrycloth robe, because as I crossed into the living room, there were two men, each with a camera aimed through our picture window. As soon as they saw me they started clicking so fast the flashes were like a strobe.

"Nathan!" I screamed. "Put something on and get out here! And, put something on, first!"

I wanted to make sure he put something on. Moments later—the two guys still snapping away—Nathan hopped down the hallway, still struggling to get the second leg of his pants all the way up.

"What the heck is . . ." he started, then found himself at a temporary loss for words. Then he recovered and said, "There's two guys taking pictures."

"That's kind of why I called you," I deadpanned.

Nathan strode over to the front door, unlocked it and threw it open. I was right behind him and as soon as we had time to focus, we froze. The driveway, the front lawn and both sides of our street were filled with cars and trucks, many of them featuring logos of radio stations, newspapers and TV networks.

"There they are!" came flooding in from several directions, and the crowd surged toward the house. Nathan slammed the door shut and relocked it as quickly as possible.

We looked at each other and said in unison, "Looks like the wait is over!"

"Are all those people and cameras and microphones out there every morning?" my funny husband inquired.

"Usually only when you're still in bed," I replied.

"I think we're about to be in the news again," he continued. "I had really hoped the last time would be enough."

I pulled the curtain aside a few inches and peaked outside, just in case we had been imagining things.

I said, "Looks like a genuine media onslaught."

Nathan joined me and said, "Of biblical proportions, I'd say."

"Okay," I said, "now that we have made with the clever quips and all, what do we do now?"

"I don't really know," Nathan said. "I am not at all happy about these people being in our yard taking pictures through the windows, but I suppose that is the least of our concerns right now."

"Agreed," I said. "What's our next move?"

"Well," he said, "first, let's make sure all the curtains are closed and get cleaned up and get into some nice clothes. One way or another, it appears we are about to meet our public."

"Then what?"

"I'm not sure, but I think whatever it is has to start with going outside. We can't go anywhere until we get past that mob."

We took our time getting ready, mostly to give ourselves a chance to get our thoughts together. I toasted a couple of bagels and poured some orange juice.

"How did this happen?" I asked, mostly rhetorically.

"Evidently, God kept us out of all of the usual build up. Instead of starting slow and gathering steam and eventually turning into something big, feels like He just decided when it was time to shoot off a cosmic starting pistol. Boom. All at once."

"What are we going to say?" I asked between bites.

"The Bible promises we will be given the words we need when we are speaking up for Jesus," Nathan said. "I think we just go out there and see how it goes."

So, we did.

Our small front porch has a railing most of the way around, with just a narrow stairway down one side. Like a Roman emperor and empress stepping out on the royal balcony to grant an audience to the adoring crowd, we quickly and quietly appeared on the royal porch.

After two or three seconds, the shock of recognition set in and the crowd went nuts. They surged forward like a giant amoeba, cameras clicking and whirring, phones held overhead, microphones shoved forward, as if clearing the way for the carrier. Thankfully, the front line held at the railings, while within minutes every possible empty space filled in from behind. All the while the yelling reached a crescendo and stayed there. Hundreds of shouted questions melded into one indecipherable roar.

Nathan had experienced this sort of thing back in the hubbub at the East Fork UMC, although not as crazy as this. Still, he learned what to do.

"Don't say a word," he shouted into my ear. "Just stand and smile, as if there was nobody there."

We did. It was very hard to do. For several minutes, the crowd simply grew louder and more insistent, screaming to be heard over the others. After ten minutes, there started to be short breaks in the wailing, but as soon as there seemed to be even a small lull, others would smell their opportunity and redouble their yelling. After another ten minutes, the noise dropped into a confused grumbling.

When it had finally gotten relatively calm, Nathan broke his silence and shouted, "If you would just be quiet and ask questions one at a time, we will be willing to give some answers."

Evidently each person there translated *one at a time* into *you go first,* as the roar jumped back to peak levels.

We waited again. But this time it only took a couple minutes to die back down.

"We will call on you, as many as we can. This is all on the record, so the rest of you can take notes," Nathan called out. "Otherwise, we're leaving."

As every hand on the property shot up, I heard my husband mutter "Let's see . . ."

Without thinking, I shouted as loud as I could, "The first question will come from Alicia Skiba, reporter from the *Muskegon Chronicle*!"

Several confused versions of '*Muskegon Chronicle*—who is that?' came from the much larger news outlets.

Nathan smiled, and we both looked out over the crowd. I didn't even know if she was out there.

"Yes!" shouted a somewhat timid voice from near the back of the mob. "Yes! Alicia Skiba, *Muskegon Chronicle*!"

"Miss Skiba, what is your question?"

The pause went on too long. I began to panic, thinking Alicia was choking on her big moment. I was about to encourage her to speak, when she did, in a much calmer, more commanding voice.

"Reverend Nathan Martin?"

"Yes."

"Reverend Jennifer Martin?"

"Yes, Alicia."

"How is it with your souls?!"

Chapter 21

Nathan

I couldn't help but laugh when I heard Alicia's icebreaking question. I didn't know she had enough exposure to church-speak to even frame such a question, much less the courage to ask it in front of a crowd of influential news colleagues.

"Thank you for asking, Alicia!" I shouted. "My soul is well! God is near! God's word, God's will and God's way are before us!"

"What more could we ask?" I heard Jennifer chime in. "All is well!"

The bulk of the crowd seemed a bit stunned by the opening exchange. Ironically, most of them had no interest whatsoever in anything to do with God. Still, after a moment's hesitation, the hands shot back into the air.

"You, sir," I shouted and pointed. "You, from *Wood TV*."

"Thank you!" he shouted in return. "Stanley Hersberger with W.O.O.D. TV. Your little church—the *WWW.God Christian Church*—which I understand has a weekly attendance of under fifty, is now number one in any measure of hits, trends, etc. on the entire internet. How do you explain that?"

"We can't," I replied.

"We have no idea," Jenn added.

"Can you give us more than that?" Stanley yelled out, not anxious to use up his turn on such a short answer.

"No," I replied.

"Only that it is clearly a God-thing," my wife corrected.

"Next, let's have the woman in the long, yellow coat," I announced.

"Thank you, I am Karen Bidwell, Faith Page reporter for the *Indianapolis Daily News*. A great many churches have tried to make headway with online church—most with little or no success. We have never seen anything remotely like this. What has been your marketing strategy and how did you create said strategy?"

"We have no strategy," I said, "except to focus all of our hearts and minds and activities on being closely connected with God, and to do whatever God wants."

"We had zero idea this was going to happen," Jenn added. "We didn't even know how to keep track of how many people were tuned in, until the numbers were already rolling in."

"Still," someone called out, "you did decide to do everything in front of a livestream camera!"

"That was God's decision," I said. "He used a devout Christian woman named Edwina Fine to get that one across to us. I guess God knows what He is doing."

"He!?!" was screamed from several directions, along with some version of, *You claim God is a man? What about women? Do you hate women? Does God hate women?*

I felt the heat climbing up the back of my neck. Even though I thought I was prepared for the inevitable slings and arrows of this highly-charged situation, I found it hard to not respond emotionally. As I formulated my response, the better thing happened.

"I'll be happy to speak to that," began my darling wife. "At Triple-W we seek to not get caught up in such discussions that can never be truly resolved. For the record, we do not believe God is male or female—God is beyond that and embodies all of the best traits we see in humanity. God loves and cherishes all people of all times and places. God plays no favorites. You may have noticed I am a woman, and I can tell you I have never experienced a more egalitarian atmosphere than I have in our little church. God calls whomever He calls, and whomever is called responds. As the Bible consistently refers to the three personalities of God as Father, Son and Holy Spirit, we are comfortable in the occasional use of the masculine pronouns. If anyone else prefers to honor God by use of other pronouns or language, we respect that and urge you to continue."

"I have nothing to add," I said, and thankfully got a few chuckles. "How about the young lady right here in front?" I had seen a very petite teenager—maybe even a tween—working her way to the front, seemingly unnoticed.

"Oh!" she said, and froze.

"What is your name and where are you from?" I asked.

"Oh, yeah . . . okay. I'm Kris Hinken, and I represent the *East Fork High School Student News*."

"Excellent. What is your question?"

"I play the piano," she said, "and I want to be good at it, so I practice a lot. So, well, I guess my question is, like . . . where did you get that piano player?"

I smiled at the mere mention of Condi and her gifts of faith and music. I was about to answer when I felt Jenn tug on my sleeve.

"Listen," she whispered.

From a crowd I had begun to fear would only bring attacks, a murmur was wafting across the crowd, followed by a scattering of applause.

"They know Condi," Jenn whispered again. "Some of them have been touched by her music."

"Let me ask you a question, Miss Kris Hinken. Would you like me to arrange a private lesson with Condi Cloverton, our devout pianist, and maybe an interview for your story?"

I have always enjoyed watching the reaction of a young girl too excited to contain all of her emotion in one little body. Kris Hinken nearly broke free of her own skin.

"I'll take that as a yes," I said. "I will set it up. I promise."

"What's with that scripture guy?" someone called out.

"Let me," Jenn said. "The Scripture Guy—he'll love that nickname—is Frank Osborn, along with his wife Sylvie. They make a perfect example of how God works. Frank has no particular training to qualify him for his ministry. He is not the person human authorities would likely pick for such an important position. But God chooses the unexpected, sometimes even the least likely. Frank and Sylvie love God without question or reservation. If God told them to run through a brick wall, they would. Now, Frank would go first to make sure Sylvie had a hole to run through without getting hurt or mussing her hair, but they would both do what God asked, no matter what. And, that's why when Frank reads scripture, millions of people just have to listen."

"Thank you, Reverend Martin," I said.

"No, thank you, Reverend Martin," she replied.

No one laughed. Maybe we're not as cute as we think we are.

"Next. The gentleman on my left in the dark suit and red tie."

"Thank you. I am Bishop Ralph Lorenz, of the *Apostolic Word of God's Reign Church* in Cincinnati, Ohio. I am also the producer and lead commentator on the television show, *God's Word Properly Explained,* now syndicated on forty-seven TV stations in thirty-eight major markets. I have spent a few hours—probably more than necessary—observing and critiquing your broadcast or podcast or whatever you call it. While much of it is harmless enough—the music is inspiring, the Scripture Guy is, again, harmless and you, Mrs. Martin, say a lovely prayer—I have grave concerns."

Bishop Lorenz shifted his position slightly, turning his side toward us and facing and speaking toward the bank of camera trucks parked on the road.

"I suppose pointing out the biblical prohibitions against females preaching or teaching will get us nowhere, as several major denominations in the U.S. already violate God's word on that. It is you sir, The Reverend Nathan Martin with whom I take serious umbrage. Per your sermon of March 10, 2018, I . . ."

"Mr. Lorenz," I finally shouted, "is there . . ."

"That is *Bishop* Lorenz," he bellowed.

"And my wife is *Reverend* Martin, sir, whether you approve or not. Now, *Bishop* Lorenz, we have agreed to answer a few questions, yet so far I cannot find a question in your speech. Have you a question?"

"Your theology is weak! Your doctrine is flawed! Your arrogance to think you can use the platform of millions of ill-advised livestreamers to preach . . ."

"That's enough!" I said, bordering on bellowing myself. "Still no question. Now, all I am going to say is . . ."

Bishop Lorenz—puffed up and red in the face—screamed, "You will have to answer to God! And, before that you will have to answer to me!"

"I will answer to God, for sure," I said. "We all will. But I am done talking to you. Our ministry at *WWW.God Christian Church* is a very different thing from what you are used to. We will not argue theology and doctrine in the effort to prove who is right. We will only do whatever God directs us to do, and say what He directs us to say. Period. If that offends you, so be it."

"You will not dismiss me!" Lorenz hollered.

"Yet, you are dismissed," I said, feeling calmer, "and if you start up again, this whole event—whatever it is—is over."

The blustery Lorenz attempted to ramp back up, but the crowd moved quickly to shut him down. They were all hoping to get their own shot at us. Even with over a hundred hands in the air, I felt my attention drawn to a particular figure. He was a very tall man, at least six-six, standing head and shoulders above those around him. He stood with his arms crossed over his chest, and had not moved a muscle throughout all of the exchanges. Before I knew it myself, I had called on him.

"I am Alexander Stevens. I am the Executive Director of the *Free Us from Religion Coalition.* You and your little church have become quite famous, Reverend Martin and Reverend Martin. Even as I decided to come here, I did not realize how influential you are. I have no questions at this time, but I am sure we will be closely associated in the very near future. Good day."

Mr. Stevens bowed slightly in our direction, turned, and disappeared beyond the trucks and vans.

Chapter 22

Jennifer

We broke up the impromptu press conference as quickly as we could. There were a few more questions, but our energy had run out. When it was obvious the questioning could go on all day, we offered to answer a couple more, and then one more, and then with profuse apologies we finally had to quit.

"God loves you, and there is nothing you can do about it!" Nathan proclaimed in his mightiest preaching voice and we dashed inside the house.

We kept the curtains drawn and waited for things to die down. Incredibly, the front doorbell rang several times, and there were a number of knocks on the back door.

"What's it going to take to get them to leave us alone?" I asked.

Nathan answered, "If they don't quit soon, I'll call Tim and have him do a drive by, maybe show some lights and blast his siren a couple of times. We might have to post a *No Trespassing* sign or something."

Just as he finished telling me his plan to involve the local cop, I risked a look past the curtain.

"They're gone," I said, "every last one of them—just like nothing went on here today."

Really?" Nathan replied.
He threw the door open and surveyed his empty yard.
"They were here," he continued. "The grass is shot. Besides, I remember it as if it was only twenty minutes ago!"
"Funny guy," I said. "What are you thinking?"
"I'm not sure. Part of me wants to strap it on and get ready for a battle royale. Another part is reminding me we vowed to take a wait-until-God's-next-move approach. Still another part of me wants to hide under the covers. How about you?"
"A lot the same as you, but I am still thinking about what went on today. Wasn't that something?"
"It was something," my husband said, "but tell me what's on your mind."
"That God is amazing! Look at all the stuff He is doing! There were people out there who have been moved! People who came here because they are thinking about—and feeling about—God in whole new ways! He has placed us in the middle of something big!"
Nathan replied, "Yes, he sure has. But, what about the scary Bishop Bombastic and scarier still Tall Man. Evidently we are going to have to answer to one of them and confront the other."
"Only if God says so," I said. "Besides, almost every big change that ever happened in the Bible came through some sort of *stirring up the pot*. There will be conflict, but as long as we keep God's will at the center of it, we don't have to worry. Do we?"
Nathan looked at me in the way he does when he is reformulating on the fly.
"No," he eventually said, "you're right. We don't. There are a few things we have to do, though."
"Like what?" I asked.
"I still have some sermon prep ahead of me. I need to call Frank and Sylvie and encourage them to keep on doing exactly as they have been doing."
"Of course!" I added, launching myself into my husband's embrace. "And, I have to spend some extra prayer time with our

God and stay extra connected for the days ahead. And, you, don't forget to call Condi! You made a promise out there!"

"Of course," he said, laughing out loud. "Kris Hinken! Didn't you just love that? I hope I didn't promise something Condi won't want to do."

I did my best bug-eyes and laughed, "Yeah, right!"

I kissed the husband God gave me and didn't think about anything else for a little while.

Chapter 23

Nathan

The days of quietly contemplating why certain things were not happening were over. Big time. Every day became a flurry of activity.

The front yard press conference resulted in a plethora of news articles and stories and special reports. Some of them were even somewhat balanced and kind of fair—attempting to tell the story of the little church that was suddenly receiving so much attention. The television news blurbs were mostly three-minute spurts of incomplete information, most of it wrong. We put Alicia to work on an accurate and honest version—complete with inside knowledge and explanation—assuming the opportunity would arise to clarify all of the erroneous stuff that was exploding about.

Then there was the Bishop Ralph Lorenz, of the *Apostolic Word of God's Reign Church* in Cincinnati, Ohio. The very next day, on his Saturday morning airing of *God's Word Properly Explained,* Lorenz launched a full-out attack, calling us *false prophets,* teaching *false doctrine.* We were clearly *wolves in sheep's clothing* and *false messiahs*—maybe even *antichrists!* For what little of it I watched, it appeared that anything I had ever said or preached, that differed in any way from whatever the Great Lorenz himself had ever taught or preached, was rock solid evidence of not only being mistaken, but evil as well.

And, what of the mysterious, scary Tall Man—Alexander Stevens, of the *Free Us from Religion Coalition?* For several days, we heard nothing from him.

We read and watched portions of the mountain of reporting—our curiosity getting the better of us—until we realized we were simply going to have to stop. If we paid attention to what all of these other people were saying, we would both go nuts and lose our focus on God. At this stage of the game, we were not about to let that occur. So, we did nothing. At least, we tried to do nothing.

Clearly, God had taken away the hedge of protection that had temporarily kept us apart from the madding crowd. Reporters and photographers of every ilk turned up everywhere we went—our home, the Triple-W church, the supermarket—snapping pictures, hollering questions, recording everything we did and said. We hid out as much as we could, but to live our lives and do our ministry we had to leave the house.

When I went to the church to prepare and practice my next sermon—something I had been doing for months in front of millions of cyber-viewers—I found myself with over thirty people sitting in the pews as an audience. The extra thirty sets of eyes were oddly disconcerting, but I plowed ahead and did my best.

Condi was soon playing to a full house! She would arrive at the church, having told no one of her plans. By the time she carried in her things and got her music arranged, the first of the visitors would arrive. When she was twenty minutes in, the pews were filled and people were standing in the back. As instructed, Condi simply played on.

I was most worried about Frank and Sylvie. How would they handle having a boisterous crowd in their face? They were not trained for this kind of thing. I decided to let them have a go of it on their own. God did promise to provide the necessary words to those who speak up on his behalf. Right? I needn't have worried. I watched on the livestream as Frank and Sylvie showed up. Sure enough, there was soon a crowd. Frank was well into a passage leading up to David's improbable selection to replace Saul as the next King of the Jews, when the audience grew noisy.

Frank looked up and bellowed, "I'm readin' the holy Word of God up here. You people are goin' to have to shut up!"

They did.

I started to accompany Jennifer to her extemporaneous prayer times. I couldn't help it. The first time she had an audience, the atmosphere was not at all prayerful. People talked out loud and set up cameras. A few even shouted out their questions. But my magnificent wife, walking hand-in-hand with God, simply prayed as only she can do. The crowd silenced. Previously irreverent noise-makers closed their mouths, and then their eyes. Not a peep was heard, except for a few sniffling tears. A few left early—either overwhelmed or doing their very best to resist. In the coming days, whenever Jennifer showed up to pray, the gathered crowd changed. Most of them were no longer moving in for the kill. They were coming for a closer experience of God.

All that said, it was Sunday services that truly amazed. Two days after the May 3rd, blow-up press conference on the lawn, our Sunday service went like any other. Despite the TV shows and podcasts and blogs and news features—even despite being followed and accosted everywhere we went—the morning worship was just as it had been; lovely, meaningful, deep and shared amongst thirty-eight people. *Excellent,* I thought. At least God is giving us some tranquility in worship.

I have always been convinced God has a sense of humor. On Sunday, May 12, 2018 Jennifer and I arrived, as is our practice, one hour before the beginning of the service. We are nearly always the first to arrive.

This day, while still a mile away from the church, Jennifer said, "What's going on?"

"I don't know," I said, also noticing the four corners of Compton Road and Williams Road were filled with vehicles.

As we drew closer, we could see the little parking lot was full of cars and trucks. The shoulders of the roads were lined on both sides with another fifty vehicles, with more pulling in all the time.

"Are we late?" I asked, rather dimwittedly.

"No, we're not late," Jennifer answered. "See the logos?"

"Oh, no. The press is coming to worship. What are we going to do?"

Jenn looked at me expectantly and grinned.

After a pause to catch up, I said, "Oh, yes! The press is finally coming to worship! What a wonderful opportunity!"

"There you go, Big Guy. Now you're seeing it."

"Okay. Fair enough," I said. "But the inside has to be packed already, and our people aren't even here . . . no, wait, I am not going to finish that sentence. I have always said the most important person in the church is the next one through the door— the one we haven't met yet. So, our people are already in the building. Right?"

"Yes, dear," she said, "you've got that right."

"Good, but we still have the problem of not having room for everyone, including the regulars."

"You let me worry about that," Jennifer said, patting me on my shoulder. "You get inside and start organizing for a super-duper worship time."

I went inside. It was a madhouse. The pews were nearly full. There was only enough space to comfortably seat a hundred, and at least twenty spots were being lost to tripods for cameras and lights. I admit, my first thought was, *Who do these people think they are? No one asked permission to do this!* Then I remembered Pastor Carl had instructed the doors were never to be locked, so the church would always be accessible. So, I gave my head a couple of good shakes and took the stage.

"Good morning, people of God!" I started. "It is so good to see you this morning!"

"He's here!" somebody shouted. "That's him!"

"Hi, I am Nathan Martin, one of the pastors here at the *W.W.W.God Christian Church*, which we like to call Triple-W."

"Pastor Nathan!" someone shouted. "What do you make of the attacks being made on your teachings by Bishop Lorenz. He seems awfully sure of himself!"

I moved into one of my very best negotiating tactics. I played stupid.

"Yes, worship begins in about forty-five minutes, and everyone is welcome! I am so glad to see you all this morning."

"There are rumors *Time* magazine is after your story! What do you have to say about that?"

"Yes, the wonderful Condi Cloverton will be playing, and worshipping, with us this morning! Thank you for asking!"

"I heard Dr. Phil—he's a Christian, you know—is trying to get you on the show. What do you . . ."

"Yes, on Sunday mornings, everything else stops, so we can praise and worship God to the best of our ability and return some of the great love He has for us. So, I am going to have to ask a couple of favors. First, please remove any and all tripods and stands from the building—we've still got plenty of time. Please no lights, flash or large cameras. If you want to use handhelds and such, fine. You can take notes if you wish, but please no questions during the service, unless they are about God or loving God or worshipping God. In that case, go on ahead. We are here to worship, and we will not be distracted. I really, really hope you all will stay."

Most did. A few packed up and left. Stands and lights and cameras were put away. The pews filled in. I saw the Tall Man enter and stand in the back right corner. It was now fifteen minutes before service time, there was no room for anyone else, and none of the usual faces were in the church. I ducked into the tiny back room to get a grip on myself and prepare to lead worship. All of my career I have wondered why people don't understand that preachers need to be left alone in the final few minutes before a service. It takes an engaged, connected, calm frame of mind to preach and teach and pray and sing and all of that. I tried to focus.

At T-minus four minutes, I walked out of the back room to have a look. At that same moment Jennifer and Condi walked into the building.

Jennifer smiled and said, "Ready when you are!"

Condi took her place at the piano. Jennifer and I started for the worship space in the front.

"Where is everybody?" I hissed

She stopped and pointed out one of the side windows. The usual congregation—the devout and faithful few of Triple-W—had encircled the church, each one holding hands with the next.

Chapter 24

Jennifer

That first Sunday when all the outsiders showed up was extraordinarily tense in the beginning. When the church members arrived they were taken aback by what they found. The scene took the old church adage of *Someone is sitting in my pew!* to a whole new level.

Art Walsh even said it out loud, "Someone has taken our church!"

"It's okay, Art," I replied. "This is going to be a big day! Please grab all the regulars you can and get them gathered in the backyard. I'll be around to explain the plan."

If only I actually had a plan.

Condi and Kevin Cloverton arrived and joined Art and Leta in the back. Janice Pohl showed up with Jane Petra, another former member of East Fork UMC. Then there was Frank and Sylvie. I felt better for some reason, with Frank and Sylvie on hand. Jeremy Clark, still not quite eighteen, drove up with his weekly passenger, the wizened Edwina Fine. As Jeremy helped her from the car, Frank ran off to fetch her a chair. It sure is nice when other people notice a problem and fix it right in front of you. Francine Cook, John and Shelley Drobena, Michelle Garner and Jeff Conway all joined the group as did the rest. Once again, just like many Sundays before, the whole team was in place.

"Good morning, everyone," I said. "I feel so much better now that you are all here. As you can see, there are some unusual happenings this morning. The sanctuary is packed to the gills and there is nowhere for us to sit."

Immediately, there was a grumbling mix of mild upset and confusion, including several questions along the lines of, *What are we going to do?* As I struggled to get my mind around my still-elusive plan, the mumbling was pierced by a loud, "Yeee! Haw!! Halleluiah!" I looked in the direction from which the exclamation came and my eyes landed on Jeremy.

"Don't look at me!" he exclaimed through a huge grin, and tilted his head down to his left.

There sat Edwina, so excited she could hardly stay seated on an ancient folding chair in a grass-studded gravel parking lot.

"I knew God was not messing around," she said. "Look at this place!"

After a quick wave of shame for our negativity rushed through the rest of us, the mood was decidedly more upbeat.

Janice asked, "What's the plan?"

I still didn't have one, but before I could speak, Jane Petra—sweet, quiet Jane, who rarely spoke up but was growing closer to God every day—made several rapid-fire announcements.

"This needs to be an especially touching service. Condi and Pastor Honey, you need to go inside and get ready to worship like never before. John and Jeff, please go get some more chairs and bring them out here. Please, don't ask why, just go get."

Off they went to do their duty.

"Frank and Sylvie," Jane continued, "please help everyone else get arranged in a big circle all the way around the church, close enough together to hold hands. Anybody who can't stand for an hour or more, be sure they get a chair. We have less than five minutes to start covering this entire service in prayer."

They all hesitated and looked at me.

"You heard the woman," I said. "It's prayer time!"

As each person sprang to their post, I saw Jane stop Michelle Garner. Michelle was so quiet I could not remember a particular instance of hearing her speak.

"Michelle," Jane said, "would you be upset if I gave you a special job?"

"Of course not," Michelle replied.

"Here's some money," Jane continued, reaching into her purse. "We're going to need way more cookies and punch."

Michelle seemed dumbstruck for a few beats, then she grinned, waved off Jane's money and took off at a run.

"I've got this!" she hollered back over her shoulder.

Recognizing our own duties, Condi and I headed inside. It was very nearly time to start the service. As I moved toward the front, I was joined by my beloved husband. He seemed under control, but was clearly wound pretty tight.

"Where is everybody?" he stage-whispered.

I knew by everybody he meant the regular members, so I pointed out a window. From our angle, it looked like the entire church was already surrounded. Just then, Jane burst in and marched directly to the front.

"If you have attended church with some regularity in your life, please raise your hands," she announced. Perhaps twenty hands went up. "Good," she continued. "I need you, you, you, you and you," she said while pointing. "We can't quite reach. Please follow me."

Without question the five draftees followed Jane out the door. My heart nearly burst with an odd mix of pride and excitement. Things were really starting to cook.

Nathan and I stepped up into the worship space and took our seats in the massive, old clergy chairs. Nathan caught Condi's eye and gave her the nod to begin playing the prelude. And play she did—a magnificent piece that grabbed an unruly, largely inexperienced-at-doing-church crowd and brought them to silent reverence. They might not have any idea what was coming next, but they knew it was going to be something.

Chapter 25

Nathan

Sometimes things just happen. Maybe that's a good thing. When I got up that Sunday morning, I had no idea anything unusual was about to take place. Yet, there I stood, in front of a packed house of strangers, with no particular plan in mind, except to stay open to wherever the Holy Spirit might lead. My prepared sermon on how to forgive others when forgiving is hard, didn't seem apropos anymore. So, I set it aside.

"Good morning, people of God!" I began. They just stared at me. "No, I mean it! You are, each and every one of you, children of God, made in God's own image. You may or may not know that . . . but God knows."

The crowd did not rebel or complain, but neither did they engage. Mostly, they squirmed.

"I hope today's worship service is meaningful to all of you. And, lest I forget, welcome to all of the millions of people who are with us on livestream this morning."

As I was contemplating my next move, I heard Jennifer chime in, "Everybody stand up, turn around and wave at the camera." After no one moved, Jennifer added, "I mean it! Nothing else proceeds until we greet the rest of the congregation."

As a couple, then a few and then the rest rose hesitantly to their feet, I called out to Jeremy, "Jeremy, what do the counts look like this morning?"

We had upgraded our computer setup twice already, trying to keep up with the flood of viewers and to keep all the information straight.

"Well, Pastor Nathan," Jeremy replied, "we have fifty states and sixty-two countries. Numbers, I am not sure. It is growing so fast I can't read it. We just blew past fifty million."

"You are waving at over fifty million people!" Jennifer announced.

The congregation looked around at each other, then waved a little harder.

"Please be seated," I said. "Let us continue our time of praise and worship."

I surveyed the crowd, panning slowly from my left to my right. I did my very best to appear thoughtful and contemplative, but the truth is I wasn't sure how to begin or what to say. I recalled something I had heard my friend and mentor Pastor Carl once say, *Sometimes when God wants to use you to say something, all you have to do is get your lips moving.* So, I simply started talking.

"The single most important task for each and every human being born into this world—born into this time and place—is the apprehension of God. To discover God. To believe in God. To understand God. To love God. To trust God. To turn one's very self—now and eternal—over to Him. To worship God. To praise God. To glorify God. To serve God. To follow God's will, God's word, and God's way. To, eventually, go and be with Him.

"There are other things that matter, to be sure: Love, family, beauty, art, music, honest, fulfilling work, good works, love of neighbor and enemy, honesty, honor, duty carried out. All good gifts from God. All good things that fit within His will, word and way. It is good to be patriotic, to toil for noble causes, to save and protect our world and our environment, to learn a great deal about important subjects, to earn a good living. The list is nearly endless, yet pales in comparison to the greatest imperative for anyone born human—the apprehension of God. To live this life without addressing the eternal question of God, is to have missed the point completely.

"There are, especially in today's world, many who will not only disagree with everything I just said, but will be angered and upset by it. It is widely considered offensive to tell anyone some things are true and other things are not. Or dare to suggest some things are wrong and some things are right—some evil, some good—always, for everyone. For some it is infuriating to hear that the human intellect is not the greatest force in the universe, and not the supreme source of morals and ethics—what is acceptable in our world and what is not. But, rather, that those decisions belong to God, who created us and everything we have.

"I know that, and it is not lightly or without trepidation I say these things. I am not enamored of anger and conflict. Yet, God is God and I am not, and neither are you, or anyone else but Him. And that is the truth. Some may consider it an inconvenient truth, but God does not require my nor your agreement on the matter. God is. It is as simple as that."

As I was framing my next thought, I saw the Tall Man rise to his feet. He moved half way across the back wall, right in front of the main door. He paused and rose to his full height, searching out my eyes with his. When he had locked me into undeniable eye contact, the Tall Man mimed the tipping of a hat, and barely tilted his head toward me. He smiled. Not a happy smile or an about-to-laugh smile, but a smile I can best describe as resolute. Then, he quickly turned and exited the building. To me, his intent was clear. The Tall Man had just thrown down the gauntlet.

Chapter 26

Jennifer

It threw him off. It didn't show much, but I know my husband better than anybody else does, and it definitely threw him when the tall guy from the *Free Us from Religion Coalition* walked out in the middle of Nathan's message.

Nathan was in a real *Prophet* mode, too. It doesn't happen every week, or anything, but once in a while he gets so close and so open to the Holy Spirit that it truly is God's words coming out of him. Happens to me in the middle of a prayer, from time to time. It is a glorious experience.

Anyway, I believe Nathan was in that place. We had all these new people in the church—some of whom did not come to church to worship, but to get a quote or a story, or even to discredit the goings-on at Triple-W. So, Nathan, being the wonder he is, shifted gears away from the sermon he spent so much time preparing and into the sermon those people needed to hear. He was in the zone and was laying out a compelling statement on the importance of God, when Alexander Stevens—I remembered his name because it seemed like he has two first names—did what he did. I think he wanted to cause Nathan trouble, without making it look like he did it on purpose. But he doesn't know who he's messing with. Not only is my husband a highly capable man all on his own, but recently he has become a powerful instrument of God. I know that. I don't think Nathan does, just yet, but that might be for the best. He's got me for that.

So, there was just a blip when the Tall Man walked out. A short pause. Nathan recovered and completed a stirring—both simple and complex—treatise on God. Perhaps it would be better described as *the case for God.*

Condi played more magnificent music. Anybody who walked into our church service thinking it was going to be some sort of a Podunk experience must have had quite a shock. I prayed. I don't like to comment on my own stuff, but I never felt closer to the Father, the Son and the Holy Spirit.

At one point Nathan took a pause and walked over to both side walls of the church, opening windows. "Let's all be silent for a couple of minutes," he said. Prayer poured into the church. In a manner of praying often referred to as *simultaneous* prayer, they were all praying different things at once. Nathan and I had never suggested or taught them how to do this. It was an emotional, moving experience.

After the service, I was surprised to see how many of the strangers and media personnel stuck around. We moved our social hour outside, picnic style. Thanks to Michelle Garner, we had plenty of punch and cookies for everybody, plus a giant urn of coffee. Regulars mixed with strangers. Questions were asked, but the mood was respectful and polite. For once the social hour actually lasted about an hour. Then, people gradually drifted away. The doers put away the chairs and cleaned up and restored the building to order.

When the rest were gone, Condi and Kevin remained, as did Frank and Sylvie. They approached Nathan and I in a manner that seemed unnaturally wary.

"You look kind of serious," Nathan said. "What's up?"

Frank answered, "Just lookin' to say our goodbyes. But, if it's alright, I'd like to say a prayer for our two pastors before we go."

"Of course," Nathan and I both replied.

In typical Frank style, he jumped right in. "Dear God in heaven," he started, "Father, Son and Holy Ghost; we pray to you today on behalf of our whole church family here at the Triple-W church, especially for these two here, Reverend Nathan and Reverend Jennifer."

I was growing rather tense and curious as to what was going on. This was not a common event. Frank seemed awfully earnest. He also was getting really good at praying out loud.

"There has been a lot of really good stuff happening here, God, and these two have done a magnificent job of leadin' and teachin' and bringin' us along. And, it was a good day today. Real good. I think there are bunch more people thinkin' seriously about you today than there was yesterday, and isn't that a wonderful thing. But here's the thing, God. This was just a start to somethin'. Somethin' real big. Somethin' you have chosen Pastor Nathan and Pastor Jennifer to do. I am not sure what it is, but I don't think they have even an inkling of how big, and maybe hard, this is about to get. Now, God, I'm just a dumb farmer, but you been teachin' me some stuff, too. You gave me the best wife in seven counties, and you yanked me right up front to read your holy scriptures. Nobody here even knows I could hardly read before, but now I can."

I started to tear up a bit. I admit I peeked and Sylvie was full-blown crying.

"I guess all I'm sayin' here, God, is if it seems you are usin' me for tellin' something, then you probably are. So, send your Holy Ghost on these two, real strong. Make sure they know the rest of us are with them. If me and Sylvie aren't right here by their side, it can only mean we're dead. And, even then, I figure. And Condi and Kevin here, wow, you really did some of your best work there."

I heard Condi gasp.

"So, whatever it is exactly, it's comin' and real soon. Get us all ready for the battle. And, just to be clear, God. We know the battle is yours, so it is already won. We just need to be strong enough to do our part. Anything else, Sylvie?"

"No, husband. You did good."

"Condi? Kevin?"

"No, Frank," Kevin said. "You did good."

"Well, alright, then. Thank you, God. Thanks for listenin'. Frank. Amen."

Chapter 27

Nathan

There are certain things I have learned, over and over again. I cannot understand why, as a pastor who has preached on God's mysterious ways hundreds of times, I cannot seem to remember the conclusion! I have preached the sermons and answered the questions about how God usually does not use the person who would be the most obvious choice—the smartest, the richest, the most powerful, the best looking, the most highly educated, whatever—to do His work or speak on His behalf. *No, sir!*, I have preached in a booming voice, God often chooses the unexpected, the untrained, the fearful, the tongue-tied to do great things and to deliver important news.

Still, it surprises me and takes me a few minutes to comprehend every time God uses a guy like Frank to speak life-changing truth. Frank—one of the best human beings I have ever known. Frank and Sylvie—the single finest couple I have ever known. And yet, when Frank prayed his powerful, straightforward prayer, it took a while for it to sink in. God had just spoken.

Frank and Sylvie and Condi and Kevin had already left by the time I started to get my mind around what had just happened. I think my darling Jennifer knew it would take me some time, so she just waited quietly by my side.

Finally, I asked her, "What do you make of that?"

"Just what he said," she whispered. "Frank's words don't usually need a lot of translation."

"No, they sure don't," I whispered back (we evidently thought loud voices might scare the moment away). "But . . ." I continued and then faltered.

"But, what, Honey?" she asked gently.

"What do you make of it?" I repeated, as if saying it again would somehow clarify my question.

I guess it did, because this time she answered, in a bigger much bolder voice, "I think we have been noticed. I think God has made what is going on here too big for anti-God forces to ignore. I think the atheists are coming for us. Not the regular, *I-don't-really-give-a-crap* atheists, but the organized atheists. The official, superior, card-carrying, academic intelligentsia, organized atheists are coming for us. Mostly for you. The Tall Man will be leading the pack. And, they mean business. They need us gone. They need us ended."

I almost responded with something sarcastic and clever, but all that actually came out was, "What else?"

Jennifer smirked. Then smiled. Then laughed. Out loud, she laughed.

"What is so funny?" I barked. "I'm kind of shook up over here."

"Me, too," she said through a still-too-big-for-my-taste grin. "I'm all shook up. I'm terrified. I am thinking a hundred thoughts at once, the good and the bad all mixed into one."

"Then stop laughing."

"No, I can't help but laugh. Don't you see, Nate? This is it. This is what the whole thing is about. All the way back to the long-closed broken down church on the corner. All the way back to the mystery man, Pastor Carl. This is the purpose of Triple-W! Don't you see?"

I saw. I just needed to ease into the magnitude of it.

"Yes, but give me a minute." She did. After a break, I started again, "Pastor Carl. The special, little church. A church that was to be powerful but never grow. The church that pretty much did everything to keep people away, except a special few. Condi and Kevin. Frank and Sylvie. Janice and Jane. Jeremy and Edwina and the rest."

"And you," Jennifer said. "You."

"And you," I replied. "You."

"Yes, You and I. We mustn't minimize it or shrink from it. God almost always puts someone at the head of the spear. And that, Most High Excellent Reverend Nathan Martin, is you."

"We use those terms to tease," I interrupted. "I don't think this is a time to be funny about . . ."

"Who's being funny?" she interrupted back. "God has chosen an ordinary man like you to be a whole other thing. Own it. What's coming will not be easy. It may be too much for us."

"Yes, us," I said. "Why am I the point of the spear. How about you?"

"Oh, I will be right at your side. Hear me. I will be strong. He has chosen me, as well. But you are at the head because God said so, and because you are the one they are coming for. You will be the symbol—the one who must be brought down."

"Then, we had better start thinking in terms of preparing for this. What do you think is coming? How bad will it get?"

Jennifer grew pensive and said, "I think it will be bad, worse than we can handle on our own. But I have no idea what is about to happen."

"Then we'd better prepare for anything. God is on our side."

"For sure," Jennifer said. "God is on our side. But it feels like He wants to use us to fight this battle. You and me, and all the others at Triple-W. I think much is expected of us."

"We will rise up and do our best," I said, "and another thing."

"What's that?" Jennifer asked.

"I don't think the other side has anything like a Frank!"

Chapter 28

Jennifer

Things went down fast after that. We started to receive incredible numbers of phone calls, texts and emails. Our little church building didn't really have an office. The phone number was just a cellphone. Usually, either Nathan or I would carry it around or just leave it on the counter at home. We had never received enough calls to worry about, but all of the sudden it rang day and night. Continuously. By the time one call was completed, the phone would be ringing again. The capacity of the system to store text messages and voicemails was maxed out several times a day. Our email account was filled with hundreds of messages each day. We couldn't begin to read them all, much less respond. We called an emergency meeting of certain Triple-W Members—Janice Pohl, Jane Petra, John and Shelley Drobena, Michelle Garner and Jeff Conway—who were savvy with that sort of thing. We also invited Alicia Skiba, who was not yet an official member of the church, but seemed uniquely qualified to help, given her reporter status.

After explaining the situation to the group, I asked, "So what do we do?"

Jeff said, "I would like to know more about the content or purpose of all these communications? What do they want?"

"It varies quite a bit," Nathan answered. "I would guesstimate about fifty percent of them want prayers for some problem or illness or whatever. They evidently feel we can offer more powerful prayers than they can."

The group nodded their heads to indicate that seemed like a good thing.

"I'll bet it is closer to sixty percent," I jumped in.

"Okay. Sixty," Nathan said. "Another fifteen percent are positive, congratulatory, go-get-'em church kind of messages."

"And the rest?" Michelle asked.

"What do you think?" Nathan asked, looking straight at me. "Fifteen and Ten or Ten and Fifteen?"

I answered, "Call it twelve and a half and twelve and a half."

"Fair enough," he said. "Twelve and a half percent are other Christians telling us how wrong and misguided and ungodly we are . . ."

"Figures," John chipped in.

"And," Nathan continued, "the final twelve and a half are atheists—some of them polite and cerebral, others spewing spews and ranting rants about the evils of religion of any sort."

"That's quite a mix," Janice added. "I think what we do depends on what you want to accomplish. If we wish to become a ministry for prayer concerns—or, more correctly, if God wants us to do that—then we power up and staff up and get to work. More phone lines, more email addresses, more phones, computers, whatever it takes. And, more people, a group of people dedicated to this stuff."

"What are the other choices?" Shelley asked, then let out a nervous giggle.

Janice kept right on going. "Probably the next likely choice, again, depending on how God is moving us, is to do nothing. Ignore it. Sooner or later people will figure out they are not going to get a personal answer, and it will stop."

"There is more to consider before we start to narrow this down," Jane offered. "I think you two pastors have left a significant part out of the mix. Sorry, don't mean to criticize. I read through a bunch of those messages and every so often there's one from media people, including some big ones. Newspapers and blogs and news sites and TV shows and magazines. They want time and appearances and even debates. I saw Oprah Winfrey's network in there! And *Time* magazine! And Dr. Phil! Who knows who all is trying to get ahold of you? What do we do with that?"

"Nathan and I have discussed that," I said. "So far, we feel like we need to avoid a big public splash."

"Too late for that," Jeff chimed in. "Our audience is already far greater than any of those people."

"Yes, I suppose that's true," Nathan replied. "But it would still be a whole other level of exposure—the kind that can easily look like sensationalism and self-aggrandizement."

"So?" John said. "Why would we worry about that?"

As Nathan was about to respond, I decided to jump in.

"Alicia? What's your take on this?"

Nathan looked a bit perturbed, but I really wanted to get the discussion on a different tack.

"Well, from what I have observed, this is the point where somebody usually says, 'Let's discern what God wants and do exactly that!'"

There were slightly embarrassed nods all around.

"That said," Alicia continued, "I have a few thoughts. First, I think one, limited way for people to make contact with us—do you mind if I say *us* . . .?

Everyone smiled and affirmed Alicia's status.

She smiled hugely and continued, ". . . we could and probably should do that. So, maybe an email account set up to receive and answer questions and provide prayers. Prayer requests could be added to a master list, and then a prayer team could pray for both individual requests and in a more general way, to keep up with the demand. Other kinds of requests could be redirected or deleted."

"The haters and the complainers need to be on the prayer list," Michelle said softly. I was so proud of her just then.

"Of course," Alicia continued. "Whatever is decided becomes a sort of protocol. I think a handful of people and a couple new computers could handle quite a bit that way. You can even answer people by letting them know they are being prayed for—without the need to craft thousands of individual responses."

"This is going to cost money," Jeff said. "Are we okay there?"

Alicia jumped right back in, "If we include a mailing address at the bottom of our email responses, all kinds of money will come in. We don't even need to mention it."

"You sure?" Jeff asked.

Alicia grinned and said, "Strangely, yes, I am sure."

Nathan spoke up, "Let's take a few minutes and pray about this. Honey?"

I prayed. It felt good and right and comfortable. Everyone else agreed and we put a plan in place. As it appeared the meeting was about to disperse, Jane spoke up.

"What about the other part? The media requests and such? It seems like a huge opportunity to get God's word out. When was the last time the media was all hot to talk about religion?"

"Nathan," I said. "What are you thinking? It's you they're going to want front and center."

I thought about Pastor Carl, and I knew Nathan was thinking about him, too. Pastor Carl was the last person who would ever seek the limelight, but he was also the last person who would refuse any request from God. He passed that on to my husband.

Nathan took a very long pause. He learned that from Pastor Carl, too. Never rush. Practice patience. Listen. Give God time to speak.

"I'm not sure," Nathan finally said. "I do know we have to do things in a way that allows time for God to be clear with us. Alicia, what do you think?"

"In addition to being open to what God wants," she began somewhat hesitantly, "I recommend we control the narrative, so to speak. There are people out there who want to seek out the truth, and maybe even to be helpful to the cause. But—and this goes double for you, Pastor Nathan and Pastor Jennifer—there will be those who are out to get you. You might even say out to get God. Putting an event or an interview or a debate in the wrong hands could turn out badly. If God . . . indicates . . . you should take any of these people on publicly, we want to maintain some control."

"Then it is settled," I said emphatically. "All media requests will be funneled through Alicia, our new Press Liaison."

Chapter 29

Nathan

I had a lot on my mind. I felt crushed under the weight of too many choices and too much confusion. I wasn't talking. We'd only been home for a few minutes, but I knew if I didn't cheer up and start some sort of a witty conversation real soon, Jennifer was going to be asking, *What's wrong? Are you okay?* And, I didn't have legitimate answers for those questions. I did not feel entirely okay, but I really had no idea what was wrong. What was I supposed to say?

"This must be very hard for you," Jenn said, handing me a Diet Coke.

She must have felt something was terribly the matter—she was willingly supplying me with the banned beverage!

She didn't wait for a response. She just kept talking. "I think it is a rare person who has ever been subjected to such an onslaught of pressures and stressors and questions and choices all at the same time. No one I've ever known, that's for sure."

"How about you?" I interrupted. "Everything that is coming at me is coming at you, too."

"That's true," she answered. "At least, almost true. We'll get back to that, believe me. But, let me finish, first. You are committed to follow God's will, but you aren't sure exactly what that is, especially when the situations and opportunities are flying in right and left! Millions of people—tens of millions of people—

are hanging all over everything we say and do. I tell you, Nathan, if I let myself stop and think about what I actually feel, I'm going to keel right over."

"You, too?" I whispered.

"Of course," she said. "A lot of them are our friends, but there are plenty who are not. You must be shuddering at the very idea of smart, powerful people gearing up to tear you and our church down to size. Maybe even destroy it! And they figure they can discredit religion, the Bible and even God if they can discredit us. I feel it, too, but they are coming after us through you. You get that, right?"

"Well, yeah, but now you're scaring me!"

"Good. Fear is motivation. And the uncertainty! Do we just keep preaching and teaching, and let the chips fall where they may? Do we answer all that mail? What about the big-time media? Do we grab the opportunity—the forum? Oprah! Dr. Phil! *Time* magazine! Who knows who else? I'll tell you this, my dear husband, you can write your own ticket. There isn't a media outlet in the world who won't put you on the air or in print, right now."

"Can that be true?" I asked.

"No, it can't be true, except it is. That's part of the rush of it all. Things that cannot be are happening anyway, right now. Things we couldn't even have dreamed just a few months ago. This must be what it felt like to go to bed just a regular nobody and wake up to find out you are Elvis, or the Beatles, or Mohammed Ali!"

"Yes!" I blurted. "But I think they wanted to be famous. I didn't ask for this. And what about you? You're an integral part of what has happened. And Condi and . . . and even Frank and Sylvie!"

"They will not be forgotten. But they will always take their cue from you, as will I."

"What if I can't? What if I don't want to? What if I try . . . and fail? What about that?"

Jenn looked at me and smiled. Jenn could communicate a great number of things with smiles. I don't know how much she was aware of what she was putting out, or if she was just so in touch with her feelings and her relationship with God that a certain smile, perfect for the occasion, would just happen. Anyway, her smile told me she was pleased. She was content. She knew she had just helped me get where I needed to be. She knew she had served her God well and had been granted surety and certainty for her soul.

"Those are the hard questions for you, aren't they Sweetheart?" she said. "But the answers are easy. God has called you to do this, and so you can. He has called you to do this, and so it does not matter if you want to. You will. You will give it your all, because that is what you have promised. As for the results—what is or feels like success, or what is or feels like failure—that is up to God. You are not to worry about the results, not before, during or after. God has reserved that to Himself."

"Pastor Carl taught me that same lesson," I said, "and here I have to learn it all over again."

"Then, God gave you Pastor Carl. Now, He has given you me."

"God is Good," I said.

"All the time," Jenn replied. "Now, are we set to go? I'm hungry."

Chapter 30

Jennifer

"I am absolutely shocked," Alicia said, "it simply does not work this way, but it did. They contacted us about a hundred times," she continued. "*Time* magazine is still bigtime. They wouldn't usually be so persistent regarding a story about unknowns. But I did a conference call with them. They want that story. I informed them I was not going to allow—how about that, the likes of me telling *Time* what I was going to allow! Anyway, I told them I was not going to let somebody who didn't really understand this complicated, nuanced story do an interview and then write a chopped-up article that didn't get to any of the important points about our movement."

"So, what did they do then, Alicia?" I asked, even though I already knew the answer.

"They offered me five thousand dollars to write the article myself! A thousand words! Me! They just wouldn't hire somebody involved in the story to write the story, but they did, right there on the spot!"

"What did you tell them?" I asked.

I told them I would have to get back to them! I wouldn't do anything like that without checking with Triple-W first. Especially you and Pastor Nathan. And, the Chronicle. I do have a writer's job."

"What did they say at the paper?" I asked.

"I was worried, but they were pretty excited. They said as long as the byline read *Alicia Skiba, Muskegon Chronicle Staff Reporter,* I should go for it."

"Excellent," I said. "As far as we are concerned, you are free to do whatever you decide God is leading you to do, just like the rest of us. We don't tell Condi or Frank or anybody else what they can and cannot do. That's part of our deal."

"Okay, but I am way new to this. I don't know what God is telling me."

"I'll bet you do," I responded. "Did you think this up yourself? Was this your own idea?"

"No. Never crossed my mind until it happened."

"Was your first thought how rich and famous you were going to be?"

After a long, contemplative pause, Alicia said, "Actually, no. I admit I did a little of that, later, but my first thought was it would be such a great story to tell, because things like this just don't come around every day."

"And?" I asked.

"And, maybe I could do something that would help you guys, and maybe even make a difference in the world."

"And?" I persisted.

"I am not sure I can say it," she said, quietly.

"Of course you can," I said, and waited.

Eventually, she spoke softly, "Maybe I could make God happy."

Alicia agreed to write that article, and she did. The whole process only took a couple of weeks. While our saga continued— more millions of views, thousands of emails, most of them getting answers from our new team of responders, and continued praise and worship—Alicia wrote her story and turned it in to *Time*. She asked Nathan and me to proof it first, but we flatly refused. This was now part of Alicia's ministry. Soon, we got word that the article would be published in the next issue, which would be sent early to Alicia.

We all agreed that, as hard as it would be to do, the core church body would gather to read it together.

The big day came. We were all in the church. I prayed a short prayer, then said, "Well, Alicia, the honor belongs to you. Let's hear it."

She tore the mailing envelope open, as excited as any child on Christmas morning. She opened the cover and found the Contents page.

"There it is!" she all-but-squealed. "*A Post-Modern Awakening*, by Alicia Skiba, Staff Reporter, *Muskegon Chronicle*," she read. "I'm so excited! I can't tell you how much I appreciate all . . ."

Midsentence, her demeaner changed completely. Her face went slack and she took on a countenance of . . . dread. At least, it looked like dread.

"Go on ahead, then!" Frank barked through a big grin.

"Shush, husband," Sylvie whispered while she grabbed Frank's arm and squeezed. "Shush. Something's wrong."

"There's . . ." Alicia started and stopped. "There's another . . . I didn't know . . . Oh my. . . I'm sorry . . . I should have known it was too perfect . . ."

"Tell us," Nathan said calmly. "Whatever it is, it's all right. We are all in this together."

"I think I messed up, bad," she said.

"Then you are in just the right place," Nathan continued, "surrounded by people who love you. Go on."

Alicia took a deep breath, choked back rapidly rising tears and said, "There is another article listed, right after mine." She read, "*Freedom from Nonsense*, by Alexander Stevens, Executive Director, *Free Us from Religion Coalition*."

As soon as she completed the sentence, she lost her battle with tears and began to sob. Alicia was surrounded with hugs and reassurances she had done nothing wrong. After a few minutes she seemed recomposed.

"Well," I said, "obviously *Time* did not choose to let you in on their entire agenda. Kind of sneaky. But, still, they published your article, and I, for one, am anxious to hear it."

"What about the one from that Stevens character?" Alicia asked, through remaining sniffles.

"We will deal with that eventually," Nathan broke in, "but it is not going to ruin our excitement for what you have accomplished. Let's hear it."

"Okay," Alicia said, took a deep breath, and started to read:

A Post-Modern Awakening by Alicia Skiba. As I write this, it is June 2rd, 2018. Just a little over a year ago—though it seems much longer—I was a young, very inexperienced freelance writer, just trying to write something I might sell for any amount of money, to, well, anybody. I had no real resume' and desperately wanted to build one. Living in Western Lower Michigan, near Grand Rapids, I was in a decidedly small market. However, after poking around a bit, I eventually came across a situation that seemed juicy enough to fit the bill.

In East Fork, Michigan—a small, upper middle-class town a few miles outside of Grand Rapids—a feud had erupted between a rich and powerful church member and the appointed pastor of the *East Fork First United Methodist Church*, the Reverend Nathan Martin. Eventually the ringleader and his cronies expanded the conflict to include the entire hierarchy of the United Methodist denomination, the second largest organization of Protestants in the United States. Accusations, insinuations and outright lies were leveled at Reverend Martin and the UMC. Like a lot of people in my generation, I was suspicious and uneasy with religion and religious claims. So, in an episode of my life which brings me nothing but shame and embarrassment, I picked up on those unfair allegations and wrote a speculative and derogatory story about the Reverend. One might assume Pastor Nathan Martin would be angry with me, hate me, do his best to discredit me and refute my claims.

However, instead he invited me to meet with him and talk. I was anxiety-ridden walking into that meeting. I assumed he was going to read me the riot act. But he did not. He was kind. He was forgiving. He was calm—even relaxed. Amazingly, he made no effort to defend himself. Instead, he showed interest in me. I had rarely, if ever, experienced this kind of treatment. When we talked about my writing a follow-up article, he didn't try to influence me at all! He said I should write whatever I thought was good and right and true.

My life was changed by Reverend Martin's reaction. I still wasn't sure what I thought about religious matters. I didn't suddenly become an active Christian. But I knew something was going on that did not even resemble the accusations being thrown about. I wrote one more story explaining exactly that, but I also withdrew from any more writing on that conflict.

Fast forwarding to recent times. Reverend Nathan Martin left the *United Methodist Church*. He and his wife, Jennifer Martin, were led by an influential, devout, somewhat mysterious man, called Pastor Carl, to reopen a tiny country church that had been closed for over twenty years. They did so. The church ordained Jennifer to clergy status. Upon the public announcement the *WWWGod Christian Church* was open, with the intention of being a small but powerful force for God's Kingdom, a first-Sunday congregation of forty-one people showed up. Several of the charter members had followed the Martins from the East Fork UMC, while others were brand new faces, moved to give the new venture a try. The first few weeks brought ups and downs, fits and starts and seeming gains and losses.

At this point it would have been inconceivable this little church on a four-corners with corn fields would be featured in an article in *Time* magazine. However, things changed. Big time. Reverends Nathan and Jennifer, along with key people like Condi and Frank and Sylvie—names millions of Americans and others around the world already know—decided to stick with their roots of a small church with powerful influence. They went online, 24/365. They catered to no one but God.

They prayed and preached and played glorious music and read scripture aloud, whenever they felt moved to do so. No schedule. No advertising. No pleas for money. Just honoring God, teaching about God, offering praise and worship. Most incredibly, they did all this while purposely not worrying or caring what others thought about it.

Then, the unthinkable happened. Perhaps unfathomable is a better word. What was happening at the Triple-W church—as it has become popularly called—became big news. Hundreds accessed the continuous livestream, not just for Sunday services, but all of the unscheduled, unannounced practices and prayer sessions and readings and music rehearsals that were too wonderful to be called just a rehearsal. How could that even happen? Hard to explain. Then the count was thousands, then hundreds of thousands, then millions. New equipment was added to keep up with the counts and locations. Soon there were people tuned in from all fifty states and dozens of countries. Twenty million, then thirty and forty and fifty million. Now, even more. What couldn't happen... happened.

Soon the world's media caught on. TV talk shows and celebrity interviewers and newspapers, blogs and magazines—such as *Time*—all wanted the story, even if they couldn't quite get a handle on what the story was. A world that appears by all measures to be moving away from religion, is all agog for a tiny church in a cornfield—and the very special people who congregate there. It appears the world still seeks guidance, inspiration, hope... and God. And, they want the *WWWGod Christian Church* to show them the way.

What does it all mean? Where is this heading? While I sure wish I could be the one to explain this phenomenal happening to the rest of the world, I cannot. Not even the esteemed (the Martins are exceptional people; unlike any I have ever known) Reverends Martin know! You see, part of their secret (if there is a secret) is their ability to engage God in the moment, doing as He moves them to do, speaking God's wishes, praising Him all along the way, and doing their best to not worry or even think about the results. 'Leave the results to God,' is commonly heard at the *WWWGod Christian Church*. So, what is next remains a wonderful mystery.

I have used up my allowed word count. I will close with this. I am not a religious scholar. I know nothing of theology or doctrine or biblical criticism. My knowledge of organized religion is both narrow and shallow. But, in ways I cannot yet explain, my life has changed. What I am focused on is new. What I care about is new. I am new. And this thing that is happening in that little building in Michigan? I am confident of this—it is a God-Thing, as unfettered by human interference as we are ever likely to see.

There was a poignant, pregnant pause, but it didn't last long.

"That was real good!" Frank exclaimed. "You shouldn't be crying over that. You did good!"

"My husband is right," Sylvie added, "even though I know you weren't exactly crying about your own article. But he's right, it is real good."

"Thank you," Alicia said between sniffles.

"It was lovely," I added. "You have done us all proud, even though you might have been overly kind and generous in your descriptions. Let me check with the group—is anybody here upset with Alicia?"

Covered in a cascade of "No!" "Of course not!" and other affirming exclamations, Alicia was engulfed in a giant group hug.

As the group sort of came back to itself, Kevin spoke up. "I love you, Alicia. We all do. But I think all of us know we are going to have to hear the other article."

Chapter 31

Nathan

"Kevin is right," I said. "Alicia, you are one of us, so dealing with things as they come along is part of the deal. Just be sure you understand no one blames you for anything this yahoo wrote. *Time* gave you space, and *Time* gave him space. That's fine. We aren't hiding from anything, and God sure isn't. Might well be God has something He wants said right now, for purposes only He knows. Alicia, do you want to read it, or would you rather ask Jennifer?"

"Would you mind, Pastor Jennifer?" Alicia asked.

"Of course I don't mind," she replied. "You just relax a little bit."

I took notice of how comfortable I had become with throwing things in my wife's direction, in full confidence she could and would handle whatever came along. That felt good.

"Maybe everybody should sit down," Jennifer started, "and let's have a short prayer." After the people had arranged themselves, Jennifer closed her eyes and said, "Dear Heavenly Father, you are our God and we are your people. Isn't that a good and wonderful thing. We aren't going to like what we are about to hear. We already know that, but to serve your purposes we need to hear it. Strengthen us in our faith, and open our ears, that we might better understand things we need to understand. In Jesus' name we pray. Amen."

Then, Jennifer began to read:

> Freedom from Nonsense, by Alexander Stevens, Executive Director, *Free Us from Religion Coalition*. I am Alexander Stevens. I have had a successful career as an attorney and corporate consultant. My degrees are a bachelor's from Central Michigan University, an MBA from the Wharton School of Business and a law degree from Harvard Law. While my ongoing career is fulfilling and lucrative, my true passion for the past fifteen years is my role as Executive Director of the *Free Us from Religion Coalition*. Our stated goal is to remove the blight of religion—most especially Christianity—from all public discourse. Of particular concern is the elimination of Christian influence on public and governmental policy.
>
> It is 2018. I am amazed and somewhat befuddled that we, as a society and as a country, still have to have this conversation. Time, enlightenment and simple logic would seem to make the demise of superstition and magical thinking inevitable. And yet, still today, we find our society continues to be plagued with such nonsense, both officially and unofficially. I do not seek the criminalization of religion, only that all expressions of it be mandated a private matter. We are fortunate to be living in a free country, and so must respect the rights of people to believe whatever they wish, no matter how misguided. However, I am convinced the world would be a better place for all the people in it, with far less religion and far more secularism—science and fact and proof.
>
> Despite how obvious this seems, we find ourselves not only still hip-deep in the battle to keep religion out of public policy, but facing evidence of a resurgence in Christian influence. After decades of slow but steady progress in limiting religious participation and church attendance, the advent of social media has served the Christian Agenda well. I say without apology: religion is foolhardy, nonsensical and dangerous. To ultimately perfect our society through humanist efforts, we must get religion out of the way.

One might reasonably ask, 'What harm can religion do? Does it not benefit our society and make the world a better place?' I will answer that.

It is easy to become a Christian. It only requires one basic principle. All you have to do is give up your ability to think. Religious belief is the death of intelligent thought. Once you give up on thinking, it is not so hard to insist we are created and not evolved, no matter how strong the evidence for evolution. With no critical thought one can call it a good thing to scare children with tales of hellfire and eternal punishment, both for themselves and for everybody they love who won't get in line with the claims of the church. Furthermore, it becomes a good thing to insist a certain book of legend and myth, a book of unevidenced claims and falsehoods, is really the work of God and therefore is always right and cannot be questioned or argued against. If one does not think, but merely relies on irrational, unevidenced belief in the impossible, and faith that an eternal, celestial, all-powerful, divine puppet master really exists and has every right to boss us around, judge us and punish us at his every whim, it becomes not only possible but easy to be a Christian. If one person believed all of this nonsense, they would be called delusional and would be treated for mental illness. But, because many people believe it, we dub it a religion.

I cannot, nor am I trying to, deny people their right to believe nonsense. But I do not want to allow my society to be infected with it. The reasons—perhaps better described as the dangers—are many. In a world growing more and more to value inclusivity, Christianity seeks to proclaim good and wonder to the pinnacle of exclusivity. We are right and you are wrong. We are in and you are out. We will live forever in heavenly splendor and you will live forever in the burning agony of hell. They won't even let us just die and be done with it.

We keep on being told religion, whatever its imperfections, at least instills morality. In fact, the claim is often made that without religion, we would have no morality. First, there is a great deal of conclusive evidence that the practice of so-called Christian morality is a dangerous proposition. I haven't words enough in this article to detail the wars and starvation and persecutions and death and suffering that has been caused over the years by religious claims and demands—but we all know it is true. Religion makes people meaner and more justified in their practice of hatred. Furthermore, we do not need to invent a god to create a moral code. Our humanity—our human intellect—is more than sufficient to determine right from wrong, good from evil and love from hate. We do not need a celestial dictator to tell us how to live a good and proper life. We human beings can, and often do, go into the world and do good for those in need, without beating them about the head and shoulders with a Bible and insisting if they ever want to live a good life like us, they had better bow down to a peasant who supposedly lived and died and lived again two thousand years ago in the Middle East. A society freed from the effects of religion stands the better chance of developing a consistent and beneficial code of living.

I have often heard it argued God is loving and perfect, and the only reason the Church is not loving and perfect is because the people who make up the Church are human and imperfect. That religion—I'm talking particularly Christianity—is often good, and has the potential to be always good. Firstly, I certainly do not deny that some good comes out of the church. It does. However, not only does the bad outweigh the good, but the good could have been more easily accomplished without the Church! But I am always willing to consider a proposition. So, what would it take for the Church to become good? For religion to become a good thing now—something we have not yet seen, but hypothetically, at least—I submit the first thing that would have to happen would for said religion to give up all supernatural claims. Smart, educated, thinking people know miracles—things that happen totally unfettered by the laws of the natural world and science—cannot, by definition, happen. Even the most befuddling events—if they actually happened—can ultimately be explained by science. As long as those who claim religion as their source of power, strength and understanding continue to believe in and proclaim the impossible, they can never be taken seriously. Furthermore, the very notion of an eternal, all-powerful, controlling authority figure who serves as judge, jury and executioner—with no human right of appeal or even argument—would have to be summarily discredited and dropped, should the religious folks expect to receive respect and credibility.

Can these things happen and even retain something that is anything like a religion? No. And so, I reject religion. I find it easy to reject. That which is claimed without evidence, can be dismissed without evidence. Religious claims—being so outlandish—would require strong evidence, and yet there is none. And so, I am an atheist. Proudly so. The *Free Us from Religion Coalition* is filled with people like me, and we will battle, litigate, debate, argue and discredit religion, and its negative effects on society, until the conversation becomes unnecessary. As our cherished freedoms ensure the right of religious people to believe and practice whatever they choose, so those same freedoms protect our right to speak out against nonsense and for science and reason.

When Jennifer stopped reading the entire group sat for a long time, stunned into silence. Not even Frank could figure out what to say right away.

Janice broke the quiet. "His article was longer than ours," she said. There were a few giggles.

"I have never heard such pointed, unapologetic criticism of God and the Church," Jane said. "Not ever."

"Doesn't that guy know God is listening?" Frank said. "Man, I'd be nervous if I was him."

"Is that even legal?" Sylvie asked.

"Yes," I said, "Stevens was right about that part. Just as the First Amendment stops anybody from trying to censure what we say on God's behalf, it stops us from trying to censure what anyone might say against Him. It's not so much about having the right to say things, but whether they should be said. We believe we are right in what we say. I am sure Stevens thinks he is right, too."

"Well, he's wrong!" Frank barked.

"Of course he is," Jennifer said softly. "Everybody here knows that. However, that does not change what we are looking at here."

"What do you think we are looking at, Pastor Jennifer?" Kevin asked.

"I admit I am not sure, except Stevens—and *Time* magazine I suppose—have thrown down the gauntlet. They're dying to either discredit us all at once, or draw us into a fight. What do you think, Nathan?"

"I think you're right. They want a fight and all the attention we have been getting lately has made us the obvious target."

"Us, yes, but mostly you," Alicia pointed out. "You are the face of our movement, and Stevens is the face of his. He wants to fight you in the most public way. It will be hard to hold him off for long. The public will want to know why you don't stand up to him."

As I pondered in silence for a few moments, Edwina Fine spoke up. "Way back in the Old Testament Goliath made the mistake of thinking he was taking on young David, and by the time he realized he was fighting God, it was over."

She was laughing.

Chapter 32

Jennifer

The articles in *Time* magazine had the same effect as throwing gas on an already roaring fire. The level of craziness jumped up a few more levels. Our already upgraded equipment could not even measure the number of views coming in. Every device we had was overloaded with emails and texts and tweets and phone calls. Even good old-fashioned snail mail exploded. The post office took to delivering several times a day. We gathered most of the membership together in the attempt to stay ahead of it, but after a couple of days we mostly gave up. We did manage to open all the envelopes and packages. They contained blessings and donations in almost equal numbers with threats and complaints. We held on as best we could, but by the fourth day after *Time* hit the public, we were overwhelmed.

Nathan returned to our little church building—I hadn't even seen him leave. He had an armload of grocery bags.

"Everybody!" Nathan shouted, "stop whatever you are doing and gather around!"

As the group followed instructions, Nathan continued yelling like a maniac, laughing at the same time.

"Ice cream! Fudge! Sprinkles! Whipped cream!" he hollered. "This occasion calls for ice cream!"

As everyone moved quickly to the table where Nathan had thrown down his wares—smiles and laughter all around—Frank yelled, "What occasion is that, Pastor?"

"This is the day the Lord has made!" Nathan replied boisterously. "Let us rejoice and have ice cream in it!"

"Okay, Honey," I said. "We're all on board for ice cream, but why the celebration?"

He calmed himself a bit and smiled. "This is out of our control," he said. "You are all fantastic warriors for God," he continued, now addressing the entire group, "but we are acting like we can handle this if we work hard enough. We can't. So, let's eat ice cream."

"Now he's got it!" giggled Edwina. "I'll take two scoops with double fudge and sprinkles. No whipped cream. I'm watching my figure."

It was the best impromptu ice cream social ever. As we finally slowed down and people each found a place to sit and try to digest, Jeremy—still the youngest of us—walked in. I guess he had gone out to try to walk off the huge banana split he had just inhaled.

"Something is happening outside," he said. "There's tractors and a big earthmover out there."

"Here?" someone asked.

"No. Across the road, in the old cornfield. I've never seen anyone do anything over there."

Most of the group started to move. A couple couldn't seem to accomplish that and stayed where they were. Soon we were pouring out the front door and lined up across our parking lot. Sure enough, right across the road three huge machines were working away.

"What are they doing?" Kevin asked, looking directly at Frank. Frank would know.

"Gimme a minute," Frank answered. A good five minutes later, after watching the iron monsters working methodically back and forth, he announced, "One's brush-hoggin'—cutting everything down—and the other is pickin' up the heavy stuff and pilin' it way back from the road. The big one has his bucket up but is draggin' a roller—a big one. They're levelin' it. There's forty acres over there and it looks like they mean to level the whole thing."

"Why would they do that, husband?" Sylvie quietly asked. "Why would somebody level a cornfield but not plow it or disc it?" Sylvie knew her stuff, too.

"Well, nobody would probably do that," he said. "About the only good it would do you is so you could walk on it. Or drive on it."

Just then Kevin rejoined the group, turning off his cell phone and putting it back in his pocket.

"I talked to my guy at the bank. He did some calling around and found out that land was sold two days ago. It was a blind sale. Can't say who owns it now."

It didn't take long to find out. We were still staring at the operation going on across the road, when a small caravan pulled up. There was a truck with *West Michigan Signs and Fence* emblazoned on the side. Right behind that was a big, black, almost limousine kind of car. Bringing up the rear was a huge truck outfitted with heavy duty drilling equipment. You didn't need a sign to tell what it was, but it did say *Riegler Well Drillers* on the doors. After they parked, a very tall man exited the car and began pointing and gesturing and giving orders. We just stood and watched, not sure what else to do. The two men pulled a surprisingly large sign out of the smaller truck and—following the Tall Man's directions—pointed the sign directly at us and started to pound the heavy metal stakes into the ground. The sign read, *"Future Home of the Free Us from Religion Coalition . . . Freeing Society through Science, Wisdom and Reason.*

The Tall Man—Alexander Stevens—had yet to look at us or even turn his head toward us. But, as soon as the sign was in place, he directed the well drillers to three spots on the property—the east end, the west and the center—and shouted, "Time is wasting! Let's get started!"

Then, he walked determinedly to the sign, framed it with his arms just like Vanna White, turned slowly toward us, and smiled.

I admit his little show hit me like a ton of bricks. *What in heaven's name was this all about?* I panicked a bit. Truth is, the Tall Man scared me. I did my best to not show my fear, but the whole group sucked in a collective breath, and an atmosphere of dread was palpable. I tried desperately to come up with a quick quip, but came up empty. Then I saw my husband moving, not away, but toward the source of our discomfort.

"Follow me," he said quietly and firmly.

He strode purposefully across the road, me at his side and the rest lagging behind, but moving.

As Nathan drew near his adversary, he extended his hand and proclaimed, "Welcome, neighbor!"

Chapter 33

Nathan

The Tall Man was trying to scare us. He was trying to establish the upper hand. He knew it. I knew it. And, truth be told, it worked. When he looked directly at us and showed that wicked grin of his, I immediately experienced a rush of some combination of fear and dread and shock. I was afraid I was going to melt down right there in front of my own church, in front of several of the most active members.

But, within seconds I flashed back to a conversation I once had with Pastor Carl. Pastor Carl was a rock. My rock. In addition to Jesus, I mean. One day we were working on the interior walls of the church—sanding and staining. I was telling him about the trials that were going on at the East Fork UMC. I admitted I was very nervous about an upcoming confrontation with my main nemesis, businessman Bob Williams. Williams had launched an all-out effort to have me removed as pastor and was willing to say and do almost anything to make it happen.

I have a question for you, Pastor Carl had said. *What is the difference between doing the right thing and doing the right thing when you are afraid?*

I remember I was framing an elegant answer, when he interrupted me. *Nothing,* he said. *There is no difference at all.* Then he just kept on sanding the wood.

I heard *follow me* come out of my own mouth. By the time I walked across the road, hoping someone was following, my fear was gone. It felt like the Holy Spirit was leading me, so I marched right up to Alexander Stevens and offered my hand. I am just under six feet tall, but I felt like I was looking up at a skyscraper. Man, that guy is tall!

"Welcome neighbor!" I exclaimed.

The Tall Man froze. It only lasted a second, but I saw it. I am not sure what he expected would happen in this moment. I imagine he had visualized a scenario in his head whereby all of us ignorant, religious folk would panic and cave at the sight of his bold action. Our response left him, at the very least, confused.

"Well . . . ah . . . good morning," he said, doing his best to crush my right hand. "I guess, technically at least, co-existing so close together could be construed as being neighbors."

"Mr. Stevens," I heard my wife chime in, "you would be our neighbor no matter how close or far you might be."

She is quick.

"So, what ya buildin'?" Frank asked.

Stevens finally let go of my hand. "Well, eventually we plan on several buildings, sort of a world headquarters for logic and reason . . ." He was recovering fast. " . . . but right now, we are turning it into an outdoor meeting place, sort of a center for rallies and such."

"I see," Frank went on, "so that's what the wells are for, gonna get some water and bathrooms in here. Well . . ."

"Excuse me," the Tall Man broke in, rather too loudly, I thought. "I am not sure you people are fully comprehending the nature of what is about to happen here. I . . ."

It was my turn to interrupt. "Mr. Stevens," I said, "you may not understand our reactions, but, rest assured, we know exactly what it is you are trying to do here."

He stepped closer to me. Too close. I'm sure using height to intimidate was a common practice of his. I stepped back, in a dramatic and exaggerated fashion. He moved in. I stepped back. His face flushed red and he burst out, "I have important things to do and a tight schedule. Good day."

He turned abruptly, marched to his car, got in and drove away. As I turned back to my people, the first thing that caught my eye was Edwina Fine holding tightly to young Jeremy's arm. She was grinning like the Cheshire Cat.

Chapter 34

Jennifer

I love my husband, and I have always been proud of him. I admit an extra level of pride as I watched the Tall Man drive away. Stevens was as arrogant as they come, but he had no idea who he was messing with. Not only was he completely oblivious to what it means to challenge God, but he was also underestimating Nathan.

After I got done admiring my husband, I noticed something going on with Edwina. When I first met her I found her to be just a sweet old Christian lady. Maybe I simply assumed that. But as the weeks and months passed, I discovered her to be insightful, wise and a real hoot.

"You seem to be enjoying yourself, Edwina," I said. "Why aren't you as scared as I was?"

"Oh," she said through a big grin, "that character can't scare an old bird like me. At my age, whatever happens, I won't have to put up with it for long. I've got my bags packed for heaven and I'm ready to go."

"Still," I said, laughing a bit myself, "you seem to be having a good time here and now."

"I am! I spent a lot of years in my rocking chair, reading my Bible and praying for all sorts of things. I still do. But it sure feels good to be out here on the front lines."

"The front lines?" Jane asked. "I guess I never thought of this in military terms."

"I don't know about military, exactly," Edwina continued, "but there is definitely a time for war and a time for peace, and I think we have a battle on our hands. I have sung the hymn *Stand Up, Stand Up for Jesus* a hundred times and now I get to actually stand up. I'm liking it."

All the others looked to Nathan and then to me.

"She's not wrong," Nathan said.

I added, "But we shouldn't forget, God loves the people we're battling with, and so should we. We all hope that in the end, everyone is closer to Him than they were before. Even Stevens."

"Besides," Edwina went on, "God will do the heavy lifting. We just need to be open to Him and do and say what He wants."

"Conduit!" Frank bellowed. "We're conduit for God!"

Nathan laughed and said, "That'll preach!"

With a sort of collective shrug of the shoulders and a few more laughs, we meandered back to our side of the road.

"What now?" someone asked.

"Nothing has changed," Nathan answered. "We pray, we answer mail, we pay the bills, we play, read scripture and sing and preach."

"We are who we are," I added, "God's people and disciples of Jesus. No bully is going to change that."

"We need to be stronger than ever, so all we need to do is stay close to God," Nathan concluded.

Edwina hugged me and then Nathan. "You're good kids," she said each time.

In that moment, I felt strong.

So, we did our best to get back to what had become our routines. However, we were still overwhelmed by the mail, email, texts—we even got a few telegrams. The sheer tonnage of prayer requests, questions, donations, accusations and threats was more than we could deal with. Our ice cream break had only put us further behind. For a few days we just tried to peddle faster. We banked the donations, answered every question we could and prayed bigger and broader prayers.

Once in a while we would take a break and wander into the front lot of the Triple-W church and sneak a look across the street.

Things were hopping over there. The wells were drilled and three portable bathrooms arrived, built on trailers and pulled into place. Wires and pipes appeared, delivering the power and water. Voila! Bathrooms.

"No septic systems," Frank commented. "They're going to have to pump those every time they fill up. That's gonna cost."

"I get the feeling these people aren't hurting for money," Janice responded. "I wonder where they get it all."

"Unfortunately," Nathan said, "the atheist movement has increasing support. More and more people around the world are turning their backs on any idea of God, and they are willing to put up their money to make the point."

"Sad," Frank said, shaking his head.

There was also a huge pavilion going up. It appeared to be a place to meet out of the rain or hot sun. It was big enough to shelter at least five hundred people. There must have been a hundred workers buzzing around the place.

As we moseyed back into the church, Edwina asked if we could have a short meeting.

Once we gathered, she said, "Now, it has been my privilege to just be a part of this mighty band of Jesus followers. It has been more special than anything I could have ever asked for. But, I hope you don't mind if I make a couple of suggestions. Seems to me certain people need to get refocused on what they are meant to do and not be so caught up in all this communications stuff. Pastor Nathan, Pastor Honey—I get a kick out of that and I'm old so I can get away with saying most anything—Condi and Frank and Sylvie, for sure and maybe some others need to get back to what started all this. We need the preaching and the praying and Bible reading and that glorious music. Now, I know you've been doing it, but not near enough. We need more of that stuff, not less."

"I agree," Janice said, "but how are we going to . . .?"

"Janice, I love you, but please let me finish, or I'll forget what I had planned to say."

"Okay."

"Now, I checked with Kevin and he said we've got all kinds of money . . . right Kevin?"

"She's right. These checks keep coming. We've got a bit over two hundred thousand banked already and another mail bag full of envelopes we haven't even opened yet."

"So, we have money," Edwina continued. "And, I was reading in the paper that unemployment around here is pretty high, and people need work . . ."

Heads were beginning to nod.

" . . . and I am sure we could get a nice crew in here to answer phones and return emails and such."

I got excited and blurted out, "Oh, I would love to train a prayer team! Call in and get a prayer, no strings attached!"

Edwina continued, "Kevin is a human resources expert, Janice can organize anything, and God seems to be sending all of this our way."

"We can't fit all that in here," Jane observed. "I know we can do it," she said, "but where?"

"There's some office space available in town that's pretty cheap," Janice said. "We could lease."

"I think it has to be here," Frank said. "Pastor Nathan, how much land do we have here?"

"You know, I have to admit it never crossed my mind to find out. I guess I just see the building and the two gravel lots as all we need."

"There's four acres," Edwina said. "Way back it was a five and then Old Man Compton kept one for his son to build a house and gave the four for the church. Of course, that was well over a century ago."

"Where does it run?" Frank asked.

"It's perfectly square, so it runs about 200 feet into the brush at the back and probably 150 feet past the lot on the far side."

"Okay. What do we need?" Frank asked. "The basics."

"Space," Kevin said. "Accessible and legal."
"Lots of phones."
"And computers."
"Furniture."
"Electricity and water."
"Bathrooms."
"Okay. Me and Sylvie are on it. Jeremy, will you help me with the phones and computers and stuff?"
"Sure."
"Then consider it done."
Amazingly, no one felt the need for any more questions. Except one.
"When will you start?" Edwina asked.
"What time is it now?"
I would have assumed that comment would come from Frank. But it was Sylvie.

Chapter 35

Nathan

I admit I was still having trouble just letting things happen. No committee meetings, no Robert's Rules of Order, no votes. It was disconcerting. And yet, it did serve as the best way to get out of God's way. When He inspired someone to get busy with something, we learned to let it happen.

Frank became a man obsessed. The same day he said he would create the space necessary to our expanded operations, he showed up with a massive tractor, sporting a nasty-looking bushhog on the front. He started clearing the rest of the church lot, and when it got dark he simply turned on the headlights and kept going. The next morning he fed all that brush into a wood-chipper and blasted the remains into a high-sided farm truck. Sylvie drove the truck and continually maneuvered it to the right spot for Frank to keep chipping without missing a beat. When she had a full load, off she would drive off to dump it who knows where. While she was gone, Frank would jump on a front loader that showed up somehow and started digging massive holes. I resisted the temptation to ask what the holes were for, and did anybody think about getting permits. Instead, I went home to work on my next sermon.

Over the next couple of weeks, a sort of race developed. It was largely—at least to the naked eye—a contest between an obsessed farm couple and the big-budget *Free Us from Religion Coalition*. At the intersection of Williams and Compton Roads—an uneventful four-corners in rural Michigan where nothing much had happened in decades—the foundation was created for what would become the battlefield for a conflict of epic—even biblical—proportions. But, at the time, no one knew that yet.

On our side of the road—right next to our beloved old church building—Frank and Sylvie's vision became reality. He created the biggest drain field I have ever seen. Attached to it were two huge septic tanks. During the process, Frank would occasionally look up, grin, and shout something like, "Only a durn fool builds something you got to pump out every other day!" Then he would put his nose to the grindstone and keep working. A new power transformer appeared. *The Riegler Well-Drillers*—the same outfit that had just drilled the wells across the street—showed up and went to work.

"Ours will pump twice what they've got over there!" Sylvie shouted gleefully.

A brand-new mobile home was delivered, at sixteen by eighty feet, the biggest one you could legally haul down the road.

"Had her special built," Frank said. "I know a guy who got us first in line. No bedrooms. Ten small offices. Turned the kitchen smaller and made it into a break room. Two half baths—no tubs or showers. Front door ramped. This will be great. God showed me what it should look like, kinda like Noah and the Ark!"

As soon as it was in place, Jeremy drove up with his father and a whole crew. They connected everything, wired, plumbed, drilled and hammered. A delivery truck from a local electronics company backed in and delivered ten of everything: computers, monitors, phones, lamps and fans.

I couldn't begin to keep track already, when a whole other building on wheels showed up.

"What the heck is that?!" I yelled before I could hush myself.

Frank came running over with another massive grin on his face. "Don't worry, Pastor, that's just the sixteen new bathrooms I had built. That's what the big drain field is for!"

"But, Frank!" I hollered, trying not to sound angry or afraid. "What in heaven's name do we need sixteen bathrooms for?"

"I have no idea!" he hollered back, "but we need 'em!" With that, he burst out laughing and ran back to work.

I went back inside the church to sit down and try not to hyperventilate. Edwina sat down beside me. I hadn't seen her arrive, but then, there was a lot going on.

"I always wondered what would happen if we church-people quit trying to slow God down," she said. "Isn't it magnificent what is happening here?"

"Yes . . . yes it is," I replied. "I think it is."

"You think?"

"Oh, I know it's great, but I admit it is a little scary. What is all this for? And, what does it cost? This is way more than I expected."

"What would your beloved Pastor Carl say?" Edwina asked. "What would he tell you to do?"

I didn't respond for quite a while. Then I said, "You play dirty sometimes, you know that?"

"Whatever it takes," she said.

"Fair enough. He would tell me I don't need to know what everything is for until God's time comes."

"I think so, too."

"And he would tell me God wouldn't make something expensive happen unless there would be resources to pay for it."

"Yes," Edwina added, "now doesn't that make things more peaceful to contemplate?"

"Not yet," I said, "but, yes, in a little while it will seem peaceful."

"Now, before you get back to work on one of those wonderful sermons you have been preaching lately, let's go out front and spy on the competition!"

A Dragon Outside the Church   147

Spying on the competition had become a daily, if not hourly, thing for the Triple-W church family. After I helped Edwina down the front ramp we joined Kevin and Condi and Jennifer, already standing on our side of the road.

"What's new across the way?" I asked no one in particular.

Condi answered, "They seem to be putting on the finishing touches."

The change across the street had been just as striking as Frank's project. Their three bathroom buildings were now fully functional—even painted and landscaped. Rows upon rows of electric boxes lined much of the property, with almost as many water spigots. It was a campground. A big one. But, the most attention-grabbing feature was the tent. For over a week there had been a constant stream of cement trucks dropping off load after load of ready-to-pour concrete. Dozens of workers proceeded to create the biggest concrete pad I had ever seen. After a few days of drying in place, there arrived a tent, also the biggest I have ever seen. No circus ever had a tent bigger than this one. It dwarfed the new pavilion that had once looked so big. The canopy was supported by three monstrous poles. It featured canvas walls all around, which could be rolled up to create an almost open-air effect. The matrix of ropes and stakes was impressive in itself.

When it was all up, at a time when most of us were staring at it in awe, I asked, "How big is that thing?"

Immediately Frank answered, "Sixty thousand square feet."

"You think?" I said.

"I know. I snuck over there around three o'clock in the morning and measured it. It's about an acre and a half."

"Wow," said most of us.

"If you had enough chairs, you could easily seat five thousand people under that," Kevin said.

The next day, the chairs arrived. Two semis filled with those hard-plastic, molded white folding chairs so popular in churches around the country.

A crew unpacked them and set them up in perfect rows. There were four interior aisles from back to front, and room to walk on both sides and the rear. The massive setup was cut sideways by two long cross-aisles, as well, creating fifteen equal squares of nearly three hundred and fifty chairs each. The spacing was generous, creating a vision of easy accessibility. The whole thing made an impressive sight of beauty, organization . . . and power.

We had been watching the process for quite a while without speaking. We were all more than a little overwhelmed. Jennifer broke the silence.

"My," she said.

"My, my," Condi agreed.

"Nice planning," Kevin added.

"So that's what over an acre of chairs looks like," Frank said.

"And every last one of them pointed right at us," Janice whispered.

At that moment a figure appeared at the very back of the huge arrangement. A tall figure. Slowly, he moved toward the front—toward us. When he finally reached the front, he paused and looked around. Seemingly satisfied with all he saw, he turned toward us and pointed. Then, he spun one hundred and eighty degrees and strode quickly away.

I was about to attempt a rally-the-troops speech when Edwina beat me to it.

"They're coming for us," she said. "Lots of them." She got a twinkle in her eye that showed how much she was enjoying this. "I am going home and pray a while," she said, and moved away.

It took a little longer for the rest of us to get our heads around the latest developments, but eventually people moved on.

"I am going to work a little more, but me and Sylvie will be in tonight to read some scripture," Frank said. "We're getting into really good stuff."

"I'm thinking I'll play a bit tomorrow, maybe in the afternoon," Condi said as she took Kevin's hand and walked away.

"I've got a few questions for God," Jennifer said. "Maybe I'll go inside right now and have a talk. Training for the new prayer team starts in a couple days."

"I'll be at home, Honey," I said without reservation. "Sermon work."

As the group dispersed, Sylvie, who moments before had a terrified look on her face, stared at the thousands of chairs for a moment. That same face morphed into a sparkling grin as she said, "So that's why we need all those bathrooms!"

Chapter 36

Jennifer

Frank, Sylvie and the rest of us finished our work. Over the next couple of weeks the two new buildings were completed. They even had concrete-block foundations put underneath. All of the new equipment and fixtures were installed, wired and plumbed into place. On the day the bank of bathrooms was finally fully functional, complete with ramps and rails and country-chic décor, Frank was beyond excited.

"Be careful with small pets and little children," he shouted, "those babies will flush anything!"

There was even instant grass. Frank had sod trucked in to surround the restrooms and the call center.

"No time to let it grow," he said.

"I still didn't know what he knew or how he knew it. Whatever it was, I guess time was running out. Whatever the purpose, we had created a lovely little compound.

We did get the call center rolling. Frank and Jeremy created the facility. It was beautiful and super-efficient. Kevin hired twenty-six people to staff the phones and computers twenty-four hours a day three hundred sixty-five days a year. I trained them for a week, and Janice organized the schedules. Kevin had to hire a firm to take care of all the Human Resource duties and paperwork. Nathan was stressing about the money until Kevin told him not to worry. He said he could hardly count it and get it in the bank fast enough to start on the next load. It was hard to believe how fast God was providing.

That gave me an idea for a name for the call-in prayer center. In the Bible, John 6, verses 1-13 tell the story of Jesus feeding five thousand people. In fact, some figure with all the children and women added in, it was probably more like twelve thousand people. Anyway, Jesus and the disciples only had two fish and five small loaves of bread they got from a young boy. Jesus started feeding all those people with only that little bit of food, and it just didn't run out! In fact, after every person ate as much as they wanted, the disciples gathered up the scraps and filled twelve baskets. It was impossible, except nothing is impossible for God.

In good Triple-W fashion, I gathered the regulars together and shouted out my idea to name the call-center. They shouted out their approval, before someone shouted out a motion and a second. Then they shouted out a unanimous vote, and the Twelve Baskets Center for Unending Prayer was born, christened and put into action.

The very next Sunday things came to a head. At least, it felt like a *head* at the time. For weeks we had been working and praying and working and preaching and working and making music and reading scripture and praying for people over the phones. Amazingly, the call volume for prayers and help was so heavy and consistent our new facility and prayer team could barely handle it. But, handle it they did. Donations rolled in and internet viewership was often as high as eighty million. And yet, for reasons I can't even begin to explain, attendance at our weekly church service remained steady. In addition to all of our working and praying and such, our other main activity was speculating. What was coming next? The folks across the road didn't do all that construction to let it sit empty.

Nathan and I arrived, as we typically do, an hour before service time and twenty minutes before anyone else. This day, the first thing to catch our attention was a new development. The world headquarters of the *Free Us from Religion Coalition* was swarming with cars, trucks, campers and tents. And people. Everywhere we looked, more people. Campsites were rapidly filling up with facilities for those who planned on staying a while. The seemingly endless space set aside for parking was already clogging up—vehicles were being parked in a growing line down the roads. Even with all of the movement and jockeying about, the irresistible focal point of the scene was the tent filled with chairs.

"My goodness," Nathan said. "There must be four thousand seats filled already. Where are they going to put the rest of them?"

"I don't know, Honey," I replied. "What I want to know is what they're here for? What the heck is going on?"

"Actually, I think I know," he answered. "The Tall Man is forcing our hand. He's always been ticked off we have been receiving so much attention—that God has been receiving so much attention. He can't stand it. His whole goal is to make religion fade away. Then we came along."

"He's blaming us for stirring up interest in God. I can see that. What did you mean when you said he is forcing our hand?"

"Not sure, specifically, but he wants a battle. He wants the world to see him crush us. He's starting by bringing in all these people, to demonstrate the world is becoming more atheist."

"How do you suppose he got all these people here, and we never got wind of it? They must have been planning this for weeks! And, they must have been arriving and setting up all night! Nobody noticed?"

"Probably the same way a lot of what we have been doing doesn't make sense."

The voice startled us. It was Edwina. I didn't even see her pull up, but there she was, right next to us, with Jeremy at her side.

"Oh! Good morning, Edwina," Nathan got out. "Didn't see you coming."

"I'm stealthy like that," she said. "I see our friend Mr. Stevens has been a busy fellow. This is a good thing, you know. Especially the mysterious side of it."

"How's that?" I asked.

"It's biblical in nature. God wants something particular to happen here. We don't know exactly what, yet, but it obviously is coming fast. And just like in many of the best Bible stories, God is using both his people and the opposition—the good guys and the bad guys, so to speak—to make it happen. You can't have David without Goliath."

We pondered for a moment. "You're not wrong," Nathan said. "Jennifer, I think you and I need to *Pastor Carl* even more than we usually do."

"Be still and listen to God."

"Do the next right thing."

"Leave the results up to God."

"Easier to say than it is to do," Nathan said, ruefully shaking his head. "I struggle so, and Carl made it look so easy."

"Husband," Jennifer said, "You don't know how long it took Pastor Carl to get to the point where it looked easy, now do you. I imagine he had his struggles earlier on, don't you think?"

"Yeah, I suppose so," he replied. "Edwina, what do you think about . . .?"

Nathan stopped abruptly when it became obvious she was no longer with us. We turned just in time to see her disappear up her ramp and into the church, with Jeremy holding the door.

"Looks like Mrs. Fine said what she had to say and is now going to church," Nathan said. "Do you suppose maybe we should join her?"

Before I could respond, Nathan's cell phone rang.

"Good morning, this is Pastor Nathan."

"It appears that my attendance will be a bit greater than yours, today," said the voice on the other end. "We have big plans for today and well beyond."

Nathan started looking around, a bit frantically. Shortly, his gazed focused on the tall figure across the road, who had a cell phone pressed to his ear.

Off balance, Nathan blurted too loudly, "What now, Stevens. Are you going to try to infringe on our right to worship?"

"Of course not, Pastor. Perish the thought. You will get no interruption from us. However, we will be watching you. All day, every day, we will be watching you. Have a lovely service. And by the way, give my regards to your wife."

He hung up.

Nathan said, "That was Stevens. He said . . ."

"I heard him. Don't let him get to you."

"I was a little shocked. At first I . . ."

"It's fine," I said. "He's messing with us. We don't need to take the bait."

"You're right, of course. We should get inside. Time to worship and sing and praise and preach."

"And listen," I added. "Time to listen."

"Yeah," he said, a little too quietly.

I turned and started for the church. The others were arriving in a steady stream that suddenly seemed more like a trickle. Nathan didn't move.

"You coming?" I asked.

"In a minute," he said. "You go ahead. Give me a minute."

I walked a few more steps, then turned and looked back at my husband. He stood, ramrod straight, still gazing across the road. In the distance, just off my husband's shoulder, stood the Tall Man, staring back.

You can't get to my husband unless you get through me first, I thought with a ferocity I hadn't felt in a long while. *Where did that come from?*

Chapter 37

Nathan

I was disconcerted. I admit it. What would soon be a standing-room-only crowd of over five thousand was sitting across the road, quietly staring at my church, which would soon be half filled with nearly fifty people. I had no idea what was going on. That's not entirely true. I understood the Tall Man and his kind were coming for me. For reasons of his own, he had decided I was his target—the symbol of everything he hated. I was the one he felt he must destroy . . . discredit. Many thousands of dollars had been spent in preparation for the attack, the details of which were still unknown to me.

    On my own, I was in big trouble. Oh, I could take care of myself. I had years of successful pastoring behind me. A great education. A quick mind, if I don't say so myself. I could debate with almost anyone. But I had never faced anything like this. Not even when the self-serving, highly motivated Bob Williams had decided to drive me from the *East Fork First United Methodist Church*—using every lie and manipulation he thought necessary to his task—did I feel this outnumbered. And this time, due to Alexander Stevens, *Time* magazine and a God-inspired eighty million online followers, the battle would be fought on a worldwide stage, with me at the center.

    So be it.

It took me a few minutes to remember this was not so different from every day of my professional ministry. I had never told anyone this, but I have a very personal experience with God each and every morning. I wake up feeling the uncertainty and the fragility of being human. My flaws are many. I think all people are glad others cannot hear all our thoughts and sense all of our emotions. The self-centeredness, the anger, the pride, the bigotry, the lust, the pettiness. Oh my, I know I am glad others don't know everything that goes on with me. In that morning-state, I am moved to ask God, *Why Me? You have called me to preach and teach your word, to lead your people. You put in my hands the power to baptize and serve at the Holy Table. Me? Really? How can the likes of me serve as your prophet, your priest, your pastor?*

I ask—sometimes out loud—*are you sure you still want me to do this?*

Each time God answers—in some form or another—*Yes. I have called you to do this. I have chosen you.*

And when I rise up to go about my day, I have become a force to be reckoned with, called and filled by God for whatever comes next. In fact, that had happened again just that morning.

"I am not alone," I whispered. "The Father has called me. Jesus has saved me. The Holy Spirit is in me. Not only that, I have Jennifer, and Condi, and lessons from Carl. And Frank. I got me a Frank," I said, laughing. "Who can stand up to a Frank?"

By the time I entered the church I felt great. Despite the stress and weirdness of what was going on outside, we had the most glorious worship service ever. I preached like I was singing the greatest song ever written. Jennifer prayed like God was sitting right across from her, moved to tears by her majestic words. Condi played the concert of her life, each note flowing into the next as if part of a heavenly being. I swear, maybe it was just in my head, but the congregation sang like the *Mormon Tabernacle Choir*, and there aren't enough good singers out there to form a decent barbershop quartet.

I was breathless by the time we came near the end of the service. I had never experienced anything like this. As I tried to form the perfect closing benediction in my mind, I was interrupted by Edwina Fine.

"And so, God strengthened His people!" she shouted, "for whatever may come!"

I was wise enough to simply say, "Amen," and exit the stage, hand in hand with my beloved wife and partner.

As the service broke up, the others were stunned, as well.

"What was that?" Janice asked.

"That was marvelous, was what it was," Jane answered.

"If that wasn't a mountaintop experience, I don't know what is!" Condi exclaimed, tears still running down her cheeks.

"I wonder what is going on across the road?" Frank said, and the whole crowd headed outside.

There they sat, all five thousand of them, plus those still standing. They didn't move a bit. Just sat and watched.

"Interesting strategy," Kevin Cloverton said. "Still, it is just a strategy. Putting on a show."

Kevin was probably right, but it was a pretty impressive show. After maybe five minutes of silence, the Tall Man appeared and stepped up to a podium in front of his crowd. His back was to us, but as soon as he began to speak it became obvious that, while most of a huge bank of speakers were oriented properly toward the seated audience, a couple of the biggest ones were pointing right at us.

"Good people of the *Free Us from Religion Coalition*— rational, thinking, educated people—I thank you for being here at this glorious event. Most of you have just witnessed—via the scientific wonder that is the internet—the ritualistic, empty-headed spectacle that just assaulted our world from the tiny little building right across the road. Let us take a few minutes to apply critical thinking to . . ."

With the Tall Man's voice blaring through the massive speakers, his message could not be ignored. He was playing his strategic cards in a very slick manner. Careful to keep his minions quiet during our worship service, he could not be accused of interrupting or infringing on our right to worship. He even kept a short *demilitarized zone* of silence. But now, in searing rhetoric, he held back nothing.

"Our stated goal is to remove the blight of religion—most especially Christianity—from all public discourse. Of particular concern is the elimination of Christian influence on public and governmental policy.

It is 2018. I am amazed and befuddled that we, as a society and as a country, still have to have this conversation. Time, enlightenment and simple logic would seem to make the demise of superstition and magical thinking inevitable. And yet, still today, we find our society continues to be plagued with such nonsense!"

As he warmed up to his task, he grew louder and more self-assured. He pounded on the key words: *Blight! Influence! Superstition! Magical thinking! Nonsense!*

He continued, "I do not seek the criminalization of religion, only that all expressions of it be mandated a private matter. We are fortunate to be living in a free country, and so must respect the rights of people to believe whatever they wish, no matter how misguided. However, I am convinced the world would be a better place for all the people in it, with far less religion and far more secularism—science and fact and proof.

Despite how obvious this seems, we find ourselves not only still hip-deep in the battle to keep religion out of public policy, but facing evidence of a resurgence in Christian influence. After decades of slow but steady progress in limiting religious participation and church attendance, the advent of social media has served the Christian Agenda well. I say without apology: religion is foolhardy, nonsensical and dangerous. To ultimately perfect our society through humanist efforts, we must get religion out of the way."

Foolhardy! Nonsensical! Dangerous!

Stevens was almost shouting, now, "One might reasonably ask, 'What harm can religion do? Does it not benefit our society and make the world a better place?' I will answer that. It is easy to become a Christian. It only requires one basic principle. All you have to do is give up is your ability to think. Religious belief is the death of intelligent thought . . .."

I have to acknowledge I was finding myself mesmerized. The man could preach! And, that is exactly what he was doing—preaching. Clearly, he espoused a different gospel than mine and Jennifer's and every Christian preacher. His was not a gospel of God—Father, Son and Holy Spirit—and the saving grace offered us by Jesus Christ, but a gospel of science and logic and human power. Still, it was obvious to me, as he drew me into his words, he believed everything he said, with a passion similar to my passion for God. This was a dangerous man.

"That is almost word for word from his article in *Time!*" Alicia Skiba's words startled me.

"I have read it so many times I know it by heart," she continued. "That's all he is doing. He is shouting out *talking points* like a politician giving the same speech for the hundredth time."

"Still," Jennifer chimed in, "he has a way of getting his point across."

"He sure does," Condi agreed.

"They are livestreaming," Jeremy added. "I've got it on my tablet. If you didn't listen to his words you would think he was preaching a sermon, the way he is going at it. No, offense, Pastor Nathan."

"None taken, Jeremy," I said.

Our conversation was cut short by the unexpected vision of Frank walking past us and taking a spot on the shoulder of our side of the road. Sylvie followed nearby, wearing plastic gloves and carrying a bucket. What made the scene odd was what Frank was wearing. He was almost engulfed in an old-fashioned sandwich sign, made of two large sheets of plywood held together by two wide straps of leather. The thing must have weighed thirty or forty pounds and hung down so low Frank could barely walk. He took his position near the road, oriented directly toward the crowd on the other side. Never had a man looked more resolute. Whatever his quest was, he was seriously into it.

The rest of us were a bit stunned, but we had learned that to live around Frank required a certain patience, so we all stood in silence and watched. From our angle, we could only read the sign on his back. It was made up of large, carefully stenciled, spray-painted letters, blue on white plywood. The sign read:

. . .
Jesus Loves You,
and
So Do We.

I wondered what the ellipse at the beginning was for, but knew enough to wait. With Frank, the answer would usually come along soon enough. For a full minute, Frank stood as still as a rock and looked across the road. Then he straightened up and did a practiced about-face. The front sign Frank had just been displaying to the atheists across the street became visible to us, and we all let out a synchronized chuckle. The sign read:

Welcome!
Clean, Free Bathrooms!
Open to Everyone!
Because . . .

With the precision and timing of the soldiers guarding *The Tomb of the Unknown Soldier*, Frank did his one hundred eighty degree turn every sixty seconds. Sylvie stood perhaps fifteen feet away. Just as still. Just as resolute.

After a few turns, I felt the need to respond. I sidled up to Frank and said, "Impressive display. Have you got a plan?"

Frank tried not to smile, but mostly failed.

"I figure it will kick in about half an hour from now."

At that moment, I was startled back into returning my attention to the events across the street.

"We will be heard!" the Tall Man screamed. "We will battle this out once and for all. We will debate for all the world to see! The people will demand it! I will meet the Most High Reverend Nathan Martin and the Reverend Jennifer Martin . . ." He paused and laughed. "They call her Pastor Honey. Can you imagine? I will meet them both in televised debate. They can run but they cannot hide! Let them prepare to defend this precious god of theirs, if they can! You and I, highly educated, thinking people, already know they cannot. One cannot defend that which never existed! I admit it! I admit it! I am licking my chops for the great debate!"

Nowhere near winding down, Stevens nonetheless had to shift gears.

"Thank you! Thank you!" he shouted to thunderous applause.

The effect was hard to handle.

"I know many of you are staying here for days or weeks! The campsites are all filled with a waiting line down the road! Most of you will be leaving, at least for a time, but don't even think about going yet! We have an exciting afternoon planned. So, I hope to see each and every one of you right after the scheduled break for lunch. For those of you who didn't bring food, there are concessions set up. See you all in an hour and a half!"

It felt wrong to stay and watch, and it felt wrong to turn tail and leave. I was not alone. The people took action. Before I knew it, they agreed we should stay together for lunch. A couple of cars left to go into town for supplies. Others went inside to prepare to serve food. Still others found quiet places to rest. Today was not unfolding as anyone had planned.

Like clockwork, Frank continued to turn. I left others to their plans and watched. As soon as Stevens dismissed the crowds, the chaos began. The bathrooms—three for men, three for women—were immediately swarmed with long lines of impatient people. I had never seen the inside of their facilities, but they didn't look big enough to have more than three or four stalls each. I moved up near Frank, to see what he was thinking. Before I could even form a question, he spoke, without turning his head to look at me.

"Each men's room has two stalls and four urinals," he said. "Don't ask me how I know that. That's six toilets and twelve urinals for a good two or three thousand men and boys. Do the math. And that's the good news. The women's rooms have five stalls each. Fifteen toilets for at least twenty-five hundred women and girls. And these people say we're dumb!"

"Probably a lot of the campers have their own bathrooms," I said, just trying to add to the conversation.

"Probably, but it won't save them."

"Save them?"

"Pastor Nathan, there is a place for fine thinkers like you and Pastor Jennifer. There sure is. But I am a real practical man. Whatever they call that event over there is about to come apart at the seams."

I smiled. The genius of Frank's plan was finally dawning on me. "They go into panic over there, and you are ready for them over here."

"Yes, sir!" he said, beaming, "and that doesn't even account for the fact that, at this rate, those pump-the-tank bathrooms are goin' to be full in three or four hours!"

"How did you figure this out before we ever knew what was going to go on over there?"

"You're the one who taught me to listen to God, right? So I did!"

"You are really something, Frank."

"He sure is," Sylvie said, just loud enough to hear.

"So when things get bad over there . . . ?" I asked.

"They have to come to us," he said through a snort. "Even if they are so much smarter than we are, they still gotta go!"

Chapter 38

Jennifer

If I am honest with myself, I have always held to a basic assumption that the people who are the smartest and have the most education are the obvious leaders in any organization or endeavor. I don't think I ever decided to believe that or even realized I was doing it. It was simply part of the world I lived in. Watching Frank and Sylvie in action, I realized I still had a lot to learn.

More and more Frank demonstrated his unique talent in sizing up—often ahead of time—what was going to take place in a given situation. Not what people might be thinking or feeling or debating, but what was going to tangibly happen. Or maybe his unique talent was listening to God about things the rest of us were ignoring. Either way, it finally dawned on me what Frank was up to.

Looking across the road at the huge crowd, I could readily see how a super-organized event, with thousands of people sitting in neat little rows, was disintegrating before our eyes. Almost immediately following the adjournment of their first session, the lines at the bathrooms were fifty people long. Five minutes later, they were a hundred, then more. The tiny concession stands were so mobbed I couldn't even see them anymore.

Every sixty seconds, Frank turned his signs. First,

Welcome!
Clean, Free Bathrooms!
Open to Everyone!
Because...

Then,

...
Jesus Loves You,
and
So Do We.

I actually began to feel sorry for them. I could see the people in the bathroom lines getting frantic, some trying to take cuts, unable to wait any longer. Others refused them and sent them to the end of the line. There was no shortage of desperate people. Moms and dads struggled with little children. I could hear the cries of *Hold it! Just a little longer! Hold it!*

A mother gripping the hands of two small children was the first to break. She sprinted for the road, dragging the kids behind her. That road was the only thing that separated her from *Clean, Free Bathrooms!* Right at that moment, nothing else mattered. Then another fled the line. And another. Then a dozen.

A voice—I like to think it was the Tall Man himself, but I am not sure—came over the speaker system and pleaded, "Please stay calm. Be patient! The lines are growing shorter!" But they were not. Across the road they came. By then Sylvie had taken up her spot in front of the brand-new restroom building, directing traffic. People entered from both ends (there was a hallway down the middle, with bathrooms on either side), straining to make it on time. Relieved, the first sixteen disappeared in a cacophony of locking doors. Then came a hundred more. Then more. Lines formed, to be sure, but they moved through pretty quickly. Frank finally put his sign down where both sides could still be seen and went to aid Sylvie. Before he reached her, he stopped next to me and said, "Be quiet and listen."

I did. I said, "All I can hear is the almost constant sound of powerful toilet flushes."

"I know," he replied, his face near split in half by a grin. "Isn't that a beautiful sound!"

Frank joined Sylvie, although he spent most of his time greeting people and shouting, *thanks for comin'!*

Sylvie's bucket turned out to be filled with cleaning supplies. After the first few uses, she started cleaning.

"I know it's difficult, but please give me a moment to check the facilities," she would say to someone at the head of a line. "We want to make sure things are nice for you."

And in she'd go, with a load of brushes and cleanser and deodorizing spray and fresh rolls of toilet paper. Only a couple of minutes later she would reappear and say, "There, things are ready for you now. Bless you."

Frank continued to meet the people. Then Nathan jumped in and did the same.

I called to Sylvie, "You're going to need some help!"

She smiled and replied, "More kits in the truck."

Sure enough, I found three more buckets filled with supplies. I took them over to the bathroom area and set two down off to the side. Then I took my cue from Sylvie and started working the bathrooms. Then Condi and Kevin both joined in.

Please let me make things nice for you. Things are ready for you now. Thanks for comin'. Thanks for comin'. Things are ready for you now. Let me make things nice for you. Bless you. Bless you. Bless you.

When I got a chance to peek, I saw Frank and Nathan and Jane and Janice and even Jeremy were in conversations with the people in line, and the people who were heading back to their side of the road. Edwina sat in a lawn chair off to the side, laughing and drinking iced tea.

It went on for hours. Most of our core congregation stayed all afternoon. We rotated positions and duties, so each person could catch some rest and have something to eat. But we kept on.

I was next to Condi when I overheard an exchange.

"Thank you so much," said the unidentified woman, hanging on to three children. "I don't know what I would have done without you . . . and your bathrooms."

"Just happy to help," Condi replied.

"It's getting pretty ripe in there," the other woman continued, "I don't know if I could be smiling as much as you are."

I couldn't help but think about how Condi's talent could take her far away from cleaning bathrooms after strangers.

Condi responded, "I guess this is just part of how God made us human beings—not everything is pleasant, but its fine. We're all in this life together, trying to get by."

"I don't know about the God part, but I still appreciate your attitude," the woman said.

"I do," Condi replied. "You and your children have a wonderful rest of your day."

"You do? You do, what?" the woman asked.

"Know about the God part," Condi said, then comically bugged her eyes out, took a deep breath, and disappeared into the next stall in need of service.

I did the same, with a bit more enthusiasm than I had just moments before.

Later, a gentleman politely thanked me for the use of the facilities, but couldn't resist adding, "The use of a bathroom is not enough to change my convictions, you know. There still is no god, nor a need for one."

"We didn't provide you a bathroom to make you believe in God," I said. "Feel free to come back anytime."

"Why, then?" he asked, "Provide us with bathrooms I mean—and why do you have so many bathrooms anyway?"

"We help because Jesus loves you and so, then, do we," I said. "And we built more bathrooms than make sense, because God told a devout farmer to do so."

Speaking the truth so bluntly created in me a wave of nerves.

"That's nonsense," the man said. After a long pause he added, "Magnificent nonsense, I must admit, but still nonsense."

"Plenty more where that came from," I said. "Have a wonderful afternoon."

I had many conversations with our guests, some polite, some not entirely and some that left me puzzled. I heard bits and pieces of discussions going on all around me. I didn't have time to process it much. The odd undercurrent was the continual awareness that—presumably—all of these visitors were atheist activists, and we were all Christians. In the moment, there was little time to think about that, but I did have time to wonder, *Who would have thought the pathway to conversation and relationship would come through the need to get to a toilet?*

One problem did arise we were not equipped to handle. Food. Many of these people were hungry, although obviously not yet starving. Evidently the food situation across the road was just as inadequate as the restroom facilities. We directed many people to the nearest food sources: a couple of nearby convenience stores and a restaurant, plus the eleven miles into town. It was going to be a big business day in East Fork, and on a Sunday afternoon, those businesses were going to be overwhelmed. Oh well. We had all we could handle right in front of us.

It was evening before the lines finally disappeared. The folks across the road had finished their afternoon of speeches and music and readings and such. The whole program seemed to consist of little more than bashing religion or extolling science and the powers of the human mind. I didn't hear a whole lot of it as we were kept busy taking care of the people. Just as sure as Frank predicted, it was mid-afternoon when the sewage filled their holding tanks, and then backed up. People ran from the bathrooms screaming. We experienced quite a rush of business until the pumper arrived to empty the tanks. As the truck maneuvered into place to do the job, Frank laughed and commented. "Billy charges double on Sundays," he said.

I didn't know what he meant until he pointed to the truck. Emblazoned on the side was **Billy's Honey Hauler.** I didn't want to find that funny, but it was funny and I laughed. Anyway, they got their system working again and the crowds thinned out. Most left, while more than a few retired to their campsites. We were finally able to shut down.

Many of our people had gone home for a well-deserved rest, but Nathan and I remained, along with Kevin and Condi, Frank and Sylvie, Edwina, Jeremy and Janice. We sat around a table in the basement of the church and picked at the remnants of the sandwiches and cold salads that had been keeping us going all day. For a while, no one said much.

"That was quite a day," Condi eventually offered.

"Sure was," her husband Kevin responded. "Not the Sunday I had planned, exactly, but it was certainly quite a day."

We were too tired to belly-laugh or guffaw, but we all chuckled a bit.

"What happened, do you suppose?" Janice asked. "I was too busy keeping up to figure out what exactly was going on."

Nathan—who had been unusually quiet—spoke up. "Jesus said His followers should feed the hungry, give drink to the thirsty and clothe the naked. He didn't mention we should *bathroom the desperate,* but I think He would be pleased."

With that, he raised his red plastic cup filled with Diet Coke in the air and said, "Here's to King Frank and his Queen Sylvie! I don't know how you did it, but well done!"

Here, here! To Frank and Sylvie!

The toasting done, it grew quiet again, until Frank said, "I want to say how much all of you—especially Pastors Nathan and Jennifer—have meant to me. I built those bathrooms cause God told me to. Can you even think what that means? Not two years ago God wouldn't of asked me to do nothin'. And if He did, I'd of refused. I'd of fought Him off. I was a sad, bitter old schlub who lived mostly on disappointment. Then God gave me Sylvie, which I didn't begin to know how to handle. Then into my life came Pastor Nathan. And things started happening. And then me and Sylvie decided to follow Pastor to this little church, and God gave us Pastor Jennifer and all the rest of you, too. All I hoped for was to help out. Didn't know what use I'd be, but I figured if God loved me enough to give me Sylvie, maybe he thought I might be good for somethin'."

Sylvie took Frank's hand and cried.

Frank went on, "So we listened and prayed and we tried to learn and see what God had in store next. I'm sure not braggin', but now I'm the kind of guy who will read scripture I hardly understand in front of the world and build Him a big ole bathroom without knowin' why. You think I didn't wonder how big a fool I was goin' to look like? I'm ashamed to say I did. Well, anyhow, I just wanted to say what a powerful God-thing you people got goin' here . . . and say my thanks."

We all sat quietly for quite a while.

Chapter 39

Nathan

It had been an amazing day. I could not get over how great our people were about adjusting quickly and hanging in until what needed to be done was done. They all expected to attend church and then go back to whatever they had planned for a Sunday afternoon. Instead, they stayed until late in the evening, serving people they had never met—people who made a point of disagreeing with them at the very deepest levels—by cleaning up after them in the most humbling of ways. Like I said—amazing.

After what seemed a long silence, my mind started working on the never-ending parade of *what's next*? Even though we were a tired bunch, everybody in the room appeared to be content.

"Thank you all for the excellent ministry you did today," I started. "We met more people and had more good conversations in one day than we could have had in a year of trying to get them around a table."

"Do you think it will do any good?" Janice asked.

"Yes," I replied. "Without question. Not that we will necessarily know what good was done. But somebody in that crowd—maybe several somebodies—is thinking and feeling something new, because some crazy Christians did them a kindness for no discernable reason. That's all we can know, for now. But, you guys sure did a great job of service and hospitality. Wonderful stuff."

"This is only the beginning," Edwina declared. "This is the first ripple of the tidal wave that is coming."

He words would have sounded frightening if she hadn't been smiling with everything she said. Her feelings on the matter became clear when she added, "Isn't it great!?"

"She's right," Alicia Skiba said.

I had lost track of her and was startled to realize she was behind me.

"I've been gathering information," she continued. "We know their immediate plan is to have small events throughout the week, with a big blowout each Sunday, similar to what happened today. They have pleaded with the people to not be put off by the food and bathroom problems, because, quote, *We will be more organized next week.*"

Frank jumped in, "Unless getting organized means building new bathrooms and a gigantic concession stand in a week, it will fall apart just like it did today."

"I agree," Alicia replied. "I am not sure what we want to do about that, but I think we need to know it is going to happen again."

This time, Sylvie didn't wait for Frank to speak up. "I'll be ready," she said. "I'll bring the buckets, only this time I think I'll double up on the air-fresheners. I think some of those atheists weren't feeling too good."

As tired as we were, that got a belly-laugh from all of us. It appeared we were now committed to another Sunday of our new bathroom ministry.

I suddenly had a thought. "What about the call center? I got so busy I just plain forgot about that. Have they been out there all this time."

"Don't worry, my darling husband. I have been checking on them from time to time. *The Twelve Baskets Center for Unending Prayer* has been rolling all day and still is. We are already well into second shift. With our livestreamed service this morning—is this still that same day?—and whatever they have been sending out from across the street, we have stimulated a record number of calls. It's going great. You should hear the prayers flowing out of that sacred trailer."

"Wonderful," I said. "I am continually amazed at the ministry going on all around me, whether I do anything or not. Thanks to all of you for that."

"Next week we need to feed them." It was Edwina.

"What?" I said, a little dumbfounded.

Edwina said, "I think it is our turn to feed the five thousand. Next Sunday."

"They sure can't feed themselves," Frank said.

This prospect struck me as a huge job we might not have to do. The logistics of feeding five thousand people could be overwhelming. Our building was small, our kitchen even smaller. How was this supposed to happen? No!

Thankfully, this all transpired quickly enough to stay in my head and not come out of my mouth. What I actually said was, "How do the rest of you feel about that?"

"I'm in," said Frank.

"Me, too," said Sylvie.

"We're in," said Condi, while Kevin nodded along.

The rest all chimed in as well, ready to go. I was about to give a Devil's Advocate speech about how hard it would be, and maybe they weren't thinking it all the way through, when I realized Jennifer hadn't said anything yet.

"What do you think, Honey?" I asked, while silently trying to will her to get me out of this.

"Well," she started, "given our lack of facilities and the strain already being put on our limited people-power, I think this will prove to be an almost impossible task."

I breathed easier, until she concluded, "Which is why I think we had better get started right away. Lots of prayer tonight and a get-organized meeting tomorrow at noon. That work for everybody?"

Amid the unanimous yeses and head nodding, I realized two things. One, I was defeated on the issue of feeding five thousand people—we were going to have to make it happen. And, two, everyone was raring to go but me. So, what was up with me? As I pondered this, Alicia spoke up.

"Before we go, there is one more thing to consider. Today it was made clear what Mr. Stevens is shooting for. He intends to debate you, Pastors Nathan and Jennifer, on national TV and livestream. He wants to duke it out in front of the world as to the very existence of God and what he considers the irrelevance of the people who believe. He has gone to great lengths and expense to force your hand, to make it all but impossible for you to refuse."

"All things are possible with God," I snapped. "I have no problem saying no to anyone but God, and that includes the idiot Stevens."

There was a wall of stunned silence. Poor Alicia seemed to shrink up before my eyes and stepped back a few feet. It was not one of my finer moments.

"Of course," Jennifer said, "of course Mr. Stevens can't force us to do anything God does not want us to do. The thing is, we don't yet know what God wants us to do. As always, we will seek His will and prepare to do whatever He requires of us. Alicia, thank you so much for doing such a good job of gathering information. You are such a blessing."

As I listened to my wife using diplomacy and a side door to apologize for my behavior, without making it look too obvious, my troubled mood took an inexplicable turn and surged into euphoria.

"I love you guys!" I exclaimed. "Each and every one of you."

I scooted over to Alicia and wrapped her in an exaggerated bear hug.

"I'm sorry Alicia, my brain quit on me for a minute there. Nothing to do with you. You are great. Don't ever change. You know what I'd really like right now?" I said more than asked. "I would like you all to gather round me and lay your powerful hands on me and pray your wonderful prayers. There's big stuff right around the corner and we all need to be ready. I need you! Come on in."

As the whole team, led by Jennifer, enclosed me in their strength and love, I heard Edwina whisper, "Now we're talking."

They prayed deeply and sincerely and so did I. I held Jennifer's hand in mine and whispered in her ear, "We can do this."

She whispered back, "I know."

Chapter 40

Jennifer

I slept the long, deep sleep of the content that night. What a magnificent day we had just experienced! When I finally woke up I had just enough time to pull myself together and make it to the noon planning meeting. The enthusiasm was palpable and all the key players willingly took on some part of the task. We decided that we would have to find a facility—a restaurant or school or someplace with a licensed kitchen—to prepare sandwiches and side dishes by the thousands, which could then be delivered as needed, for immediate consumption. We even thought we had a line on a refrigerated truck, which would make the whole thing easier and safer. By 1:30 we had dispersed, each on a quest to procure some part of the whole shebang.

As we try to take Mondays off, Nate and I were relaxing at home, getting a couple hours of needed respite and just beginning to think about supper plans, when there was a knock at the front door. Nate snuck a peak through the far curtain.

"You'll never believe this," he whispered. "It's our archenemy."

"Bob Williams!" I responded. "You have got to be kidding me. What can he want?"

Bob Williams was wealthy and well-known in and around East Fork, Michigan. He had almost single-handedly driven my husband out as pastor of the East Fork UMC. He lied. He demonized. He manipulated. And, he lied some more. He insulted me so graphically that my husband, a good and civil man, punched him in the mouth. That part wasn't so bad. He even found a way to tie up most of the church's funding, forcing the hierarchy of the *United Methodist Church* to remove Nathan from his position and make plans to send him elsewhere. Before that could take place, we quit, to found our new church. Despite the fact it all turned out great, the man who waged a vicious campaign against my husband was standing outside my front door, and I was not inclined to let him in.

Nathan opened the door and let him in.

"Good evening, Bob," he said. "Come in and sit down."

"Thank you," he replied, and took a seat.

Nathan sat down directly across from Bob, while I settled on the couch, off to one side.

"I must say," Nathan began, "of all of the things I might have predicted would happen today, a visit from you was not on the list."

"I imagine not," Bob replied, "given our history."

"Yeah . . . history," I said with more than a little snotty in my voice.

"I have come to regret some of the things I did and said," Bob continued, "and I am sorry for those things. I did have some legitimate concerns, but . . . ."

"Let me interject," Nathan interrupted. "If you are here to rehash or revisit old business, I would rather not. We have moved on to new things."

"Yes, of course. You are right. I did not come here for that. In fact, I have heard some pretty amazing things have happened in your new venture. That must be very exciting."

"It is," we both answered.

"Then what is the purpose of your visit?" Nathan asked.

"Mother is quite ill."

That caught us by surprise. I am ashamed to say, of all the assumptions I had flying through my head, none of them considered Bob might actually need some help. It was especially shocking that it was about his mother. She had been something of an ally to us. She eventually put an end to the worst of Bob's shenanigans, making it clear in the process she was deeply disappointed in her son.

While I was still thinking it through, Nathan replied, "I am so sorry to hear that. Is she going to be okay?"

"No, I don't think so. We are looking into every possible treatment, but the doctors are not optimistic. That's kind of why I am here."

"How can we help?" Nathan asked. "Are you looking for pastoral care or help with arrangements?"

I was a little astounded how quickly Nathan could drop the animosity of the past and move on to being the caring pastor. On second thought, I wasn't surprised at all. This was my husband we are talking about.

"No . . . no, that's not it. Although I am truly grateful you would be willing. No, Pastor Karen, your . . . um . . . replacement . . ."

"We know who she is," I replied, trying hard to put kindness into my voice. "She's good."

"Yes, she is," Bob said. "She has been great with Mom. I think we're in good hands there."

"Then, maybe we should stop guessing and let you tell us," Nathan said, while assuming his *patient* pose.

It took a minute, but Bob finally started. "Right now, my mother loves me. I know that, but it is also a that she sees me as a disappointment and a pale version of my father."

"Bob, sometimes . . ."

"Let me finish. What I say is true and I can't do anything about it if I don't face it before it is too late. A couple of your people were in our supermarket today, and the restaurant, inquiring about large quantities of food and supplies—even kitchen space. Everybody is talking about the huge crowd that was out here yesterday. In fact, the whole town was busy. I'm not sure I understand what all is going on, but it seems you folks have become an international sensation and quite a lightning rod for attention, both wanted and unwanted, I hear.

"Yes, that's kind of an understatement," I added. I wanted to add a whole bunch of other stuff but decided better of it.

"Anyway," Bob continued. "It seems you have committed to provide food to the very people who are here to hurt you. Five thousand of them, I hear."

"We have," Nathan said quietly.

"So, I was thinking, maybe you would let me do it."

"Do what, exactly?" I asked. I was proving myself a little less patient than my husband.

"Feed them. All of them. All your people and all the ones from across the street."

"Thank you for the offer, Bob," Nathan said, "but this can't be a business opportunity. It has to be . . ."

"Free!" Bob interrupted. "Completely free. Sandwiches, sides, cold drinks. Free, all day, until the people quit coming."

"That's quite an undertaking," I said.

"I can do it!" Bob jumped in. "I have the connections, the equipment and the crew. I've been thinking about it all afternoon. We'll set up in three locations, maybe four. One on your corner—there's still room even with all you have going on. Another one will be kitty corner from your church—there's land over there and I know the guy. And I just happen to own a piece of land on the back side of whatever that atheist place is. That will pull the crowds apart instead of together. I can get the permits. I'll close some of our businesses for the day, so I can get the workers. This is the kind of stuff I do!"

As Bob wound down, we three sat in silence for a long pause.

"What would we do?" I asked.

"As far as the food goes, you don't have to do anything except say yes. Please say yes. I think you should concentrate on the churchy stuff—sorry, that didn't come out right. The spiritual stuff. Talk to them. Pray. I heard about that whole bathroom scene. Sounds like you'll have to do that again, right?"

"You sound overanxious, Bob," Nathan said. "Why do you want to do this? Why do you want it so bad? Is this just to impress your mother?"

Bob paused for a moment and took a deep breath, before he began, "I hope you can see your way to cut me a little slack here, because the truth is, I am not sure. Exactly. It started out to be that. I admit. Who wants their mother to be disappointed in how you turned out? But here's the other thing. Mom is not wrong about much. Maybe she's right about me. You two are the last ones who are going to believe me, but I really want to be a good man. I haven't shown it very well. I know. But, I believe in God. Really, I do. Something doesn't sit right with me with all these atheists trying to convince others to forget Him. I'm not sure what it is, because I don't understand this stuff very deeply, and I don't pretend to get your strategy of taking care of and feeding the atheists, but you seem to be on top of the God stuff . . . maybe I want God to think I'm okay, too."

Bob's eyes grew misty. "Now I'm just embarrassed. Do you think maybe you could let me work this out while we're getting the job done?"

I was about to encourage Bob along this new line of thinking and feeling, when Nathan spoke up.

"There will be certain conditions."

"Name it," Bob responded immediately.

"It can't say *Williams* anywhere. No signs for any of your businesses or family. The people who matter will know—you couldn't hide it if you tried—but you don't make any kind of splash."

Bob gulped audibly and asked, "What else?"

"You put up big signs that read *Free Food to All Comers!* And, you put up small, tasteful signs at every food station that read something like: *Courtesy of the East Fork Ministerial Association of Churches; God loves you and so do we.*"

Bob smiled and said, "I'll do every bit of that, for one thing in return."

"Go on."

"My Mom can spend as much of that day as she wants inside of your church, where there will be good people around her while I am working the event."

"Done," said my husband.

"Done and done," replied a smiling Bob who I could barely recognize as the same man I used to know.

After a few pleasantries and goodbyes, he left.

"So, what do you think of that?" I asked Nathan.

"Seems too good to be true, but, then in recent weeks and months God has provided all kinds of miraculous events."

"That's for sure," I answered, feeling relieved. "Who'd a thunk it?"

My beloved walked over to me and took me in his arms. I expected one of his great kisses.

Instead, he said, "Besides, with the food task in Bob's hands, we will have more time to set up and prepare for the Great Debate."

"You mean, we're doing it? Debating the Tall Man?"

"Unless you disapprove. I reckon God has not lined up miracle after miracle—and involved literally tens of millions of people on some level—to not do a Big Thing. I believe the debate may well be the Big Thing."

"I do not disapprove," I said. "I'm all-in. Now what?"

"We get Alicia involved. There will be lots of Who, What, When, Where and How. Ground rules and format. Alicia can represent us in the negotiations. We'll have to meet with her to make plans."

"God will get us through," I said.

"Of course," he answered. "But, God will help us get through the planning, preparation and strategizing, too. We don't want to be either naïve or unprepared. Stevens won't be pulling any punches."

"Fair enough. When do we get started?"

"Tomorrow. Right now, we're going to notify the others that Williams is taking care of the food, and then you and I are going out to dinner."

Chapter 41

Nathan

Jenn and I met with Alicia, without any of the other church members present. I just had a feeling we needed to be able to brainstorm and kick some ideas around without committing to anything right away. That can be hard to do with too many people. Besides, it seemed Jenn and I would be the ones on the hotspot, so I wanted to be real sure the arrangements were something the two of us could be comfortable with.

We arrived at a pretty simple plan. We would suggest the debate be between Jenn and me on our side, and Stevens and another person of his choice on the other. Western Michigan University is in Kalamazoo, Michigan—less than an hour's drive south of us. They have a good Journalism Department there, so we decided to suggest the department head as a moderator. We went back and forth for a long time on whether to request a format of three-minute speech/one-minute rebuttal, three-minute speech/one-minute rebuttal or three-minute speech/three-minute speech, one-minute rebuttal/one-minute rebuttal. In the end we decided to just let Alicia work it out in negotiations with the other side.

We figured the speeches would be in response to questions asked by the moderator. The big sticking point concerned the questions. What questions? Prepared by who? We really didn't come up with a solid answer and decided to see what the Tall Man had in mind. We were probably going to have to compromise here and there, anyway.

My biggest concern over the Great Debate was location. Where should this thing happen? Particularly, should it be a place big enough to house a large audience? If so, who should be allowed onsite? I wanted this to be a time of thoughtful discussion, done in complete sentences and finished thoughts. I had considerable dread over the idea of a partisan audience screaming and applauding and booing and hissing. Obviously, the event would be livestreamed and broadcast on TV and radio. That was largely the point. I instructed Alicia to try to negotiate a small, in-studio sort of setting. If we were going to speak for and about God, I at least wanted the opportunity to offer clear and understandable information.

When we had discussed all that could be discussed, I said, "Alicia, just take the ball and run with it. Find whoever is negotiating for the other side and have a meeting. We'll know a lot more when we find out what they are thinking."

"I will," she replied. "But, I am still nervous about disappointing you. I can't know how this is going to turn out."

"Nobody knows exactly what's next," Jenn answered. "You don't need to worry a bit. We will accept whatever happens as God's will."

"Okay. I'll get back to you as soon as I know something."

Chapter 42

Jennifer

Life went on. Busily. *The Twelve Baskets Center for Unending Prayer* was busy all the time. Even the overnight shift received increasing calls, many from parts of the world where the sun was already up. We had to add five more prayer partners to keep up. Kevin Cloverton assured us money was still piling up, so we hired freely. I truly loved the training program that had evolved, helping the new people to recognize what the callers were really seeking—which was often not exactly the thing they said it was—and providing Holy Spirit-filled prayer on their behalf. I had discovered seemingly everyday people often turned into sincere, profound prayer warriors.

Through all of the busy weeks we continued our core activities. Nathan still honed his sermons in the church, at random times. Condi played her beautiful music as she felt moved to do so. I prayed from time to time, for minutes or hours. And Frank and Sylvie continued to work their way through the Old Testament, always filled with wide-eyed wonderment. Each week they brought their various questions to Nathan. At the beginning of each subsequent session, they would excitedly provide the answers to last week's questions. I had to admit, it was a masterstroke in teaching Bible 101.

The livestream was being watched by so many people we were never sure of accurate numbers, but it had to be well over a hundred million. We had long ago accepted that as a normal thing and no longer wondered, *How is this possible? Because God said so*, seemed to suffice.

On Thursday, trailers and equipment began to arrive to various sites around the four corners. We smiled when we realized much of the stuff had big blank spots on the sides, where the names of various Williams-family enterprises were covered up. We stayed out of the way and let them prepare.

Nathan and I were settled in and feeling relatively relaxed on Friday evening, when there was a knock at the door. It was Alicia.

"Come in. Come in," Nathan said. "Have a seat."

I got her a beverage and gave her a few moments to catch her breath. She appeared more than a little shaken.

"Well, Alicia," Nathan began. "I'm guessing something has happened. Tell us about it."

"Stevens is doing his own negotiating," she said. "I just spent over an hour with that . . . guy. I can live the rest of my life without doing that again."

"I'm so sorry," I said. "That wasn't fair. We should have gone with you and . . ."

"Are you kidding!" Alicia blurted, "I kicked his butt!"

Unfortunately, Nathan was caught in the middle of a mouthful of Diet Coke, most of which he laughed onto the front of his shirt. Alicia giggled.

"I need to explain," she continued. "I am not exactly sure how things turned out."

"Go ahead and tell the story," Nathan said. "I'll just sit here and dry out for a while."

"He accepted the meeting, but he seemed disappointed to be talking to me. He made a couple cracks about you not facing him yourselves, but I told him I was the decision-maker on this event and he ought to get serious. Then he tried to bully me a bit—that guy can't go two minutes without speechifying against religion and for his massive intellect. Anyway, I informed him my beliefs where not germane to the conversation at hand and we should get started on making arrangements for the debate."

"I'm impressed," Nathan said. "So how did the negotiations go?"

"I'm not sure. That's where it got interesting. He whipped out a sheet of paper with a full-blown plan for the debate. Number of people, date, place, time, panel of questioners, the whole bit. Huge auditorium. Twenty-five hundred people. Panel of nationally known newscasters, in exchange for broadcast rights. Livestream prohibited—he knows who has the numbers there. Before I could say much of anything, he moved on as if the format was settled and pulled out his list of approved questions."

"Wow," I said. "I can only imagine what that looked like."

"Well, I can only imagine most of it myself," Alicia said. "I didn't get to read most of it."

"You don't have the questions?" Nathan asked, his voice straining a bit against an increasingly brittle smile.

"Nope. That's where the butt-kicking came in. The first question was offered in a debate-style format, something like, 'Be it resolved that the society of the United States, and the world, would be better off without the influence of Christianity and other ill-conceived religions.' He explained to me—as if I am some kind of idiot—he would be arguing the affirmative and you would be arguing the negative. When I saw the next couple of questioned started with phrases like, 'In spite of the provable, demonstrable truth of science, how can one rationally hold the belief that . . .' and other stuff like that."

My head spinning, I really wanted to jump in with some comments, but I thought better of it. Alicia was doing fine. Nathan must have reasoned the same, as he said nothing.

"So, I handed everything back to him and said, 'None of this is happening.' Just like that! At first, he sat there and stared. So, I stared back. He was pissin' me off!"

This time, it was me who laughed.

"Finally, he said, 'This is the plan. If the Reverends Martin want this forum, they will have to abide by it.' I didn't even have to think before I responded, 'That's fine. We have no real need to do this anyway.' I almost kept talking, but somehow I was on my feet and heading for the door."

"You go, girl!" I nearly shouted. My attempt at sounding cool came out lame.

"What did he do?" Nathan asked, shooting a grin my way.

"He chased me out the door, and down the hall and out the front door. He was hollering about how we weren't finished yet and I had better get back in here. I kept going and he yelled about how I was failing to do my job and the Martins will be upset. As I got in the car and slammed the door, he was into 'Please! Please' and stuff like that. Then I came here."

"Holy Cow!" Nathan said. "You handled that like a real pro. Good job!"

"That's for sure," I added. "I'm glad we weren't there to mess it up. You did great!"

"I hope so," she said. "But I'm not at all sure where that leaves us. It's true I failed to get a negotiated agreement."

"That will come," Nathan said. "I think this leaves us with the upper hand. Stevens is obviously desperate to get his day in the sun. And, to hear you say it out loud reminds me we really don't need to do this, at least not his way. We can wait as long as need be. Sounds like he can't."

"So, what do I do next?" Alicia asked.

"Wait," I said. "Just wait. Patience is not only a virtue, it is our best weapon."

"Okay. I'll try," Alicia answered with a shake of her head. "I hate to admit it, but I kind of want to give the Tall Man another shot."

"You'll get your shot," Nathan said. "For now, who's up for pizza?"

Chapter 43

Nathan

When I was in training to be a pastor, one of the many tasks required of us as candidates was to interview six experienced pastors. The idea was to ask questions about what it is actually like to be a pastor—the day-to-day stuff nobody teaches you in college or seminary. Of course, the end result was to be a *reflection paper* written about the responses. Most of it I forgot long ago, but a few things stuck. One old guy told me to always double-knot my shoes and pee one last time before entering the sanctuary for Sunday service. I have always followed that advice. Another told me the biggest mistake a lot of pastors make is to try to do new things and improve the church they are serving. He said, *The people don't want to change and they don't want to improve, so just shut up and keep your head down and this job will be really easy.* That advice I do not follow.

I remember one other piece of advice, coming from a woman. I considered her an old pastor at the time, but I now realize she was younger then than I am now. Anyway, she said, *Don't try to pack too much information into one sermon. The people can only follow so much, and you are going to need lots more sermons.* She continued, *Preparing for Sundays is like watching telephone poles when you are doing sixty down the highway; you see one coming, and it seems a ways off, then you get there and whoosh, it's gone. Then you look up and here comes another one.*

I thought of that because, suddenly, it was Sunday again. And, quite a Sunday it was. Nothing about it was normal, except nothing had been normal for many months.

Once again, the crowd across the street was huge early and growing by the minute. I had to hand it to Stevens, whatever he was doing to turn out the people was working. Once again, our usual group of devout people arrived for worship. It remained a mystery how it could remain so constant. One would have thought attendance would grow—or even shrink—but it did neither. Except this week we had one special guest. Martha Williams. Once again, our now-massive computer system showed millions upon millions of viewers tuning in for the service.

There were some recent changes. Our crew was dressed for a day filled with hard labor, and mounds of bathroom cleaning equipment and chemicals were stacked at the ready. I chuckled a bit when I noticed three full cases of air fresheners. The most noticeable additions were the four food stations, created by one Mr. Bob Williams. One was on our property, another was kitty-corner from us and there were two way off in the distance, off the backside of the atheist property. It was obvious that Bob planned on splitting the traffic flow, so as to avoid gridlock. The man knew what he was doing. Each station had all the agreed upon signage and was backed by refrigerated trucks ready to dispense free food in record time.

As I was admiring the setup, Frank snuck up beside me. "I don't see where they did anything to improve the bathroom or the food situations," he said. "Looks like maybe more people than last week. Even if they don't want to do business with us, the people will be streaming over soon enough."

"Frank," I asked. "Would you think less of me if I admitted to you I am really enjoying some of this?"

"Thank God!" Frank burst out. "I thought it was just me!"

As we shared a laugh, we heard announcements coming over the sprawling PA system from across the road. "Please make your way to your seats! The program will begin soon! Please be seated." The flow of the traffic changed, as people began to consolidate.

"Well, Pastor," Frank said, "almost time for worship."

I was about to reply when I was interrupted by another announcement. "Please be seated. Thank you. We are happy to see you all here today, another great crowd. You may see other offerings nearby," the voice on the loudspeakers continued, "but all your needs for food and bathroom facilities will be met right here on the complex. Thank you for your cooperation!"

Frank laughed. "Don't bet your lunch money on that," he said. "Pastor? Let's go to church!"

Go to church we did. We had a wonderful service, still in our little island of privacy. Each Sunday I wondered if God had decided to take the protective bubble away from our little Triple-W building, but so far we were still in our small group, except for the addition of Martha. She did look thinner and older than the last time I had seen her, but she seemed to be feeling fine. In fact, there were times she appeared to beam.

After the service, Martha said, "That was quite lovely. Our new preacher at East Fork First UMC does a fine job, but, Reverend Martin, I do appreciate your succinct and straightforward style. That was a fine message."

"Why, thank you, Mrs. Williams," I said.

"Mrs. Williams! For heaven's sake, Pastor. Call me Martha. And, Condi," she continued, "I had almost forgotten what it was like to hear her play. Just magnificent."

"We are blessed to have her," I responded.

"Losing her was a great loss to First Church," Martha said. "But, then, I suppose we had reason to expect some sort of punishment."

Before I could think up a response, Jennifer joined us and Martha went on, "Oh, Mrs. Martin, may I have a word with you. Oh, I am sorry, I understand it is Reverend Martin now."

"Yes, thank you, it is," Jennifer said, "although around here they tend to call me Reverend Honey."

That left Martha speechless, but not for long.

"I suppose there must be a story behind that. Be that as it may, I just wanted to say I have rarely heard such inspired prayer. I generally hope for prayers to be over with as soon as possible, but I could have luxuriated in your words for hours. Splendid."

"Those are very kind words, Mrs. Williams," Jennifer said.

"It is Martha, dear. Just Martha."

"Very well . . . Martha."

"Now," Martha continued, "What has gotten into that son of mine?"

She stopped talking and waited for a response, as if her single-sentence question clearly stated all she wanted to know.

"What do you mean?" I asked.

"Come now, Reverends Martin, surely you have noticed my Bob is suddenly doing things he has never done before. He has an army of employees and friends out there with enough food to feed an actual army. I've not seen him do that before. And, all the signs say Free. I think we can all agree that is not the expected behavior of the Williams family."

I was glad to see a glint in her eye and the hint of a smile.

"So, I ask again, what has gotten into Bob?"

"Holy Spirit got him, sure as shootin'." It was an obviously eves-dropping Frank.

"What does that . . .?" Martha started.

"I think maybe he had a *come to Jesus* moment," Sylvie chimed in.

"Maybe both!" Frank said through a belly laugh. "Come on Sylvie, we got to get out there and advertise *Clean, Free Bathrooms!*"

As they moved on their way, Martha exclaimed, "Would somebody please explain to me what they are talking about?"

I was about to say something brilliant when we were interrupted once again. Evidently, the regular members of the congregation were keeping a pretty close eye—and ear—on Martha.

"Good morning, Martha," said Edwina Fine. "I assume I may call you Martha, as I have seen a few more years than you. What Frank and Sylvie Osborn—two of the most devout Christians I have ever met—are saying in their no-nonsense manner is your son has been moved by faith to become a better man. He wishes to be less of what he has always been and more like the man God wants him to be. Robert will never again be quite the same."

"How do you know this?" Martha asked, more in wonderment than challenge.

Edwina smiled. "It will have to suffice to know that I know."

"And you can take what Edwina says to the bank!" I finally got a word in edgewise.

Chapter 44

Jennifer

After that remarkable exchange with Martha Williams, we all headed outside to see what was happening. The huge crowd across the street was mostly settled in their seats, with quite a few left standing. Our side of the road was in a quiet state of waiting.

The Tall Man was rhapsodizing away, with yet another version of his philosophy of science, logic and the universal superiority of the magnificent human brain. The flip side of that, of course, was the nonsensical approach of people stupid enough, inferior enough and weak enough to *need* an invented god to absolve them of their responsibility to think and make decisions for themselves. It had gotten to be standard stuff.

After a good hour and a half of this, two things happened. First, Bob—perhaps I mean Robert—Williams sauntered over and approached Nathan.

"You sure about this? The hungry crowds, I mean? We've got a ton—actually way more than a ton—of food and haven't given anything away so far."

"It's coming," Nathan said. "Soon."

"I'm sure you're right," Williams said, but he didn't sound too certain.

"Hang on," Nathan said, "I'll get you a timetable. Frank! Can you come here a minute?"

"Sure, Pastor. What's up?"

"Bob here wants to know when the traffic is going to start up. What do you think?"

"Well, you see how the parents with little kids and the old men are starting to sneak out to the bathrooms? They're gettin' antsy. The speaker is too carried away with himself to realize he is about to lose the crowd, but he's smart and he's about to figure it out. It's already half past noon. If he doesn't stop talkin' in twenty minutes, they're bustin' loose anyway. Then, bathrooms first, then food. Mr. Williams, you best be ready to fling the hash in no more than twenty-five minutes."

I spoke up. "Frank, Mr. Williams wants us to use his first name. From now on, he's Robert."

"Well, Robert," Nathan said, "best get the hash ready."

Robert's face grew determined, and he took off at a run, to rally his troops. Frank smiled and trotted over to get his bathroom crew ready. Nathan and I just stood still and held hands.

Then, all of the sudden, the tone changed. The Tall Man was hollering louder than usual. It took us a minute to focus on his words.

He shouted, "The Most High Reverends Martin don't seem to want to meet with me! They don't seem willing to explain their positions or defend their so-called god! I have to wonder, *WHAT ARE THEY AFRAID OF!*"

The crowd applauded and cheered and jeered.

"I have set everything up! A place to meet! Television coverage! A fair and civil exchange! All they have to do is show up! A chance to make sense out of their nonsense!"

The crowd roared.

"All laid out for them. All the work done! And yet, no agreement! Is it that they have nothing to say! Do they lack courage!"

Now the crowd was beginning to laugh.

"Really, I don't know what else I can do for them! Do they expect me to carry both sides of the debate!"

The mob started to laugh and hoot and holler again, but with a strange wave of silence rolling from the front rows to the back, they hushed. It took me a minute to see why. My husband was striding determinedly across the road. He reached the other side, hopped the ditch and jumped up and onto the platform. He moved to within a foot of The Tall Man and his cherished microphone.

"May I?" he asked.

Stunned, Stevens mumbled into the microphone, "What? May you what?"

"I would like a few words with your people. May I?"

"You can't just march up here and demand . . . ."

My husband is smart. Instead of looking sharply up at the much-taller Stevens, he leaned into the microphone and said, "Surely you are not afraid to let these good people hear a few words from an idiot like me."

"Of course not. I am not afraid of anything. Speak . . . if you must. Please be brief. It is time for our break."

"Thank you. Good afternoon, everyone," Nathan spoke firmly and boldly. "I am the Reverend Nathan Martin. I pastor—along with my wife the Reverend Jennifer Martin—that fine little church across the street—the *WWW.God Christian Church.* I represent that church, but mostly I represent God."

There were a few groans and one guy started to heckle, but those around him shushed him up quick.

"Mr. Stevens here thinks it important we publicly debate matters of science and religion. He's probably right—he's a really smart guy. I will be happy to do that. Next Sunday. In my church at 2:00 in the afternoon. My wife and I on one side and Mr. Stevens and anybody he chooses on the other. No planned questions. Only what we pose to each other. Each side gets three minutes and the other side gets two minutes to rebut. Then switch turns. Simple. Two hours. A moderator just to keep order. I promise we will not say a word when it is not our turn. I will trust your representatives to be honorable enough to do the same. We will livestream it to the world. Mr. Stevens may arrange for two TV networks of his choosing to set up and broadcast the events. That will leave room for each side to invite twenty-five visitors, who will have no voice, no vote, no anything except to witness and listen. The rest of you can sit right here and watch it on these big screens, or watch it from anywhere you please. That is the deal. I will be there, ready to go. So will Reverend Jennifer Martin."

Nathan took a beat and looked up at The Tall Man. "I sure hope you show up, Mr. Stevens. Otherwise it is going to be a lot of hoopla over nothing."

"Well, I don't think . . . I don't . . . we'll need to . . ."

While Stevens stuttered and mumbled, Nathan belted out loud and strong, "We are now adjourned for one and a half hours! Clean restrooms and free food are available for everyone!"

Stevens stood on the platform muttering—my valiant husband still next to him—while the huge audience evaporated into a mad scramble across the streets in every direction.

"Score one for our side." It was Martha.

It was hard to see much at that point. The crowds stormed the bathrooms and concession stands, seemingly coming from every direction. The facilities owned and operated by the *Free Us from Religion Coalition* were busy, too, but thousands of people showed no hesitation in taking advantage of Frank and Sylvie's free restrooms or Robert Williams' free food. Biblically, it might have been described as *like locusts*.

Despite the crowds, I did my best to keep an eye on my husband and his nemesis, the Tall Man. I was so proud of Nathan. Serious, ethical Christians are often at a disadvantage when it comes to public discourse and, especially, debate. Sometimes the problem is even true when we are in disagreement with other Christians, perhaps of the not so ethical variety. Anyway, it is part of who we are and what we do. We aren't to lie or cast false aspersions. We aren't to denigrate or condemn or call names or demonize. When the other side, the opponent, or even the enemy feels free to fight dirty, it can be tough. It is hard to win a battle when the other side is blithely using weapons we will not use.

Nathan had just found a powerful and clever way to turn the tables on the Tall Man without resorting to foul play. Sure, he pinned Stevens into a corner in front of thousands of his own followers, but he didn't lie or call him any names.

Anyway, Nathan and Stevens remained on the platform for quite a while, facing each other. Nathan had to tilt his head sharply up to maintain eye contact, but he didn't flinch. Neither spoke. Each one sizing up the other, it seemed to me. Eventually, Nathan extended his hand to Stevens. Stevens glanced around to see if he was being watched. He was. Slowly and reluctantly, he brought his hand up to Nathan's and shook. They both gave a curt nod, spun decisively around and walked away. The lines had been drawn.

Chapter 45

Nathan

I don't know what got into me. Actually, I do. The Holy Spirit set me in motion and gave me the words. After the confrontation on the platform, I exited in the wrong direction. It was like when I get off an elevator at the wrong floor. I walk around for a bit and then get back on, so it isn't obvious I made a mistake. So, I kept walking, right through the crowd and, front to back, across the *Free Us from Religion Coalition* property. As I approached the rear property line, I couldn't help but smile. Hundreds of people swarmed one of Williams' food outlets. Almost as quickly as they approached the counter, they retreated, hands filled with bags of food and cups of soft drinks. They were smiling and laughing. *This is great! Thank you!* and various other exclamations of happiness rang out.

"Hey! Aren't you the pastor from across the street?" one man called out. "Hey look! It's the guy!" responded another. Soon I had some fifty people encircling me.

"Yes, as a matter of fact. I am Nathan. Nice to be with you all!" I tensed a bit, waiting for whatever would be next.

"What's with all the free food?!" a young mom trying to keep track of two kids blurted out, "I mean it's great . . . thanks and all . . ."

"Yeah, thank you," another joined in, "but I think she means . . . why?"

The small crowd realized that the question posed was a bigger deal than it might first seem. They got quiet—an oasis of calm in a sea of noise. I paused and took a deep breath.

"Because God loves you. And, because of that, we love you, too."

"You make it sound simple," the mother said.

"It is," I replied.

"There is no god!" a different man said, perhaps remembering the purpose of their rally.

"And, still, He loves you anyway."

"That does not answer the question!" yet another man screamed.

"Yes," I said, "it does."

"This makes no sense," he retorted. "You are just saying stuff!"

"And yet the people are fed," I said. "How are the sandwiches?"

"Good," a little girl piped up. "Mine's ham! And, I got chips!"

"What do you say?" exhorted her mother.

"Thank you!" both kids shouted. "This is fun!"

"Out of the mouths of children," I said.

"What do you want out of this?" one of the angry men spat out. "You can't buy us off with a sandwich!"

"I want to say we don't want anything in return," I said, "but that wouldn't be entirely true."

"Thought so!" he said. "So, what is it?"

"I want you to experience in some small way, that God loves you, and so do we. That's it. Nothing else."

The man wilted a little, but came back strong. "It's just a sandwich and a bag of chips."

"And a apple and a cookie!" the little boy corrected.

"And juice!" giggled the girl.

"Times about six thousand people!" added someone who hadn't yet said a word.

"And, still," I said, "we really don't want anything from you. We don't even need to be thanked, although that is nice. It is simply what we do. Now, if no one minds, I think I will get one of those lunches myself."

It took me awhile to work my way back to our side of the road. I walked and ate my lunch—which was really quite good— and had a few more conversations. I was challenged several more times, but grew more and more comfortable in supplying responses. Some of the people were rather blunt and even aggressive, but they stayed civil and I never had the feeling things could get out of hand. In the end, I was glad for the experience. It made me much more aware of who I was dealing with.

I found Jennifer helping with the bathroom detail. Again, there were good conversations going on all around the church grounds.

"Hi, Honey," I called out. "I was gone longer than I intended, you doing okay?"

"Sure," she replied, "nothing better than the unending opportunity to clean restrooms! Strangely, I kind of mean that."

"Well, don't let me interrupt," I said. "I am going inside and sit down for a little while. There's a lot going on."

"Tell me about it!" Jenn shouted, then took a deep breath and ducked quickly inside a just-vacated stall.

When I got inside, I found several of the regulars catching some break time. Among them were Martha and Robert Williams.

"Hello, Pastor Nathan," Robert said. "I came in to check on Mom, but I was hoping to run into you, too."

"Here I am," I replied. "How is the feeding frenzy going?"

"Great! This is one of my best days ever. The people are all excited, the crew is doing a great job, and the food is holding up, so far. We've sure been pumping it out."

"For the record," I said, "you have done a fantastic job. I don't think I've ever seen so many people served so quickly."

"Thank you," Robert said. "With that bathroom operation you've got going there, we're sure filling them up and emptying them out!"

"Oh, Robert," Mother Martha said, "don't be crass." But she was laughing.

"I am coming a little late to the party," Robert said. "What exactly is going on here, and what happens next?"

"I'm not sure anybody knows exactly what is going on," I said. "But, in short, our little church operation here has gotten a lot of attention, locally, nationally and even around the world. The wonders of the internet. We have millions of people paying attention to everything we do. It's a God-thing, for sure, because it simply could not have happened otherwise. Someday I'll tell you about all the unexplainable—mostly wonderful—things that have been going on."

"So, who are all these people across the street?"

"Atheist activists."

"Really?"

"Yeah, really. They are very organized and well-funded and passionate about eliminating any religious influence on society. Evidently, as word about what God was doing here spread, it *poked the bear*, so to speak. This atheist movement decided to target us as an example to the rest of the world. Sort of discredit us or expose us or something. So, they bought land and set up right over there."

"What's next?" Robert asked.

"I'm not sure, but I think I just forced their leader, a big, tall, smart, rich guy named Alexander Stevens, into accepting terms for a livestreamed and televised debate, right here, in this building, at 2:00 p.m. one week from today."

"Holy cow," Robert said. "This thing has really taken off! Are you up for all this?"

"All I know is Jennifer and I are committed. If Stevens shows up, it's on! I'm not sure if I am up for it, as you say. I'm nervous. But, one way or the other, this will be another God-thing. So, we'll just prepare as best we can and then hold on for dear life."

"Wow," Robert said. "I'd be terrified out of my mind . . . not that you need to be afraid. You're good at this stuff. Anyway, if there is anything we can do to help, just say so."

"Well," I said, "you have already done way more than could be expected. Truly you have. You shouldn't have to do another thing, but there is going to be another huge crowd . . ."

"You can stop right there," Mother Martha interjected. "You have more than enough to worry about. You need not think one more minute about feeding next week's crowd. My son, Robert, is on the case."

Chapter 46

Jennifer

Despite the extraordinary happenings of that penultimate Sunday, it was hard to think about anything but the rapidly approaching, new, Sunday. Everything was different now. Even though rapid change and daily, abrupt differences had become the order of the day, this was even more . . . different.

The debate was on! The task at hand was nebulous and unclear. The idea of defending the faith in front of millions—some friendly and some on the attack—was daunting, to say the least. What did the Tall Man have in store? What strategy would he employ? And, what the heck were we going to say?!

Thanks to Nathan's bold move, we at least had some ideas to build around. We knew we would be on home turf. At the very beginning of this adventure, Pastor Carl had told us the new church in the old building would be a small but powerful force in the world. He had certainly been right so far, and now having the church as the site of the Great Debate seemed proper and comforting. The live crowd would be small and equally divided. This seemed good. While we had the massive livestream audience, Stevens had the large numbers of people attending in person. We assumed the facility across the street would be packed for the debate. Balancing the crowd inside the church seemed like a good solution all the way around.

We knew that discussion topics would come up during the debate. With no way to anticipate what challenges might be coming, we could only prepare by solidifying our core beliefs and values, and strengthen our confidence in God to equip us and guide our words.

There were lots of tasks to be done, including some of the pragmatic and tangible variety. There would be crowds. How would we handle the logistics of having thousands of people on site, when only a few dozen could come inside? We still needed to think about bathrooms and food. Which of our church family would be tending to the needs of others, and which would be in the twenty-five to be invited into the pews? We needed a moderator. Stevens would be sending in crews from two TV stations. Who was going to set that up? The questions were many and the immediate answers few. We set up a Monday evening meeting at the church, with all of the regulars invited. We also set up a private meeting for Tuesday, with only Nathan, Alicia Skiba and I. We would also be having many, many meetings with God.

An hour before leaving for the Monday meeting, Nathan and I talked.

"Well, Honey, what do you think?" Nathan asked.

It seemed an odd question, as we had been talking constantly for days.

"I'm not sure what you mean," I said. "Think about what, exactly?"

"The big picture, I guess," he responded. "We've been snowed under with things and stuff and facts and assumptions and other people's problems and . . . everything related to Stevens and his crew. So, I thought maybe we should pause a minute and see what we're thinking."

"Okay. I'll try. I have been thinking about the things Pastor Carl said and wrote before he left us with this situation. He set us up. Most of the time I mean that in a good way. He told us what kind of church this would be, and he was right. Even when we tried to take it down a different path, we came back to Pastor Carl's vision. Small? Why is the church so huge, only no new people show up for church on Sunday? Powerful? So many livestream views we can't even begin to count them anymore. Hundreds of prayer requests every day. Money appearing whenever we need it."

"So well known, the organized enemies of the Universal Church of All Christians has chosen to target us," Nathan whispered, more to himself than to me.

"Yes. Exactly. And I am beginning to think we have no reason to be surprised."

"Really?" Nathan replied. "I have been surprised almost every day for months!"

"Yes! Me, too! But, that's my point. The things happening are in line with what Pastor Carl said. And, frankly, with what the Bible says. All things are possible with God. Sure, we didn't know specifically that Condi would show up and become maybe the most listened-to musician on the planet. Or people would become obsessed with listening to my prayers or watching you practice sermons!"

"That's nothing, compared with Frank the Bible Teacher!" Nathan interjected, followed by a big, satisfying belly laugh.

"That's for sure," I said, "and, we sure didn't know who the boogeyman would be, or that he would be so tall!"

After a short pause, Nathan said, slowly and calmly, "Not near so tall as Goliath."

"Huh?" I said.

"When you think about it," he continued, "David didn't know who Goliath was until the time came. He didn't know how powerful Goliath was or how skilled a warrior, or, how tall. David had simply made a habit out of trusting God and obeying His will. When Goliath showed up, he was just the next thing—bigger than the rest—but just the next thing."

"Yeah," I said, picking up the thread. "And before that, the prophet Samuel somehow knew to pick David—over all the better, more sensible choices—to succeed Saul as the next king. I think

Pastor Carl is a lot like Samuel. God used Samuel to choose David, and He used Pastor Carl to choose you."

Nathan looked me deep in the eyes and said, "And you."

For the first time, and with a confidence I had never felt before, I replied, "And me."

We accepted that as kind of a watershed moment, and didn't talk about it anymore. It was time to head over to the church for the organizational meeting. I was sure the meeting would be long and complicated and bogged down in details. I gathered my energy and patience for what promised to be a taxing evening.

When we all got settled, Nathan asked if anybody had anything to say before the meeting started. He does that quite routinely, as a way to see if he has left anything off his agenda. This time Kevin Cloverton took the opportunity to speak up.

"Yes. Thank you, Pastor Nathan. It seems to me we are meeting tonight to deal with things that will be different this Sunday, because of the debate. We need to have the church service in the morning. We've got that down pat. I think we just keep the extra people—the TV crews, the moderator, the people from the other side, etc.—out of the building until we finish at about 11:30. That gives them two and a half hours to set up. If they don't like it, too bad. We need to keep the bathrooms running and feed the crowds. I understand Bob Williams is going to handle the food again—they did a fantastic job yesterday—so we can quit worrying about that. So, all we have to do is pick twenty-five people to sit on our side in the sanctuary, and schedule others to handle the bathrooms for the two hours the debate is on. The lines should be short during that time. Everyone is excited to see the debate."

John Drobena spoke up. "Can we rig a big screen out by the bathhouse, so people outside can keep track?"

"That's a thought," Kevin said. "Jeremy?"

"Sure."

"Okay, good. Do that," Kevin continued. "The only other thing that seems out of the ordinary might be crowd control. I can see people who were not invited trying to get in. I suggest all of those who feel able—out of the group of twenty-five who are selected to attend in person—handle any control issues right up until time to start the debate. Then they can all file in and take their seats. That should work and might look impressive, too. Now all we need to do is pick the twenty-five and we should be set."

After a long pause, Janice—longtime secretary to my husband—spoke up.

"Nicely organized, Kevin, but it seems like a rather complete plan for a first comment. If you don't mind my saying."

"Not at all," Kevin answered. "I have three reasons for doing this. One, I felt called to do it. Two, we can start with this and make any adjustment the group sees fit. Third—and very important, I think—Pastors Nathan and Jennifer are faced with a challenging, unique task that virtually no one has ever had to do before. I think we need to respect that, and take care of all the other stuff, so they focus on what they need to do. We all need to do our parts. Once the debate starts, we can't help them. So, we need to do it ahead of time."

The group murmured for a bit, then grew quiet.

Frank called out, "Sounds fine to me. Let's pick the twenty-five and then get on with this."

"Well, who's going to pick?" several people asked.

"May I make a suggestion?" Jeremy Clark asked.

"Go ahead."

"I'll work bathrooms, no problem. But I think we need the best supporters of our church and our pastors to be there. The ones who have been working hard for a long time. The ones who are the best at praying. And, I think this makes sense, the ones all those millions of people following our church online recognize. The TV stations are bound to do crowd shots."

"Kid makes sense," Leta Walsh said. "So, who would that be?"

"I keep records of what goes on," Janice Pohl said. "As a starting point, and in no particular order, I would say: Condi and

Kevin. Frank and Sylvie. Edwina. Art and Leta. I am sorry in advance for saying this . . . me. Jane. Francine, Michelle and Jeff. John and Shelly. And, without a doubt, Jeremy."

"That's a great start," Kevin said, "although I was prepared to volunteer for bathroom duty, so Condi could have a spot. Any nominations from the floor?"

"I think Joe and Susan Caulket would be a plus," Jane Petra offered. "They have been quietly involved in church activities from the beginning."

"Got it," Janice announced.

"I know this is kind of a point of personal privilege," said Edwina, "but I have a friend who for a long time helped me to keep the church officially a church. Could I have an extra seat?"

There was an immediate murmur of consent, so Janice wrote it down.

"I think the rest of us should take care of things—the bathrooms and crowd control and such—while the debate is going on," said Stan Goodrum. "We are all anxious to be in on the event, but it is important things go smoothly."

"Are the rest of you okay with that?" Kevin asked the remainder of the group. All indicated they were on board. "Then," he continued, "we are still seven short of our quota. Suggestions?"

I raised my hand.

"Yes, Pastor Jennifer . . . you don't really need to raise your hand."

"Robert Williams asked us to watch over his mother while he is working the food operation. I think, even though she is kind of new here, we should offer her a seat."

"Got it," said Janice.

"That leaves six more spots," Nathan said. "How about Jennifer selects six of her best prayer warriors from the Twelve Baskets prayer team. We hardly see some of them, but they are back there praying night and day. They are a huge part of Triple-W."

All agreed, loudly.

"I move we accept the whole plan!"

"Thank you, Frank," Kevin said.

"Second!" shouted several others.

"Any discussion? Hearing none—while not pretending this is anything like Robert's Rules of Order—all in favor say Amen."

Amens filled the room.

"All right then. How about the inside-the-debate group move to the back of the sanctuary and work out any details. The bathroom patrol and crowd control group move to the front and do the same. I will assume Pastors Nathan and Jennifer, along with Alicia, will work out the business of the debate, itself."

"Oh, my!" I blurted. "We forgot a seat for Alicia, and she is sitting right over there!"

Alicia laughed. "That's okay, Pastor Jennifer. Things are happening really fast."

"Well," I continued. "You obviously have a seat. I will choose five from the prayer center, instead of six."

"Thank you for catching that," Kevin said. "Now let's adjourn to our groups. When you have finished, you are free to go."

Chapter 47

Nathan

Time was flying by. After an unexpectedly short, but productive, meeting with the whole congregation on Monday it was already time for our Tuesday meeting with Alicia. Jenn and I sat with her, this time around the dining room table as there were notes to take and diagrams to create. Before we started talking business, Jenn prayed for guidance.

"Alicia," I said, "why don't you just start by telling us what you know and what you are thinking. We'll get it organized later."

"Okay," she replied, "but there is only so much to say. There are plenty of unknowns."

"That's for sure," Jenn said, almost too softly to hear.

"First off, that was quite a coup you pulled off, Pastor Nathan, taking over Stevens' microphone like that. You bought us a favorable setup that wasn't going to happen otherwise."

"Thank you. It was very spur of the moment."

"Well, it worked. Here's what I know. The moderator situation is taken care of. Gloria Jackson is a journalism professor at Western Michigan. She has agreed to moderate. As it turns out, she won't have much to do with questioning. Still, there are announcements and introductions to make, plus keeping track of, and enforcing time limits."

"I hope that goes better than the presidential debates," Jennifer interjected.

"I think it will," Alicia said. "I got the impression that Jackson is a tough cookie, and a bit of an eccentric. Anyway, the

211

timing job will also include bringing us in and out of commercial breaks."

"Commercial breaks?" I said. "I never thought about that. There will be commercials?"

"Yes. I have communicated four times with the other side. They are actually negotiating for which two TV stations will get the broadcast rights."

"Broadcast rights!?"

"Yes, and it appears we have lost control over that. The only assurance I have from them is any revenue will be split fifty-fifty with the church. I give them credit for that."

"Who will be advertising?" Jennifer asked.

"I have no idea. The stations will be selling the air time." Alicia said. "This is the downside. Your brilliant move to force the terms of the debate did not include negotiation of details. We're committed to doing something that is morphing every day."

"Do we just let it happen, then?" Jennifer continued.

"Mostly yes. However, I think we need to consider the possibility Stevens and his *Free Us from Religion Coalition* are creating commercials as we speak."

"Can they do that?" I asked.

"There is nothing to stop them, and I have not seen much evidence of decorum or fair play in their actions, so far."

"So," I asked, "should we be making commercials?"

"No," Jennifer interrupted, "but we should buy air time."

"Do you want to elaborate on that?" Alicia asked.

"Not right now. But get with Kevin and buy us some air."

"Okay. Will do."

"What next?" I asked.

Alicia explained, "The setup will be simple. Two chairs on either side of the platform, separated by about six feet. I am borrowing a nice set of chairs, so they all match. The moderator will be on the floor, right in front of the platform, facing you and away from the audience. That's it. Keeping it simple. They agreed, except they demanded the old wooden cross, that will be in the background the whole time, be removed or covered up."

"And?" I asked.

"And, "Alicia said, "I told them they agreed to meet in a church, and a church has a cross, and if they couldn't live with it, then don't show up."

"Good girl!" Jennifer said.

"They're still coming," I said.

"Oh yeah, they're still coming," Alicia said. "They are really wound up about this. They are not backing out now."

"Excellent. What else?" I asked.

"I am writing a script for the moderator. She wants it by Thursday. Now that we have established there will be no prearranged questions, the debate itself is going to happen organically."

"Is that a polite way of saying *flying by the seat of our pants?*" Jenn asked.

"Yeah, kind of. But, not entirely. Forgive me for talking about what you are probably already doing, but I have a few suggestions. First, think about what your purpose is. What do you hope will come out of this? Why do you think God set this up?"

"Keep the main thing the main thing," I said.

"Right. If your main goal is to defeat Stevens, then you plan one way. If you seek to glorify and/or obey God, that's another. And, if you want to convert people to Christianity, that's still another."

I found myself looking at Jenn, and she was looking at me.

"Also, remember who your audience is. You will have believers, who are already supporting you and are used to churchy talk. Lots of those. They will be watching to see if you defeat the other side. However, you will also have lots of people who are the exact opposite of that; unbelievers who haven't spent much time thinking about God or church—they will be watching curiously, wanting to know what is going on—and rabid unbelievers who have thought about it and have rejected God and are opposing His Church. Who do you want to talk to?"

"My guess is you won't let me say *all of them,*" Jennifer said.

"Nope."

"Clearly," I started, "we want to reach all of them. But, I get your point. I think the middle group is the first priority, those who are unbelievers, but still have open minds. After that, the staunch unbelievers. People need God, even if they don't know it. The people who already believe have fewer true needs. I hope what we do will hearten and inspire them, but they will be all right."

"There are two more categories," Jenn said. "We should move the other three down and make room for God at number one. If we are speaking on God's behalf, we want Him to be pleased with what we say."

"Of course," I said. "Of course."

Jenn continued, "The other one is Christian people who want to catch us saying and teaching something they consider wrong, so they can be right."

"Where would you put them on the priority list?" Alicia asked.

"Last," I said.

"Last," Jenn said.

"Okay, then let me say this. You are both pastors and I am not. Obviously, you are going to do what God moves you to do, and you are going to decide what should be said. But, for your consideration, I would . . ."

Alicia picked up her notepad and read:

One: Say everything clearly and distinctly without too much church-speak and technical jargon.

Two: Emphasize the benefits of being a faithful Christian. Curious people want to know why they should consider a life of faith.

Three: Paint a picture of the kind, loving, accepting place the church is for so many of us, while admitting it has not always been that for everyone.

Four: Don't try to defeat the Tall Man. Diffuse him or redirect him, but don't try to beat him. I have heard you say both that one cannot prove God, nor can one disprove God. If you are both trying to prove your side and disprove the other's, it will turn into no more than a "he said/she said."

And, Five: Adhere strictly to the rules of the debate, especially time limits. This will tend to force him to do so. People who watch debates react negatively to anything that looks unfair. The whole thing about a debate is to make arguments fairly.

"That's my list."

"Thank you," I said. "There are a couple of things in there I never would have thought of."

"Yes, thank you," Jenn added. "You must have put in some real work to get all that together."

"I should confess. I visited my old high school debate coach for help. She seems a lot smarter now than she did when I was seventeen."

"This will be very helpful," I said. "We can work the information into our preparation time."

"Is there anything else?" Jenn asked.

"You'll have to think about what to wear. The clerical stuff you wear sometimes could work, but it might be kind of heavy handed. Stevens will be in a suit, for sure. So, suits are good. Pastor Jennifer, as far as I know, you will be the only woman on stage, so, if you wear a dress or skirt you have the extra worry of being careful how you sit. The camera is even worse for that than in person. Or, you could dress casually and throw the balance off with the unexpected. It would make it look like you're not trying too hard."

"I guess I'll have to think about that," Jenn replied. I could almost see her mind running through the inventory in her closet.

"I hadn't wondered until just now," I said, "who is going to be sitting with Stevens?"

"Total mystery," Alicia answered. "I have tried to find out but I am not hearing a thing."

"How do you think Stevens will play this?" Jenn asked.

"We can't be sure, but every time I have heard him speak he says largely the same things. I believe we can expect more of the same. He, and his type, have carefully structured arguments against God that they think are irrefutable. They insist certain premises cannot be argued. Therefore, anything that does not precisely follow the laws of physics and nature—things that cannot be scientifically proven and explained—do not exist or are simply wrong. Miracles do not exist and cannot exist. From that starting point, logic is used to extrapolate anti-God positions on almost any subject. If this can't be true, then this can't be true either."

"So, anyone who doesn't agree with them is ignorant, crazy or lying," Jenn said, quietly.

"Exactly," Alicia said. "And they are very good at pointing out where they believe you have gone wrong."

"We do the same thing," I said. "We declare that because God exists and because Jesus incarnated on earth and lived, was killed and came back to life, that this is true and this is true and that is true."

"Yes, we do," Alicia affirmed. "Remember that when you respond to his accusations."

"What else?" Jennifer asked.

"The other biggie is the notion that science and religious faith are incompatible. You simply cannot believe in both at the same time. They will pound that day and night."

"I believe in science," I said.

"Me, too," Jenn added.

"Me, three," Alicia said and laughed. "Remember that, too. Mostly, I would suggest you read Stevens' article from *Time* magazine. Maybe several times. He will almost certainly surprise you with something, but most of what he has to say is right there in that article. He's written a couple of books, too, but I would ignore those. Most of it is just a longer-winded version of the article.

That's it. I am not even sure how accurate some of it is, but it is all I have to offer."

"Thank you, Alicia," Jenn said. "I think you have helped us a lot. I have already told Nathan I expect him to take the lead on this. I will speak up when he throws the discussion to me."

"And?" I asked, eyebrows raised.

"And . . . I guess I will talk whenever else I get the urge," Jenn admitted. "No. Moved. I will talk if and when I feel moved."

"Good," I said, "that has worked out very well many times before."

"So, are you two feeling ready?" Alicia asked.

"No . . . and yes . . . and no," Jenn said.

"Yeah. Like that. Me, too," I said.

"As long as we put God in the pilot's seat, we'll be fine," Jenn continued.

"Yeah," I said. "Like that."

Part 2

Debate Day

Chapter 48

Jennifer

"Ten minutes! Ten minutes!"

Mostly to escape the hubbub and chaos, I moved to my seat on the chancel platform and sat. The previous couple of hours had been both anxiety-provoking and surreal. Nathan and I had arrived for church service considerably earlier than usual. The big day had arrived and we weren't sure what to expect. So, we tried not to expect anything.

We were greeted by sights of people who had been up a lot longer than we had. The giant tent of the *Free Us from Religion Coalition* was rapidly filling with what already looked to be a record crowd. Robert Williams' massive food operation was gearing up. Our beloved little church building was surrounded by trucks and vans equipped with satellite dishes and mounds and miles of other electronic equipment and cables. The caravan on one side bore the name and logo of *CNN*. Everything on the other side was emblazoned *CBS News*. I had assumed the local stations out of Grand Rapids or Kalamazoo would be on board, but these were the big boys. By the time we arrived, Frank had been holding the TV crews at bay for two hours. They demanded to enter the church immediately to begin their set up, but Frank wouldn't allow it. He had told them dozens of times, *When Pastor Jennifer says*

"Amen" sometime around 11:30 you can get in, but not a minute before. If you can't set up in two and a half hours, you might as well go home now.

I don't know how we got by for so many years without a Frank. By ten minutes before the regular service time of 10:30 a.m. there seemed to be people everywhere. The only ones we didn't see were the Tall Man and his minions. They were all across the street getting ready for whatever preparatory events they had in mind.

Still, only thirty-six people entered the church and sat for services. Nathan and I made thirty-eight. Thirty-eight, surrounded by thousands.

Just as we were about to begin, Robert Williams burst in and exclaimed, "Don't worry! They're pouring in from everywhere—parked down all four roads for over a mile! Don't worry! I got my best guys scrounging more food from everywhere. A lot of them are Christians!" Robert left as fast as he arrived.

As we walked up the aisle to start worship, Nathan had whispered to me, "I wasn't worried until he showed up."

As we had started the service just over three hours ago, the pressure was growing. There was so much going on around us. How were we supposed to relax and engage in worship? Then, during the very first hymn, I saw Frank moving about the sanctuary, tapping certain people on the shoulder and beckoning them to follow. Turned out all those people distance-walking from their vehicles were already lining up at the bathrooms. So, the worshipping congregation became even smaller.

We had a wonderful time of worship. Condi played beautifully, touching hearts and glorifying God, as always. Jeremy reported that even our super-souped-up equipment couldn't keep track of the number of views. Nathan preached a marvelously spot-on sermon from the seventh chapter of Judges. In it, Gideon, the leader, is about to lead an army of thirty-two thousand soldiers into battle with a much larger and more powerful enemy. The Midianites had over one hundred and thirty-five thousand soldiers.

But God wants Gideon to have faith in Him, not in his own army. Before the big battle, God tells Gideon to send home twenty-two thousand men, leaving him with only ten thousand. Gideon obeyed. Then God decided even ten thousand were too many, because they might think they won the battle on their own. So, God tells Gideon to send home all but three hundred men—three hundred to fight a hundred and thirty-five thousand Midianites. Gideon obeyed, and went on to easily defeat the much larger Midianite army, who were no match for God. Now, it seemed as if we were in that mode. Thirty-six of us. After Frank raided the pantry, there were maybe twenty-five. Soon, there would be only two.

After all that, I prayed for quite a while, asking for no more than to be servants of God—His instruments in this world. There was a moment of perfect union between God and His people. Then I said *Amen,* and all heck broke loose.

Chapter 49

Nathan

"Five minutes! Five minutes!"

I looked up to the front of the church and saw four chairs. Only one was occupied, as Jennifer had taken her seat on the outside of our little dyad. My chair waited, beckoning me forward. But, the two on the other side were empty. We had seen no sign of anyone from the atheist encampment. Not only was there no one on the platform, but their carefully marked section for twenty-five spectators was bare, as well. It momentarily crossed my mind that perhaps they weren't coming, but I banished the thought as quickly as it came. If they showed I had to be ready. If they didn't show, it really wouldn't matter.

We had maybe ten seated in our gallery. I especially noted Edwina Fine, flanked by her buddy Jeremy Clark on one side and an elderly woman on the other. I had met her briefly when they arrived. All I could remember now was her first name was Geneva. A lone chair and small wooden table were set up on the floor in front of the platform, with three microphones arranged in a tight bouquet on the table. The two big, flashy ones prominently displayed the logos of *CNN* and CBS. The little plain one was connected to our in-house sound system. At the table now sat Gloria Jackson, the moderator. She was pulling things from a book bag and arranging them in front of herself. I purposely chose to not speak with her before the debate. Technicians were swarming the place, hollering last-minute instructions to each other. Alicia was doing her best to ride herd on all the confusion, and I decided to simply leave it to her and try to stay focused.

Staying focused was almost impossible. The activity inside the church was nothing compared to what was going on outside. We had gotten used to five or even six thousand people thronging around our four corners of Williams and Compton Roads. The last time I had dared to go outside and look, it had swollen to fifteen or twenty thousand, or more, with no end in sight. The roads had ceased to exist as a barrier of any kind—the crowds had simply taken over, filling in all the available space. All new arrivals could do now was approach from one of four directions, park way out there somewhere, and walk toward the crowd. Thousands of phones were tuning in to the livestream. It was just after I thought, *even Frank's bathrooms are never going to handle this,* I realized I had to go into *whatever happens, happens* mode and hope nobody got hurt.

"Three minutes! Three Minutes!"

I moved to the front, kissed Jennifer on the cheek, and took my seat. The word had obviously gotten to the rest of my people that time had about run out. They filed in and filled in the empty spaces. All the chairs filled, all the spaces accounted for. Ready.

"We are live in fifteen seconds! Ten! Five, four, three, two, one! We're live."

A guy standing near the front with a shoulder-mount camera, focused on Gloria Jackson's face.

"Good afternoon," she started, "I am Gloria Jackson, Chair of the journalism department at *Western Michigan University.* It is my pleasure—I think—to facilitate the long-anticipated debate between representatives of the *Free Us from Religion Coalition—* an organization based on the belief that science and logic can better serve society than can religion—and the pastors of the now world famous *WWW.God Christian Church.* I say *I think* because I find myself in the unexpected conundrum of having only one side show up for the . . ."

Jackson stopped talking as a man I had never seen before walked past her and stepped up onto the platform. He was impeccably dressed in a very expensive suit. He said not a word. He simply moved to the two empty chairs and removed one of them. He just as silently left the stage, taking the chair with him. As he retreated, a line of people appeared. In orderly fashion, silently and making eye contact with no one, twenty-five people came down the aisle. The men were dressed in well-cut suits, accessorized with perfectly chosen ties. The women wore varied types of clothing: skirted suits, pant suits or dresses. The only thing they had in common was everything looked like it came with high-end price tags. The effect was clear. These were people of wealth, education and status. They filed to their seats smoothly and without misstep. With no discernable signal, they sat in unison. They had arrived.

As soon as butts hit seats, the Tall Man appeared in the back of the room. He moved to the front, steadily but slowly. His suit looked to be even more expensive than the others. Having arrived near to moderator Jackson, he actually stopped, turned one hundred and eighty degrees to face the cameras, and bowed. He then turned, moved alongside the moderator's desk, and offered his hand. She stared at it a moment and then shook it. Stevens smiled to the camera. He mounted the stage and offered his hand to Jennifer, and then to me. Of course, we shook his hand, but we did not rise. Maybe if he weren't so darned tall. Finally, he moved to his seat and sat down. He had given his permission to begin.

"Mr. Stevens," Jackson began. "I do not appreciate this delay of the proceedings. If you were a student in one of my classes, this would cost you an entire grade. Can I safely assume you will follow the agreed upon parameters the rest of the way?"

Stevens just stared back at her. I don't think he was prepared to have his momentum stolen so soon after he achieved it.

"Mr. Stevens, I have asked you a question. I require an answer."

"Yes," he eventually replied. "Yes, of course."

"Very well. Let me continue. Again, I am Gloria Jackson. The rules of the debate are unusually simple. There will be no questions proposed by me, or by anyone else, except the people on stage. There is no overriding topic or title of the debate, except that all concerned understand it is between those who are believers in the Christian faith, and those who are distinctly not. The pattern will be three-two-three-two. One side will have three uninterrupted minutes to say whatever they want to say, and the other will have two uninterrupted minutes to respond. Then the side which just gave a response will have three minutes to make another statement, on any subject, and the other side will have two minutes to respond. At roughly the halfway point, I will declare a twenty-minute break. I will strictly enforce the time limits and the no-interruptions rule. I mean strictly. As such, Mr. Stevens' first two three-minute sessions will be trimmed by one minute, as he has already caused wasted time."

"Wait just a minute!" Stevens began, "I will not stand . . ."

"I am subtracting, Mr. Stevens."

He finally wised up and stopped talking.

"Now," Jackson continued, "I have identified the organizations represented here. Let's meet the particulars. Mr. Stevens, will you please introduce yourself and state your main purpose for being here. You have no more than three minutes."

"Thank you, Ms. Jackson. Good afternoon to all who are in this tiny room and, especially, to the many millions of you who are with us via television or livestream. Welcome to what I suspect will be a highly important event. My name is Alexander Stevens and I . . . "

As Stevens started to speak, I was keenly aware of my JC Penney slacks and favorite sport shirt. At least Jennifer looked lovely in her best dress, as long as no one checked the brand name—or lack of one. *Focus!* I brought my attention back to what Stevens was saying.

". . . I am an attorney, author and entrepreneur. My Bachelor's degree came from *Central Michigan University*. I have an MBA from the *Wharton School of Business* and my Juris Doctor degree is from the law school at Harvard. I never finished lower than third in any of my graduating classes. For several years I dedicated my professional time to a variety of successful ventures, such as real estate development, tech start-ups and the writing of emerging technical law, including test cases before many state and federal courts. I once argued a case before the *United States Supreme Court.*

"During all of this I was recruited to be a member of an exclusive think tank called *New Renaissance*. The purpose of *New Renaissance* was, and still is, to explore ways to create a better, more effective society, both in the U.S. and globally. I have always been an atheist—I simply never understood how a thinking person could believe that stuff—but for many years I was not an activist about it. However, my work with the think tank made it more and more obvious how many of society's problems could be traced back to religion. Wars. Genocide. Hatred. Bigotry. Irrationality. Classism. Sexism. Even Poverty. Just scratch the surface and look for a cause, and you are likely to find at its foundation, religion."

"Thirty seconds, Mr. Stevens!"

"So, about fifteen years ago I co-founded—with my good and like-minded friend, the late, great Dr. Cynthia Landers—the *Free Us from Religion Coalition*. While there were already several fine organizations gathered around the ideal of replacing religious, superstitious thought and practice with educated, thinking, logical models of belief and behavior, none were formulating or implementing desirable change in the comprehensive manner I envisioned. We began by . . ."

"Time is up!"

Stevens held up an index finger to signify, *just a moment* and said, "We began by doing a systematic search and review of pertinent literature, to see who . . ."

"Stop talking, now, Mr. Stevens!"

Once again, Stevens raised his index finger and said, "Nearly finished. I . . ."

The room exploded in a mushroom cloud of sound. I could see the people in the audience gasping, covering their ears and, some of them, shouting. But I couldn't hear anything amidst the roaring blanket of noise. Then, just as suddenly, it was over. Gloria Jackson held high over her head—thankfully well above the microphones—an airhorn, evidently drawn from her book bag.

After a thirty-second wait for people to realize what had happened and check their eardrums, Jackson said, "Thank you, Mr. Stevens. Representatives of the *WWW.God Christian Church*, you have three minutes."

I started. "Welcome to everyone who can see us and hear us this afternoon, no matter who or where you are. I am Nathan Martin and I am the Senior Pastor here at what we like to call the Triple-W church. We want everyone, everywhere, to know God loves them. That's why we're here. Seated next to me is my wife, and our other pastor, The Reverend Jennifer Martin."

Jennifer took over. "Good afternoon. I'm Jennifer and I am, indeed, married to Nathan. More to the point today, I am the Minister of Spiritual Growth and Formation at our church. We are here to help people either discover God or move closer to Him. Welcome."

An awkward silence ensued. The moderator said nothing, so eventually I leaned into my microphone and said, "The end."

"Oh! I'm sorry," Jackson said. "Very well. Mr. Stevens, you will propose the first topic. For this first cycle you will have no more than two minutes. Exactly." She tapped her trusty airhorn to make her point. "You may begin."

"Thank you. Theoretically, the purpose of religion is to somehow make the lives of people—humanity, and the society made up of all the people—better. Nearly every society that has ever existed on earth has developed—I would say invented—some system of belief in gods or goddesses or other supernatural beings that could help them or strengthen them or protect them. Christianity, which we are discussing today, shares its roots in that anthropologically explainable desire for a higher power, to handle the things the people felt they could not handle. Shortly, we will get into how—in these post-modern times of scientific advancement, enlightenment, understanding of human psychology and the development of the human mind—the need to invent a god has been rendered not only meaningless and irrelevant, but damaging to humanity.

"For now, let me begin by narrowing the discussion to this core idea, that religion is good for people and society. In the next hour or two, I—rather, we—will demonstrate just how damaging religion has been to society. That, not only has religion not lived up to its promises of a better life and a better world, but has actually caused much of the suffering with which humanity must contend. We certainly should know better by now."

"Thirty seconds!"

"Thank you, Ms. Jackson. That will be all for the moment."

"Very well. Pastors Martin, you have two minutes to rebut."

My mind worked furiously. Before he even finished, I was recalling bits of several different arguments and rebuttals, all of which held interesting potential for disarming and counteracting The Tall Man's opening argument. I was convinced he had cut his time short to limit my time to get thoughts organized. I stole a quick look at Jennifer. She was looking at me expectantly. On the way back to center, my gaze caught Edwina's eyes. She winked at me, of all things. She winked and then gave an almost imperceptible shake of her head. *Don't do it,* I imagined her saying. I opened my mouth and out came, "I cannot respond, because Mr. Stevens' premise is inaccurate and false. Responding to a false premise would be fruitless. Thank you ... the end."

"Are you sure? Pastor Jennifer Martin, would you like the rest of your allotted time?"

"No, thank you," Jennifer said, smiling beautifully.

"Well, all right, then. Pastors Martin, you have three minutes to propose another topic."

Looking over at the Tall Man, I could see him almost licking his chops, getting ready to pounce on whatever we might have to say. I decided to make an abrupt change from the predictable order of things.

"We find faith in God and belief in the validity of science go together very nicely. I consider myself a scientist. Before attending seminary, I earned a Bachelor's Degree in Molecular Biology. My knowledge of science helps me to better understand the wonderous ways in which God has created all things. Jennifer?"

"Yes," Jennifer responded, "thank you, Nathan. While I am not teaching right now, I am certified to teach science at all levels, middle school through senior high, and did so for several years. Not only did God create all things in magnificently complex ways, but gave us the intellectual power to figure it out and explain it. That is what science is. It is in no way incompatible with belief in God. Sure, it is easy to latch on to a biblical event and hold it up to the scientific method and conclude faith and science can't mix, but that is shallow observation. Nathan?"

"Thank you, Jennifer. Firstly, let's admit there is ongoing debate about some of these things within the Christian community. For some it is important to believe in and try to prove a literal six-day creation-of-the-universe story, only six thousand years ago. While I honor their right to do that—and there are ways to make that explanation work—we do not share that belief. The Bible was never intended to be a science textbook, or a systematic history textbook, or a math textbook. It is Holy Scripture . . . it is what God wants us to have and know. Of course, when someone like our Mr. Stevens here wants to set science at odds with religious belief, they will always pick out the most dramatic example—even if it is not a consensus Christian belief—and run it up the flagpole to mock and ridicule. To look at it more thoughtfully and deeply, might not support their already-decided argument."

"One minute!"

"The other difficulty with the science/religion debate is the question of the miracles, both biblical and, sometimes, present day. While we human beings, and the world in which we live, is confined to the laws of physics, nature, mathematics, and so on, God, the creator of all the things we are trying to measure and understand, is not. On very rare occasion, God chooses to break into our existence and make something happen that—by scientific measure—cannot happen. That is a miracle. A miracle does not rewrite or eliminate science, but, in a particular moment only God can create, the limitations of science are set aside. All things are possible with God. Thank you."

"Time! Mr. Stevens, you have two minutes to respond."

Almost sputtering, he jumped right in, "Smart, educated, thinking people . . . oh, I know you have your degrees to point to, and such . . . one might be capable of learning things and passing tests and such, and still not be truly . . . effectively . . . thinking. Anyway . . ."

Alicia held up another hastily written sign. It read "Good. Off balance!"

". . . smart, educated, thinking people know miracles—things that happen totally unfettered by the laws of the natural world and science—cannot, by definition, happen. Even the most befuddling events—if they actually occurred at all—will ultimately be explained by science. As long as people like Mr. and Mrs. Martin here can claim religion as their source of power, strength and understanding and continue to believe in and proclaim the impossible, they can never be taken seriously. It is easy to become a Christian. It only requires one basic principle. All you have to do is give up your ability to think. Religious belief is inevitably the death of intelligent thought. Once you give up on thinking, it is not so hard to insist we are created and not evolved, no matter how strong the evidence for evolution. With no critical thought one can call it a good thing to scare children with tales of hellfire and eternal punishment, both for themselves and for everybody they love who won't get in line with the claims of their particular church."

"Thirty seconds!"

"Furthermore, it becomes a good thing to insist a certain book of legend and myth, a book of unevidenced claims and falsehoods, is really the work of a god and therefore is always right and cannot be questioned or argued against. A thinking, educated, scientific person would never submit to an idea, a line of thinking, a belief system, that must not be questioned!"

"Time! Thank you, Mr. Stevens. You now have two minutes—this will be the final time that you will lose a minute—to introduce another topic."

"Thank you. Let's see if we can get to this in another way. At the *Free Us from Religion Coalition* our stated goal is to remove the blight of religion—most especially Christianity—from all public discourse in the United States of America. Of particular concern is the elimination of Christian influence on public and governmental policy. It is 2018. I am amazed and befuddled that we, as a society and as a country, still have to have this conversation. Time, enlightenment and simple logic would seem to make the demise of superstition and magical thinking inevitable. And yet, still today, we find our society continues to be plagued with such nonsense, both officially and unofficially. I do not seek the criminalization of religion, only that all expressions of it be mandated a private matter. We are fortunate to be living in a free country, and so must respect the rights of people to believe whatever they wish, no matter how misguided. However, I am convinced the world would be a better place for all the people in it, with far less religion and far more secularism—science and fact and proof."

As Stevens droned on, I noticed Alicia waving a handwritten sign at me. It read: *Word for Word!* I nodded and tried to pay attention.

"Thirty seconds!"

Stevens continued, "I say without apology, religion is foolhardy, nonsensical and dangerous. To ultimately perfect our society through humanist efforts, we must get religion out of the way . . . the end."

That last thing got Stevens a chuckle from both sides of the audience. I don't like it when the other guy gets the laugh, especially when it helps to smooth over the audacity of what he just said.

"Thank you for your punctuality, Mr. Stevens. Pastors Martin, you have two minutes to respond."

"Thank you," I said. "While I happily support our country's doctrine of the separation of Church and State as a matter of governance, all of human existence will always be—must be—permeated with the question of God. Who is God? How is God? What does God want for us . . . and from us? How can we, must we, relate to God? Mr. Stevens cavalierly characterizes faith in God as superstitious, magical thinking, even nonsense, because he thinks of God as a made-up human construct. A construct to be debated and changed, molded and rewritten, even to be accepted or rejected as a human creation. He does not know God is real. God exists, not only when we believe it or will it, but all the time. God's existence is not dependent on our agreement or lack of agreement. God . . . is. Once you know that, everything changes. Thank you."

"Pastor Jennifer Martin, you have forty-five seconds remaining."

"Nothing right now. My husband said all that needs saying."

"Very well. Pastors Martin, you now have three minutes for a new topic."

"Thank you," I said.

Before I could continue, I noticed Janice had tiptoed up to the stage and handed Jennifer a note. I lost my concentration and couldn't quite remember what I was about to say. I started to sweat.

Chapter 50

Jennifer

As I finished scanning the note, I looked up and saw Nathan, who appeared to be in a bit of a trance.
"Excuse me!" I said. "Nathan, may I handle this one?"
He just smiled and nodded, vigorously.
"I have received word that the crowd outside is now estimated at over thirty thousand, most of them with devices tuned in to us right now. There are a couple of news choppers out there, getting the overhead shots. Hey camera people!" I shouted to those who were running the indoor network equipment, "are you guys getting this?"
I was beginning to have some fun.
"Yes, ma'am," one of them answered. "We are showing the overhead shot right now!"
"Hey! Let's hear it from you people outside!" I hollered at the top of my lungs.
There was a tremendous roar that I'm sure could be heard for miles.
"Now, only the Christians," I yelled.
Another roar, nearly as loud as the first.
"Now, only the rest of you—our honored and beloved guests!"
The new roar was nearly indistinguishable from the first.
"All right, all right, all right! Now we're having a good time. I want to talk privately with only my Brothers and Sisters in Christ," I continued. "So, nobody else listen."

I couldn't help giggling at my own cleverness.

"Brothers and Sisters, I know there are way more people out there than we planned on. So, space and water and food and all of that must be running short. I am asking you to take good care of our guests. Back away a little and give them some room. Share any food and water that you have. Help with the little ones who might be getting upset. And bathrooms! Let's cooperate by making an open path to the bathrooms. Let's remember that we didn't come here just to argue. We came here to be the kind of people God wants us to be, and the kind of people we claim we are. Hey camera guy! Is anybody moving out there?"

He watched a little before saying, "Yes, ma'am, they actually are!"

"Thirty seconds!"

To our guests, I shouted, "I hope I don't offend anyone by saying God bless all of you. Fact is, God loves you and so do we, and there isn't anything you can do to stop that!"

"Time is up! Mr. Stevens, you have two minutes to rebut."

"Rebut!? Rebut what? I want a clarification here, Ms. Jackson, and I don't want this to come out of my two minutes. How can I offer rebuttal when she didn't say anything! There was no substance there! No attempt to advance her case. What am I supposed to do with that?"

"Very well," Gloria Jackson replied. "The rules state that the speaker may use his or her time to say whatever she wants to say. Pastor Jennifer, did you say what you wanted to say?"

"Yes, thank you," I said. "I am satisfied with what I said, which, I might add, was filled with relevant, even essential, content."

The Tall man looked like he was about to pop a cork.

"Now she's arguing out of turn!" he whined.

"Mr. Stevens," Jackson replied, "you opened the door by questioning her right to decide on her own content. Your two-minute rebuttal starts now. Proceed."

"Well, then, I guess I will just have to respond to informal, emotional claptrap with some informality of my own. This is exactly the kind of nonsense that one might expect when someone is trying to defend a position that is indefensible. When you have no facts or logic or rationality to work with you might resort to deflection and storytelling to try to appear as if you have something to say. It is the product of weak minds and weak philosophy. I will not attempt to rebut a nonsensical argument."

"Very well," Gloria Jackson said. "I have been notified that we will now have a three-minute commercial break. Everyone please remain still and silent until we return."

It was an odd feeling to just sit there, but Nathan pointed out that there was a monitor we could see if we turned sharply to the left. For what I guessed to be sixty seconds a Roman Catholic promo ran. I couldn't hear it but they had the closed captioning on. It seemed to be a standard plea to return to the one true church and find God's favor in the process. It was nice. It was followed by our new best buddy, the Tall Man, ranting with his now-familiar message filled with words like *superstition, nonsensical, irrational* and *backward*. Halfway through the words morphed into *intelligent, educated, logical* and *wise*. I guess he was getting back to talking about himself. The final commercial in the segment was filled with a *Built Ford Tough* spot highlighting the virtues of the all new version of the best-selling F-150 line of pickups. This whole experience grew curiouser and curiouser. The ads ended with Gloria Jackson looking a little confused.

"Very well," Jackson eventually said. "Mr. Stevens, you have three minutes to introduce a new topic."

"Thank you. I think we can all agree that religion makes extraordinary claims. It makes sense to me that anyone making extraordinary claims should be prepared to offer extraordinary evidence for those claims. And yet religious people—the Church—not only fail to produce extraordinary evidence, but offers no convincing evidence at all. If one does not think, but merely relies on irrational, unevidenced belief in the impossible, and faith that an eternal, celestial, all-powerful, divine puppet master really exists and has every right to boss us around, judge us and punish us at his every whim, it becomes not only possible but easy to be a Christian. If one person believed all of this nonsense, they would be called delusional and would be treated for mental illness. But, because many people believe it, we dub it a religion. So, I say this about the core of religion, the foundation on which it is based—religion's very premise, one might say—a god. I am confident there is no god. Period. I am confident all religion is extrapolated from a single, false, demonstrably wrong premise. That there is a god. If I am to be convinced otherwise, then this god will have to present him or herself to me! Come on, so-called god! I am waiting! Show yourself! Show up! Now!"

The Tall Man was on his feet, his arms raised high over his head, his eyes glaring at the ceiling as if it might open up and reveal, perhaps, God. It was obviously an act. A drama for the crowd. He held his pose for what seemed a long time, then lowered his arms to his sides. Still looking upward he shouted, "No?!" Then, he lowered his gaze to the small audience before him and said, "I thought not." He sat.

"Time! Reverends Martin, you have two minutes to rebut."

Nathan jumped right back in on this one.

"Thank you," he began. "I am a little bit stunned to hear our esteemed opponent present such a logically flawed argument. If there is no god, as Mr. Stevens believes, then there is no god to respond to his demands to appear. If there is a god—an all-powerful God who is the creator of all things and the sole arbiter of how things really are—as I contend, then that God is not about to be bullied into doing the bidding of the likes of Mr. Stevens. Or, anyone else, for that matter. So, if God does or does not exist, God will not appear on demand. Therefore, this little drama proves nothing. The specific fallacy committed here is called a False Dichotomy. Perhaps Mr. Stevens will take note and try to avoid the same mistake in the future. Thank you."

"Thank you," said Ms. Jackson. "Reverends, you now have three minutes to present a new topic."

I looked at Nathan, checking to see if he was ready to take over. He smiled and nodded his head, so I relaxed and looked around the room. Everyone in the sanctuary—our side and their side—was completely engaged. It was quiet enough to hear the proverbial pin drop. No one wanted to miss anything. Amazingly, the only noise I could hear from outside was the faint sound of a helicopter hovering. I wouldn't have imagined that thirty thousand uncomfortable people could be so silent. Inside, all were gazing intently at Nathan, waiting for something to be said, except Edwina. Eyes closed, head down, she was deep in prayer.

"Thank you," Nathan said. "Thanks to all of you in the room and to all the thousands outside . . . a decent-sized roar responded to the mention of the outside crowd . . . and to the many millions out there in cyber space. It is remarkable, to say the least, to think about . . ."

"Here we go again," Stevens stage whispered, loud enough for all to hear.

"Mr. Stevens, that will be your final interruption!" Jackson declared, loudly. "Reverend Martin, your three minutes begins again, now."

I enjoyed seeing The Tall Man get his comeuppance, especially for messing with my husband. We sure lucked out when Alicia recruited Gloria Jackson to be our moderator.

Nathan started again. "It is remarkable, to say the least, to think about all of the thought and attention so many people are giving to Godly concerns. No matter what side each of you fall on, it is good to consider God.

Now, Mr. Stevens is about to point out the many failures of some Christians and the Church—over the centuries and, somewhat, still today. He will list the too-many religious wars and The Crusades, The Inquisition, witch-hunts, sex scandals, and the violence toward the Jews, and others, over the years. He will point out that the Church has often been bigoted in its treatment of women, minorities and people of other faiths. Unfortunately, he is right about those things, and probably some others he has on his list. As a Christian pastor in a Christian church, that reality grieves me. I am sorry. The Church has much to answer for, and I hope we can do much better from now on. We are sorry. We repent and ask forgiveness.

However, we mustn't throw out the baby with the bathwater. The evil done in the name of religion is not actually done by that religion, or by God, or in the service of God. The evil is done by perversion of that religion, by perversion of God's word, will and way. By supposedly Godly people who have lost their way—God's way. It is much like the evil done by bad politicians, bad governments, bad cops, bad teachers, bad youth leaders, bad . . . anything. And yet, few of us would say we should have no government, no police protection, no schools and no youth programs."

"One minute!"

"In a world without religion, the fanatics and perverters of religion would be gone, but then so would the religion be gone, along with people of faith, and their many important works. Done right—as it most often is—religion is not only a positive force in this world, caring for the needy and trying to make the world a better place, but is also the beacon of information and the source of help in the greatest of earthly tasks . . . coming to grips with the existence and realities of God.

"In closing, you might notice most of the truly awful failures of Christianity are buried in the history books. We are getting closer to being the Church that God would have us be. Let's not give up now."

"Time is up!"

I marveled at my Nathan. I have always been proud of him, but in recent times and, particularly, in this moment on such a big stage, he simply seemed so focused and devout and open to God's call on him—whatever that might be. It gave me shivers.

"Mr. Stevens, you have two minutes to rebut."

"Thank you, Ms. Jackson. I was going to get into this later, but my opponent has cleverly tried to get ahead of the damage this particular topic does to his arguments and his attempts to defend the indefensible. Religion and the Church have, indeed, done incalculable damage—in the past and still today—to the men, women and children of this world! Mr. Martin has barely scratched the surface on the most egregious examples of war, crusades, witch-hunts and the like. We could use our whole two hours just detailing not only the failings of the Church, but the proactive damage-producing actions of the church as well. The Church is guilty of crimes—legal, ethical and moral—against humanity, womanhood, reason and science, attacks upon medicine and enlightenment, the rights of the LGBTQIA community, and on and on. The continual attacks on the full inclusion of all people are enough in themselves to discredit the Church and the practice of Christianity as positive influences on human society. Mr. Martin would like us to accept a hardy *we're sorry* and move on. We cannot."

"Thirty seconds!"

"It might be one thing if these offenses were all in the past and the religious community had seen the error of their ways and started down a new path. But, we don't see any evidence of that, do we? Denying same-sex couples the right to marry, based on a few phrases in an outdated, irrelevant book of questionable origin. Telling women what they can and cannot do with their bodies. Shaming people for wanting to proactively use birth control to make their lives more livable, when every day they face . . ."

"Time is up!"

Stevens looked like he was about to explode, face red and eyes wild.

"How can I be expected to stop, when . . ."

"Your two-minute rebuttal has expired. You now have three minutes to bring a new topic."

The Tall Man gathered himself and seemed to recognize he was losing his cool. He sat quietly for a moment and took a deep breath.

He said, "I believe we have established I can say anything I want with my three minutes. Is that correct?"

Gloria Jackson smiled and said, "Yes, Mr. Stevens, that is correct."

"Excellent. As I was saying, religion, Christianity, the Church, call it what you will, has done and continues to do great damage to large portions of society. People often ask, 'What harm can religion do? Does it not benefit our society and make the world a better place?' I will answer that.

"The reasons—perhaps better described as the dangers—of Christian thinking are many. In a world growing more and more to value inclusivity, Christianity seeks to proclaim exclusivity to be a good and wonderful thing! *We are right and you are wrong*, they proclaim. *We are in and you are out. We will live forever in heavenly splendor and you will live forever in the burning agony of hell.* They won't even let us just die and be done with it. Religion makes people meaner and more justified in their practice of hatred and exclusion. Furthermore, we do not need to invent a god to create a moral code. Our humanity—our human intellect—is more than sufficient to determine right from wrong, good from evil and love from hate. We do not need a celestial dictator to tell us how to live a good and proper life. We human beings can, and often do, go into the world and do good for those in need, without beating them about the head and shoulders with a Bible and insisting that if they ever want to live a good life like us, they had better bow down to a peasant who supposedly lived and died and lived again two thousand years ago in the Middle East. A society freed from the effects of religion stands the better chance of developing a consistent and beneficial code of living, something at which the Church has failed miserably.

"What would it take for the Church to become good? For religion to be a good thing now—something we have not yet seen, but hypothetically, at least—I submit the first thing that would have to happen would be for said religion to give up all supernatural claims."

"One minute!"

"Furthermore, the very notion of an eternal, all-powerful, controlling authority figure who serves as judge, jury and executioner—with no human right of appeal or even argument—would have to be summarily discredited and dropped, should the religious folks expect respect and credibility.

"Can these things happen and even retain something that is anything like a religion? No. And so, I reject religion. I find it easy to reject. That which is claimed without evidence, can be dismissed without evidence. Religious claims—being so outlandish—would require strong evidence, and yet there is none. And so, I am an atheist. Proudly so. The *Free Us from Religion Coalition* is filled with people like me, and we will battle, litigate, debate, argue and discredit religion, and its negative effects on society, until the conversation becomes unnecessary. As our cherished freedoms ensure the right of religious people to believe and practice whatever they choose, so those same freedoms protect our right to speak out against nonsense and for science and reason. I cannot, nor am I trying to, deny people their right to believe nonsense. But I do not want to allow my society to be infected with it."

"Time is up!"

Chapter 51

Nathan

I shot a glance to Jennifer, letting her know I was ready to go. More than ready.

"Among people who attend church weekly, forty-five percent do volunteer work each week. Only twenty-seven percent of non-church-attenders did the same. Religious people participate more in community groups, have stronger relationships with their neighbors and spend more time engaging with their own families. Church attenders donate an average of nearly three thousand dollars a year to charities, versus seven hundred dollars for people who don't go to church. Those same church-goers give twenty percent more money to secular charities than secular people do! Sixty-five percent of weekly church attenders give time, labor, money or goods to the poor each week! Churches and religious organizations give more money to needy people around the world than the U.S government gives in foreign aid! I love the Gates Foundation. They give billions in international aid every year. Isn't that great! But members of synagogues and churches give over four times as much!

"Do you want me to go on? Oh, I can go on!" I was getting a little lathered up, but it felt good.

"Thirty seconds!"

"Religious Americans adopt children at two and a half times the rate of non-religious people. The rate is even higher for hard-to-place children. Religious Americans do most of the daily hard work of settling refugees and asylum-seekers. Religious hospitals treat twenty percent of the nation's hospitalized patients."

"Time! Your three minutes begin now."

"Good. I am just getting warmed up. In most U.S. cities, religious organizations provide over half of the emergency shelter beds. Local congregations provide over one hundred and twenty-five thousand alcohol-recovery programs, and almost as many programs for the unemployed. Food pantries? Delivered meals? Food trucks? Soup kitchens and free meal programs? Baby pantries? Help with gas or prescriptions? Church! Church! Church! Church! Church! Church! Church! I have personally assisted the churches I have pastored in giving away over two hundred and fifty tons of food to those in need. How many tons of food has the *Free Us from Religion Coalition* given?

"Are you tired of this yet? I'm not. Churches give free space to boy scouts, girl scouts, garden clubs, book clubs, and for music lessons and youth sports and yoga instruction and dance recitals. The list is endless, but I am starting to wind down."

I quieted myself and looked to Jennifer.

She laughed and said, "Drink some water, Honey."

She smiled, and went on, "Nathan is very passionate about Jesus' call on us to love and help the poor. Normally he just lives it out, but today he is forced to talk about it. I will add only a couple of things. Mr. Stevens, a word of friendly advice, don't try to argue the accuracy of the things my husband just reported. You would have to argue with The Pew Research people and such. The facts are the facts. And, just so you know, the research also shows that the recipients of all those marvelous feeding, caring, loving programs are by over ninety percent not members of the religious group that's doing the giving. Your claim that religiosity bears no fruit for society couldn't be more wrong. If you are the man of measurables and facts and science you say you are, you should do the research and then admit you were mistaken. The end."

I love my wife.

"Mr. Stevens, you have two minutes to rebut."

"Thank you, Ms. Jackson. I am not sure how to respond to such an onslaught of unvetted facts and figures . . . I suppose . . . I mean . . . the *Pew Research Center* is a reputable organization . . . if these claims are, indeed, being quoted accurately and in proper context . . . but, in any case, I do not concede that religion itself or an irrational belief in a god is in any way necessary to these kindnesses and charitable work. Mrs. Martin, . . ."

"Reverend Martin!" I bellowed before I could stop myself. "My wife's title is *Reverend* Martin, not Mrs. Martin, and I think you know that."

"Very well, then," Stevens said with a condescending smirk. "If titles are so important to you . . ."

I let the Tall Man get to me. Score one for him.

". . . I will be happy to comply. Reverend Jennifer Martin, I am sure you agree that secular, non-religious people do good works and could match these numbers you have quoted, without the need of a mythical god, who . . ."

"But they don't!" Jennifer shouted.

I was immediately both stunned and thrilled.

"Excuse me!" Stevens exploded. "Ms. Jackson! This is my rebuttal time and I will not accept this interruption! What are you going to do about it?"

Gloria Jackson looked hard at The Tall Man, and then at me, and then at Jennifer, and then back to Stevens.

"Nothing," she finally declared. "You opened the door by addressing her directly and by name. Don't do that if you do not expect a response. You have thirty seconds left in your rebuttal."

"This is not fair!" Stevens replied. "You are obviously not as unbiased as you have claimed to be. I think it is clear to all concerned that you have a preferred outcome to these proceedings and you are using your position to try to make those outcomes occur. I don't know if there is any mechanism by which I could lodge an appeal, but if there was you can be sure I would do so immediately following the conclusion . . ."

"Time is up! You may proceed with your three-minute segment. This will be the final topic before the break."

I am a little ashamed to admit how delighted I felt at that moment. Stevens was losing his cool, pitching a temper tantrum in full view. I snuck a peak at Jennifer, who was smiling serenely. I could feel an unabashed grin on my face when Edwina caught my eye. She was glaring at me and subtly shaking her head *no*. That caught me off guard, so I straightened up and tried to bring my face under control.

I watched The Tall Man's countenance change before my eyes. He sat back in his chair. His face softened, his brow dewrinkled. He smiled. He even chuckled a bit.

"Boy, that was uncalled for," he said. "Ms. Jackson, I apologize. I allowed myself to get ruffled and took it out on you. I was wrong. We are discussing some very important things here—things that influence our society in powerful ways—and I can get pretty excited about that. It is obviously no secret I believe some of the religious beliefs and practices held by the Reverends Nathan and Jennifer Martin—and millions of other people—are damaging to our society and human kind in general. I absolutely believe that and will continue to work to mitigate the effects of religion in our culture. But, in my enthusiasm, perhaps I am prone to temporarily forget Reverend Nathan and Reverend Jennifer are truly good people who are motivated by only the best intentions. Misguided, in my mind, but certainly not bad or evil. If I have said things, or applied tactics in any way that would seem to indicate differently, I sincerely apologize for that as well. The end."

For a short time there, I had almost let myself forget just how good this guy is at what he does. He quickly sized up a situation that was trending against him and turned the tables. I admired his ability to recognize and reign in his own emotions in such a short time and change the narrative to make himself sound eminently kind and reasonable. All of the sudden Stevens was back in a superior position. As I was pondering this, I heard Gloria Jackson speak.

"Very well," she said. "That leaves the Reverends Martin with a two-minute rebuttal before the break."

Before I could react, I heard Jennifer.

"Thank you, Mr. Stevens. I appreciate your apology and gladly accept it. I think I got a little wound up, too. I am sorry for that. Let's cool off. The end."

"We have reached the break!" Jackson firmly declared. "Everyone back in your places in twenty minutes!"

Immediately some guy who seemed to think he was in charge yelled, "Everybody hold on. Set up for interviews! Three minutes of commercial time, then back live for the interviews!"

I followed orders and turned back to the monitor. Of all things, there was first an invitational commercial presented by the *United Methodist Church*. Kind of ironic, being as they had pretty much run me off. Then, all of the sudden the monitor turned to the familiar. There were a few seconds of me preaching, followed by a beautiful close-up of Jennifer deep in prayer. I laughed out loud at the next vignette. It was Frank bellowing his excitement and amazement at some bit of scripture that he had just read, as Sylvie gazed at him with total admiration. The piece concluded with Condi at her best, the music as stunning as it was beautiful. Alicia and Jennifer must have spent a little extra as the spot went on for at least two minutes. Once again, they had achieved the powerful message of simplicity—no pleas, no requests, no bombast—just a small group of people hopelessly in love with God.

Chapter 52

Jennifer

Foolishly, I thought taking a break meant actually taking a break. Silly me. Reporters and men with shoulder mount cameras charged the front of our little sanctuary. They had twenty minutes of airtime to fill and they were not going to waste a bit of it.

"Mr. Stevens! Mr. Stevens! Can we get a word please?!"

"Reverend Martin! Reverend Martin! Both of You! Can you answer a couple of questions?"

Both CBS and *CNN* must have had extra people sitting out in their trucks, because we were rushed by four teams—each made up of one reporter armed with what seemed like a larger than needed microphone and a cameraman shouldering a huge camera. The reporters were made up of two men and two women. All of the camera people were men. It quickly became apparent each news network hoped to get exclusive interviews with both sides of the debate.

Exclusive was not going to happen and soon enough reporters from both networks stood in front of The Tall Man and, just a few feet away, a different team confronted Nathan and I.

"This is Phyllis Grey, of *CBS News*. I am here with the Reverends Nathan and Jennifer Martin, who are halfway through a historic debate . . ."

248

A Dragon Outside the Church 249

"Roger Stout, *CNN*!" shouted the other reporter.

"As I was saying," Phyllis Grey went on, "we are at the halfway point of this historic debate on Religion vs. Secularism. Pastor Nathan, if I may call you that, we are being told the people tuned in to this event are too many to count. Off the charts. What is your reaction to that?"

I watched my husband take all of five seconds to compose an answer, before the *CNN* guy shouted, "Who do you think is winning!?"

"I won't answer any questions," Nathan said, "until the rudeness stops."

Then he waited.

"Yes, of course," said Phyllis.

"Yeah, sure," said Roger Stout.

"Okay then. I am pleased conversation about God is drawing so much attention. It is, of course, the most important question of our lives. The notion of who is winning is unanswerable. What would winning look like? Who is keeping score?"

Even as he spoke, I knew my husband wanted desperately to win. So did I.

"Isn't the whole purpose of a debate to choose a winner, Mrs. . . . Reverend Martin?" Roger Stout asked.

"Not this one," I said.

"Then what's the point?"

"The point," Nathan answered, "is to provide as many people as possible with the knowledge and at least basic understanding of God. To know that His promises are still good and the saving grace of Jesus Christ is available for everyone. For us, that is the point."

"But," the reporter for CBS interjected, "is not this process also giving the other side—the atheistic/intellectual side—the chance to openly attack your beliefs and discredit religion?"

"Yes," I said, "but that's okay. We want people to hear the different arguments and opinions. We don't want anyone to lack information. We believe people are capable of making their own decisions. Now, if you will excuse me, I really need to take a break."

I turned and walked away.

"Pastor Nathan," the reporter from *CNN* started, "what do you think about your opponent's tactics so far? It seems that . . ."

As I walked away, I could no longer hear the interview. I felt bad about abandoning Nathan, but I needed to use a rest room before the debate restarted. As soon as I stepped out of the building I was greeted by an amazing sight. People everywhere. People in every direction as far as I could see. There was no evidence at all of an intersection of two roads. Only people. Looking across the street I could see the top of the Free Us from Religion tent, but everything else was obscured by the massive crowd. It did appear that the thousands of chairs were completely filled by those fortunate enough to get a seat.

I was going to have to fight my way to the bathrooms. As I shouldered my way into the crowd, I heard:

"There she is!"
"It's her!"
"God bless you, Pastor Jennifer!"
"There are no gods! Can't you see that yet?"
"Thank you for sticking up for God!"
"Quit filling people's heads with foolish lies!"

And, on and on. As I got a little closer to the facilities, I heard a welcome bellow.

"All right! All right! Clear a path! The pastor is coming through! Step back! All of you!"

Thank God for Frank. *Everybody needs a Frank*, I thought. *Wait a minute,* I thought, *wasn't Frank sitting inside?*

"Frank!" I shouted. "Thank you. I only have a couple minutes and I really need to use one of your lovely bathrooms!"

"They aren't real lovely right now!" he shouted through a big grin. "We've been hit pretty hard out here!"

"But you're making it, I bet," I shouted.

"You bet your sweet bippy we're makin' it!" he laughed. "Come on, let's get you to the head of the line. You and Pastor Nathan are doin' great!" he added.

"Thank you," I replied. "I am not quite sure if we are saying the right things, but we are doing our best."

"You sound way smarter than that idiot . . . sorry . . . that Stevens guy."

"Thank you, Frank. How are you and Sylvie doing?"

"You kiddin'! It's like we were born for this . . . like we're finally doin' somethin' that matters!"

"You are Frank! You are."

I pretended not to notice Frank's eyes misting up, and he got me to one of the bathroom doors. Afterward, I stepped out into a world that had changed. It was quiet. Dead silence. All the many people were still there, talking and gesturing and moving around. But, I did not hear them. It was as if I had entered the *Cone of Silence* from the old *Get Smart* TV show. The only other person inside the Cone was Edwina.

"Quite a day, isn't it," she said. "How are you holding up?"

"Pretty well," I answered. "Nathan and I are good so far. Do you know what is happening right now?" I asked.

"Not exactly," she said. "I felt God telling me to come here to talk to you, so I did. I have no clue as to how this is working, but it is nice to have a bit of quiet."

"I admit to being a bit worried. I just don't know if we are saying the right things. How is all of this going to turn out?"

"What would your beloved Pastor Carl tell you about that?"

I looked into Edwina's eyes for a long moment before saying, "You don't miss anything, do you?"

"I pay attention."

"You sure do. Pastor Carl would tell us to do our best to say exactly what God wants us to say, and leave the results up to Him."

"Once again, Pastor Carl sounds smart."

"Yes, he sure does. So, this message from God. What does He want you to tell me? I hope we haven't been running down a wrong path."

"Oh, my, no. God is pleased. You are doing a great job, so far."

"I got mad a couple of times."

"Yes, you did. But, Jesus was angry a few times, as well."

"Well, I'm no Jesus."

"Of course not, but you recovered quickly and humbly. Well done."

"Thank you. Now, what does God say?"

"Go to the change-up."

"Go to the change-up?"

"Yes, go to the change-up."

"Fine, but what does that mean?"

"Are you familiar with baseball?"

"Yes, of course. Nate and I are faithful Detroit Tiger fans. I know what a change-up is. It is to switch things up suddenly. Mix in a slow pitch among the fastballs, to throw the hitter off. Catch them by surprise."

"There you go. You two have done a great job so far, but now it is time to go to the change-up. As soon as you get back inside, just say those words to Pastor Nathan. Then, we'll see what happens."

I started to speak, but Edwina interrupted me with a shush and a reminder I only had a couple of minutes to get back to the stage inside. We walked together. The way in front of us stayed clear and quiet, so we walked unimpeded. As soon as we passed a spot, the area behind us immediately filled up with a flurry of noisy people. Mysterious ways.

Once we got back inside, Edwina took her seat next to her friend Geneva. I got quick high fives and encouraging comments from several members of the church family. With barely a minute to spare—I was highly aware of moderator Gloria Jackson's penchant for punctuality—I joined my husband, already seated on the stage.

"I thought you had finally run away from me," he said.

"No such luck, buddy boy. You're stuck with me."

It was an old joke, no longer funny but somehow reaffirming.

Nathan started to speak, but I interrupted him.

"Edwina said that God told her to give us a message."

He grew silent and focused on me, just as I had hoped he would.

"There is no time to explain. The message is simply, 'Well done so far. Now, it is time to go to the change-up.'"

Nathan just stared at me for what was probably no longer than ten seconds, but it was more than my fragile patience could stand.

I repeated, "Well done so far, now it's time to . . ."

" . . . go to the change-up," he finished.

"I don't know exactly what that means," I said.

"That's all right," he said. "I do."

Chapter 53

Nathan

"Welcome back to the debate between Alexander Stevens, representative of the *Free Us from Religion Coalition*—an organization based on the belief that science and logic can better serve society than can religion—and the pastors of the now world famous *WWW.God Christian Church*, the Reverends Jennifer and Nathan Martin. I am Gloria Jackson, the moderator for today's event."

While Gloria spoke, I had a moment to look around. Not a soul had left. The sanctuary was still packed. Stevens looked as if he had had a few moments with a makeup artist. He was looking cool and crisp. I refocused as Gloria Jackson continued.

"At the conclusion of the first session, the Reverends Martin had just completed a two-minute rebuttal period. It is now their turn to offer a new topic in three minutes. Please begin."

I spun in my chair to face Jennifer. I took her hands in mine and said, "Let's pray." She immediately closed her eyes. We sat there, praying . . . silently. As the seconds ticked by, I admit I was highly aware of the awkwardness of praying silently while being watched by millions of people, many of whom had no idea what was going on. I wrestled with my self-consciousness and attempted to focus on actually praying. I felt a bit of sweat forming on my forehead and back. I did my best to ignore it and press on.

"One minute!" Gloria called out.

I lifted my eyelids just the tiniest bit, to steal a glimpse of Jennifer. She looked so serene I couldn't tell if she was about to smile or fall asleep. I wished I could pray like her.

"Thirty seconds!"

I finally relaxed into the prayer, just before I heard, "Time is up!"

"Amen," I said.

"Amen," said Jennifer.

"Mr. Stevens," Gloria chimed in, "you have two minutes to rebut."

"Rebut! Rebut what? I don't know what in the heck that was supposed to be, but it sure wasn't part of a proper debate! How am I supposed to respond to that?"

"With the ninety seconds you have left, Mr. Stevens," answered Gloria.

The Tall Man did his best to collect himself and formulate a response. Eventually he smiled and said, "Actually, I don't think that demonstration requires a response. It speaks for itself. The end."

"Very well. Mr. Stevens, you have three minutes to introduce a new topic."

"Thank you, Ms. Jackson. Religion is a necessity for the weak mind. Yes, I said that out loud. Religion is a necessity for the weak mind. In today's developed world, especially where a least a modicum of democracy, freedom and self-determination are allowed, we have grown over the decades to recognize and value the power of the human intellect. And by intellect, I mean the human mind in all its facets. Intelligence? Absolutely. Living in the modern world requires knowledge and information and education and the ability to process such into new and innovative thoughts. Additionally, the mental capability to make decisions and plans and pursue new initiatives, even if others oppose you, takes a strength of mind and power of the self to progress and move forward. The mature, confident mind of the self-actualized person is necessary for society to move forward. We need a society that rewards the bold thinkers. Key to this process is the ability for thinkers to take responsibility for themselves. To make decisions, try new things, sometimes succeeding and sometimes failing, with the strength and courage to accept the victories and own up to the failures. People need to make their own decisions and have the strength to claim them!"

"One minute!"

"The weak-minded need religion, and religion makes the mind weak! Check your brain at the door of the church! We will tell you what to think! We will spell out what your morals will be! We will teach you what the Good Book says! All you have to do is obey! For crying out loud they say it out loud themselves—*Turn your life over to Jesus*! *Follow*! *Let go and let God do it*! And best of all, whatever happens, the responsibility will fall on an imaginary god, and you can take your weak mind home and relax. As I said, religion is a necessity for the weak mind. So go ahead, sit there and pray when you have nothing meaningful to say."

"Time is up! Reverends Martin, you have two minutes to rebut."

My mind was racing. Not too surprisingly, I was fighting a rising tide of anger. Just how insulting could this Stevens guy be? I was also trying to remain in change-up mode. What would that look like in the face of this? As was growing more common all the time, Jennifer came to the rescue.

"Mr. Stevens is a funny man," she said through a magnificent smile. "He hurls insults at us, and people like us, for over an hour now, trying to accomplish I don't know what. He doesn't have to be mean and disrespectful to make his point, but he is doing it anyway. It is a tactic we have not reciprocated with, by the way, even though it would not be very hard to do. Are we breaking down? Are we weak-minded? Are we angry? Well, a little."

She got a nice chuckle from the crowd on that one, and some nodding heads, even on Stevens' side of the room.

"One minute!"

Jennifer continued, "I think it might be important for Mr. Stevens to hear this. God still loves you. Always has and always will, no matter what you say or do. Nathan and I love you, too, and so do most of the people of this church. Right, Honey?"

She caught me by surprise, but I recovered quickly. "Yes, of course. Alexander, when all this is over, please feel free to come by. We have a lot to share with you."

"And," Jennifer interrupted, "a kind word to Mr. Stevens. Don't try to match wills, and minds, with my husband. He is a force to be reckoned with, all by himself, and he's not working alone. Just a word to the wise. The end."

"Time is up! Reverends, you have three minutes to introduce a new topic.

"My wife gives me too much credit. I am learning every day that she is the more spiritually powerful one between us. But, she does remind me of a story.

Most people know something of the story of David and Goliath . . ."

"Oh, for crying out loud," the Tall Man muttered loudly, not even trying to keep his voice down. "Now it is story time."

"Mr. Stevens!" Gloria Jackson exploded. "You will keep your tongue when it is not your turn. Reverend Martin, you now have four minutes. Begin again."

"Thank you. As I was saying, the Hebrews—God's chosen people—were at a military standstill with the dreaded Philistines. Instead of a bloody battle that would kill thousands on both sides, a fight between champions was proposed. The greatest warrior from each tribe would fight to the death, to determine the winning side and the losing side.

"Goliath came forward to represent the Philistines. He was immense—over nine feet tall. He wore armor so heavy most men couldn't even pick it up. He could throw a spear too big for most men to carry. He was a battle-hardened killer. He bellowed out challenges to the Hebrews to produce an opponent. He mocked their God. All of the greatest Hebrew warriors—including King Saul—were afraid to face Goliath. They refused. A boy—maybe fifteen or sixteen years old—stepped up and volunteered. And they, the King and all, let him enter the seemingly hopeless battle.

"Now, when Goliath first saw his adversary, he laughed. He saw this skinny little teenager, with no armor and no weapon except a boy's slingshot, and he laughed. He mocked David and he mocked David's God, but, he took no pity. He prepared for what he assumed would be a quick kill. However, Goliath was fatally shortsighted. He looked and saw nothing but a puny, human boy. However, the boy David was already a man of God. He had walked closely with God and prayed to God and listened to Him. As a young shepherd in the wilderness, David had faced the lion and faced the bear, standing in the breach between them and the flock he was defending. In those moments of great fear and greater danger, the shepherd boy trusted God to protect him and lead him to victory. David killed the bear. David killed the lion.

"Now, on a far bigger stage, David faced Goliath. As he looked across the field of battle, he saw Goliath for what he truly was—a mere human being. A mere human being obliviously marching into battle against the omnipotent, almighty God, hopelessly outmatched. As David loaded the single, smooth stone into his sling, he was confident the battle was already won. We all know the rest of the story. The end."

"Thank you, Reverend Martin," said Gloria Jackson. "Mr. Stevens, you have two minutes to rebut."

"Thank you, Ms. Jackson," Stevens responded, "but, I have no rebuttal. How can one rebut the telling of a fable meant to entertain children? What would be the point? I suppose one might surmise that the Reverend Martin is trying to paint a picture of me as the big, mean Goliath, intent on bullying the poor, naïve pastors, without being aware I am actually facing off against an all-powerful God. But, I do not believe in such a god, or any god, so this has no meaning to me. So, I will simply let it go by, without refuting his point, as it is too ridiculous to dignify with a rebuttal."

"Thank you for your non-rebuttal," Gloria Jackson said with a smirk. "You now have three minutes to introduce a new topic."

"Thank you. Before this event concludes, I want to read some things *into the record*, so to speak. These thoughts were authored by intelligent, educated, thinking people—who are atheists—about religious people. They are in no particular order.

> People who believe in a god or gods are the same as little children who believe in Santa Claus or the Easter Bunny . . . They are self-deluding fools, damaged by indoctrination into a set of beliefs that make no sense . . . Christians are gullible . . . All gods are human inventions, like elves, fairies, unicorns, the Loch Ness Monster and Bigfoot . . . Religious practice is such a monumental waste of time, effort, talent and resources that could be put to constructive use . . . Religious people are generally well-meaning, but not very bright . . . The potential for improvement in human existence is handicapped by those who cling to antiquated superstitions . . . Believers are too weak to handle their own problems and take responsibility for their own actions . . . They can't think for themselves, so they invent a god to think for them . . . Christians suffer from mass delusion . . . They decide on what they want to be true, and then try to make the evidence fit . . . Religious people are being conned, and they let it happen.

These are but a few examples of relevant comments," the Tall Man said. "There are many more, but I think this makes the point."

"One minute!"

"Perhaps I will close with one other comment. I find this particularly interesting. It goes, *Intelligent, educated, thinking people do not believe in any god. Therefore, those who believe in a god must not be intelligent, thinking people.*" Stevens sat silently for a long moment, looking as smug as a person can look.

"I guess that's it," Gloria Jackson announced. "Reverends Martin, you have two minutes to rebut."

I wanted desperately to attack Stevens' argument at a logical level. He had created another false dichotomy and otherwise simply listed a bunch of subjective and opinionated comments. However, I had been advised to *go to the changeup* and I needed another approach. Once again, Jennifer beat me to it.

"Mr. Stevens," she said, directly to our adversary, "how do the concepts of diversity, inclusion and the open-minded sharing of thoughts and ideas figure into the things you just listed?" She smiled her most brilliant smile. "I will give you the rest of our two minutes to answer. Thank you. I really want to know."

"This is unusual," Gloria Jackson stated, "but, go ahead Mr. Stevens. You may answer."

The Tall Man did not react quickly or well. He was clearly flummoxed and had to search for an answer. My wife is as sharp as they come.

"Well," he finally started, "in today's society . . . as we seek to progress toward a kinder and more egalitarian . . . society, diversity, inclusion and open-mindedness are of paramount importance. People will have differing backgrounds and cultures and will therefore have differing ideas and opinions, of course. And the acceptance of that is necessary to fruitful debates and discussions, resulting in a more fair and just society."

So far, he was making our point for us—that he and his ilk were not practicing what they were preaching.

"In this case, however," he pressed on, "one does have to acknowledge not all ideas and concepts are necessarily equal."

"Thirty seconds!"

"What I mean to say is, that, in some cases . . . one must discern whether an idea or a set of beliefs—even fairly considering the diversity and inclusion concerns of the moment, and, I must say, somebody has to decide if this admittedly different information or material is going to contribute positively to the task at hand . . ."

"Time is up! Reverends Martin, you have three minutes to introduce a new topic."

Chapter 54

Jennifer

"Thank you, Gloria," I said.

I realized I was kind of taking the reigns from my husband, but I felt moved to speak.

"The Good News of Jesus Christ—complete with all its promises of forgiveness, mercy and salvation—is offered to everyone. All people in all times and in all places. It does not matter who you are, what situation you were born into or what you have done or not done in your life. God's promises are offered to all. Now, I admit, there is much debate over who accepts God's offer and who does not, and what exactly that means. That's why there is so much disagreement, both inside and outside of the Church. But still, God values everyone. God loves everyone. It is especially important to note God does not rate people as to who is more important than the next. In fact, biblically, God seems to have a bit of a preference for the least of us—the poor and the powerless. But, in the end, every person is a child of God, made in God's own image.

"Evidently, Mr. Stevens and his ilk, disagree. Despite giving lip service to the importance of diversity, inclusion and the open-minded sharing of thoughts and ideas, Mr. Stevens has announced that he is capable of discerning who ought not be included and to whom he need not listen. He is comfortable taking a whole class of people—in this case, one point seven billion Christians—and telling us that we are not needed and our ideas and beliefs are not needed. No inclusion. No diversity. No sharing of ideas. We have invited him to our church. We have not been invited to share with his group."

"One minute!"

Nathan took the warning announcement as a cue to break in.

"Mr. Stevens!" he began. "Mr. Stevens! Ms. Jackson! All the people in this room—right, left, back and front! All the many people outside on this wonderful day! All the people in the state of Michigan and the entire U.S.A! And, all the people in the world! Hear these words! God loves you, and so do we!"

Nathan looked me and winked. In unison we shouted, "And there is nothing you can do about it!"

As I sat there giggling, Nathan concluded, "The end."

It took but a fleeting glance to see the Tall Man was not amused.

"Thank you, Reverends Martin," Gloria said. "Mr. Stevens, you have two minutes to rebut."

He simply sat and stared. After ten or fifteen seconds, Gloria Jackson said, "You may begin, Mr. Stevens."

"I have begun. Thank you."

He continued to sit and stare. He did his best to not move or change expression. Forty-five seconds later, Gloria stated, "One minute!"

As the second minute wound down, I once again had to admit to myself, *this guy is really good.* He had very quickly devised a way to respond by not responding. I couldn't be sure how the viewing audience would perceive what was happening, but I think he was successfully making his point.

"Time is up! Mr. Stevens, you have three minutes to introduce a new topic."

"Thank you, Ms. Jackson. Before we run out of time, I wish to make clear my position—and the position of the *Free Us from Religion Coalition*—on what we believe our country ought to do about the problem of organized religion. We are absolutely convinced religion in public life is a detriment to society, all based on absolutist claims that cannot be proven. Still, we recognize that the U.S. Constitution does not allow the outright criminalization of religious practice. Therefore, it is our goal to enact the following. One, that all religious symbols, such as crosses, statues, menorahs, etc. be kept, by law, from the public view. We should not be assaulted with visions of such things from our roads and sidewalks and such. Two, that all public properties be free of religious practice and symbolism, including local parks, national parks, schools, libraries, townhalls, courthouses and all other public properties. Three, that religions be banned from advertising, forcing religious material on the population. We believe there is adequate precedent for this. Four, we will seek legislation designed to outlaw faith claims and religious associations in political campaigning. It is patently ridiculous to allow such things to be a part of our system of governance. Five, we hope to lead a cultural upheaval in which religious expression and claims will simply be rejected as foolish and dangerous. When friends and co-workers and siblings and moms and dads and grandmas speak up to put down religious nonsense before it can take root, we will be able to create a society largely free of it."

"One minute!"

"Thank you, Ms. Jackson, but I believe I have finished."

I saw a look on my husband's face that told me he was ready to go.

"Thank you," he said. "Not coincidently to what Mr. Stevens just said, I would like to make our position on atheism abundantly clear. To claim there is no God is, in itself, a religious statement. It is an absolutist claim that cannot be proven. To base an entire system of belief on such an unproveable proposition is unfathomably reckless, especially when the resulting opinions enter into public life. Therefore, we really should enact the following. One, all atheistic claims, especially attacks on religion, should be banned from public discourse. Two, attempts by atheists to limit the expression of religion in any way should be dismissed as baseless, as their foundational premise—that there is no God--cannot be proven. Three, atheistic attacks on religion should be classified as hate crimes, as condemning large groups of people based on unproven claims is a clear form of bigotry and intimidation. And, four, we seek to create a culture in which religious belief and faith and practice are perceived as positives in both the public and private sectors of our country. Not that Church and State should be mixed—they should not. Rather, that people of faith are viewed as having the good judgement, moral fiber, confidence and altruistic nature that will equip them to be powerful leaders. The end."

"Thank you. Reverends Martin, you have three minutes to introduce a new topic."

"Thank you, Ms. Jackson," I said. "First, I would like to clarify what my husband just said about what should be done about the problem of atheism. We don't actually want most of those things to happen. We believe all people have intrinsic value, and have a right to their thoughts and opinions. It is interesting, though, is it not, how one group of people can rail on and on about how another group cannot positively prove their claims and beliefs, all the while demanding agreement about their own claims, which are also unproveable. It is true one cannot scientifically prove that God exists. To know for sure that God exists requires faith. However, to insist God does not exist also requires a leap of faith in one's own opinion. The existence of God cannot be disproved.

"So, all can rest assured we will not be pushing for laws to punish atheists. We will, however, continue working on the part about people of faith being viewed as having good judgement, strong moral fiber and an altruistic nature. Done properly, faith in God produces those qualities, and we will not sit quietly by and listen to Mr. Stevens—and others like him—disparage us based on their own assumptions and prejudices. The end."

"Mr. Stevens, you have two minutes to rebut."

The Tall Man was quiet. He turned toward Nathan and I and, not so subtly, shook his head at us. The look on his face gave out a clear *poor, delusional, stupid children* kind of vibe.

Finally, he said, "I am filled with the urge to continue this particular argument, but I am sure the audience is growing as weary as I am of this nonsensical reasoning. To claim something exists demands proof. To claim something does not exist does not. If you claim there exists a purple unicorn, you are going to have to show proof of the purple unicorn. Until someone can prove the existence of said unicorn, it is safe to assume there is no such unicorn. Enough said. The end."

"We will pause at this point for a three-minute commercial break," Gloria Jackson said. "Please remain seated until we come back live."

Chapter 55

Nathan

I felt pretty good as we went into the commercial break, although I must admit I was beginning to feel tired and less sharp. The tension of being on high alert for so long was draining my energy and concentration. Still, Jennifer was doing a great job. She rescued me a couple of times and made some strong points of her own. As I was thinking this through and trying to gear up for the final push, I was interrupted.

"You two are doing a wonderful job," Edwina said.

"Thank you," I replied, "but aren't you supposed to be seated?"

"I am very old. I don't really know what I am doing," she said through a knowing smirk. "Things are about to wrap up," she continued. "Don't worry about that scoundrel Stevens. Remember you have maybe the largest audience in the history of audiences. Say what needs to be said."

"Happy to," Jennifer chimed in. "Now, what would that be exactly?"

Edwina laughed and then laughed some more. When she calmed down, she said, "I have not been given that part. I believe that will be coming directly to the two of you. Just be ready."

With that, she spun around as fast as an elderly woman can be expected to spin and returned to her seat. I looked at Jennifer and smiled what I hoped was an encouraging smile. That *biggest audience in the history of audiences* line threw me off more than a little.

"You and me, Babe," was all the brilliance I could muster, but it seemed to work. Jennifer replied, "You and me, and God makes three . . . or five!"

She was still giggling at her own clevertude when Gloria Jackson broke back in with, "We are live in ten, nine, eight . . ."

"We're back!" she continued after reaching the end of her countdown. "Welcome to the final segment of the debate between Alexander Stevens, representative of the *Free Us from Religion Coalition*—an organization based on the belief that science and logic can better serve society than can religion—and the pastors of the world-famous *WWW.God Christian Church,* the Reverends Jennifer and Nathan Martin. I am Gloria Jackson, the moderator for today's event. Here is the rest of the agenda. We will have one last round of topics. Mr. Stevens will introduce and the Reverends Martin will rebut. Then, the Reverends will introduce and Mr. Stevens will rebut. At the conclusion of those two rounds, each side will have six minutes for closing remarks. At that point, this historic event will be concluded. Are there any questions? Hearing none, let us proceed. Mr. Stevens, you have three minutes."

"Thank you. I have been accused of being exclusive in our dealings with Christians. Perhaps so, but I think with good reason. Religious thought and talk is not an intrinsic, unalterable part of who and what a person is. It is more about what a person thinks and does. Thinking, educated people are not objecting to the person, but to what they do and say! I believe it to be perfectly appropriate to debate—and even refute—ideas and propositions that are introduced into the public sphere. We at the *Free Us From Religion Coalition* fully support today's values of inclusion, diversity and acceptance, and teach such values as integral parts of the perfected society we seek to create. Expanding on that idea, I must register my concern and my distaste for the habit Christian groups have of proselytizing. In a society that not only allows but encourages people to form their own dreams, beliefs, practices and morals, these Christians insist everyone needs to believe what they believe and act how they act. They are right and everyone else is wrong, and they are not going to give up until you admit they are right, even when they are not! For crying out loud, sometimes they even show up at your front door, spouting platitudes and forcing pamphlets down your throat! It ought to be illegal!"

The Tall Man paused and took a deep breath. He seemed to realize he was getting carried away.

"Perhaps I am reliving some of those unpleasant experiences right now. I apologize if I have become overly enthusiastic. However, I stand by the content of my statement. I am sure most people share in the experience of being accosted by a Christian fanatic, who is intent on convincing, scaring or even threatening a person into accepting their beliefs about God and Hell and punishment—to do as they say is the only way to avoid eternal suffering. It is one thing to believe nonsense. It is another to force those beliefs on others. We believe our society will be greatly improved when this practice is unacceptable. The end."

I think Stevens was beginning to tire, as well. He was no longer using every last second of his allotted time.

"Thank you, Mr. Stevens. Reverends Martin, you have two minutes to rebut."

"There he goes again," Jennifer chimed in. "The end."

"Very well. Reverend Nathan Martin, do you have anything to add?"

"Yes, thank you," I said. "There he goes again, advocating the use of the law to punish people who refuse to agree with him. The funny part is, he still can't seem to see what he is doing. The end."

"That brings us to our final round of *propose and rebut*. *W.W.W.God Christian Church*, you have three minutes to introduce your final new topic."

"Thank you," I began. "A relative of mine once exclaimed—I'm sure I was in the middle of pontificating on some theological topic or another—*Christians are all a pain in the butt! You think your way is the only one that is right, and you just won't shut up about it.*

"He was right. In the last sixty years, or so, we have developed a culture that glorifies individualism. This is largely good, as we live in a country that values freedom and individual rights. However, we have gone too far. Today, one of the greatest social crimes a person can commit is to suggest that something is *right* or *wrong*. To do so will create a response of: *Who are you to decide what is right?* and *Don't tell me what to do!* My favorite is *Don't judge me!* This biblical concept has been bastardized to mean, *I can do whatever I want and you'd better keep your mouth shut about it.* In our country, it is okay to believe whatever you want, so long as you don't suggest it applies to everyone.

"I am aware of how what I am about to say sounds to the unbeliever. I *do* know the only way that is true and right for everyone. It is not my way. It is not something I made up or decided upon. It is not something I created, but rather something I know. God exists. God sits in His heaven. As sinners living in a broken world, on our own, none of us could ever go to be with God. But, he loves each and every one of us too much to let that be the end of it. So, he sent his Son to pay for our sins. God invites, implores and woos every person—all races, genders, nationalities and types of sinner—to accept the saving grace of Jesus Christ. In exchange for Jesus' sacrifice on the cross, *faith* is the one thing God requires. We can spend a lifetime arguing the details, but this I know to be true—only Jesus saves."

"One minute!"

"What if someone you love is having a delightful picnic on the train track? You see the train coming and they don't. What do you do? You get them off the tracks! You tell them about the train. If they don't listen, you convince them. If they still don't move, you scream and jump up and down. If that is not enough, you grab them and pull them off those tracks! You would never say, *I love them too much to risk offending or angering them.* You would never watch them be destroyed and then say, *It's a shame they were killed, but I sure did love them.* No...you have no choice but to get them off the tracks. Even if they are upset at first, they will be grateful when they finally recognize the danger of the train. I know the need for salvation to be as real as an oncoming train. Therefore, I will try to be an even bigger pain in the butt this year than I was last. I'm sorry. I have no choice. I love you. The end."

"Thank you. Mr. Stevens, you have two minutes to rebut."

"Thank you. It won't take that long. First, I believe I have successfully discredited this god nonsense throughout this entire debate. Second, I do appreciate Reverend Martin admitting that he is a pain in the butt. The end."

He got a big laugh out of that one. Touche'.

"Well," Gloria Jackson started, "this has been quite a day so far. By coin flip at the last commercial break, it was determined that the Reverends Martin of the *WWW.God Christian Church* will make the first closing statement. You may divide your six minutes as you see fit. Please begin."

Jennifer and I had already agreed I would go first and she would offer our last words.

"A friend once said to me, *If I ever became interested in religious stuff, I would try out all the religions and pick the one I liked best.* A fellow philosophy student once argued, *The best* thing to do would be to look at all the religions, and combine the parts you agree with into your own unique religion. My favorite relative truth expression is *You might have your truth, but I have my truth.*

"The following story didn't happen, but it could have. A large, locked, wooden box appeared in a downtown park. On the side was printed *Frog*. A woman stared at the box, before saying, *A frog in a big wooden box is ridiculous.* She concluded, therefore, that there was no frog. A man said, *It makes no sense that a frog would be in a wooden box. Maybe a hamster.* He believed, therefore, there was a hamster in the box. Another man said, *I hate frogs. I would prefer there be a puppy in the box.* Soon he believed the wooden box did indeed contain a puppy, and proceeded to tell his friends what a lovely puppy it was. A committee came by and agreed the wooden box could not possibly contain only a frog, as that would be unfair to other animals. They issued a position paper explaining that the box clearly contained all species of animals that had chosen to reside in the box. There was a woman from the next town over, who had no occasion to visit that particular park. She convinced everyone she knew such a box did not exist at all, as she had not once seen it. Another couple proclaimed they would never believe in the mythical frog of the wooden box, as there was no scientific data to prove its existence. They added that *only an idiot* would believe in such an unproven frog.

"Without warning, a man returned with a big key, and unlocked the box. Out came a frog.

"The key Truth in life is that God exists: Father, Son and Holy Spirit. Through scripture, prayer, revelation and the work of the Spirit in my own life, I know this to be the Truth. I cannot prove it. But, I know it. It is not true because of my beliefs or my feelings. It is simply and always the Truth. Most importantly, it does not cease to be true because of someone's unbelief or disagreement or desire for something else to be true. I know many believe that my confidence in this Truth is mistaken. I understand. But please remember, if there is a frog in the box, there is a frog in the box. Belief otherwise will only mean that you will be surprised when the frog is revealed."

Jennifer took over.

"I have always been blessed with a good life. Maybe good is the wrong word—I always had a comfortable life. I had a stable family. I had parents who loved me and cared for me. I had my own room and, eventually, my own phone and access to one of the family cars. In high school I was a decent student, but my main focus was on the social aspect of being a teenager. The right clothes, the right clique, the right parties, the right boyfriends—all of that. Despite those advantages, I often felt empty or alone or just treading water, waiting for life to begin. Still, I continued to live out the *cool* lifestyle, until something else came along. It did. Early in my senior year, I became pregnant with my daughter. The boy dropped me flat. A couple of good friends stuck by me, but most moved on to more carefree things. My parents were disappointed, but rallied quickly to support me. I carried, delivered and kept my daughter. Life was hard, but I had help. I did feel guilt and regret. Guilt that I had let people down. Regret that the life I had planned would now go very differently. When the baby was about a year old, I started thinking about life more seriously. I questioned my own beliefs, habits, assumptions and behavior. I thought about all the stuff I had heard in all those childhood Sunday School classes and church services. I say heard, because I don't know that I learned anything way back then—I was mostly not paying attention. But, as a very young mother, I thought about it. Then I read scriptures and prayed about it, a little at first and then a lot. God was pulling me in. God was wooing me. The Grace of God, coming in the shape of what I later learned was the Holy

Spirit, grabbed hold of me and reeled me in. I accepted Jesus as my Savior, and everything changed. I never felt alone again. I never felt empty again. I never felt guilt or regret, again. I never again felt that, if I could just tread water long enough, life might finally begin. Life was now. Life was new. Life was full and abundant. Life was meaningful and filled with hope. Oh, to be sure, life still was not easy. But even in hard times I knew I would get through. God gifted me with strength and perseverance. He made me tough. I raised my daughter into the fine, good, productive person she is today. I went back to school, earned my degrees and had a marvelous career. Eventually, I found the kind, upstanding, devoted man who is now my husband. And, my spiritual life grew into a strong and loving relationship with God—Father, Son, and Holy Spirit. A God-focused life. I am not sure which is the cake and which is the frosting, but my next life, my eternal life, was comfortably and assuredly settled as well. Whenever I am done here, my eternity with God in His own heaven is certain. Done deal.

"I know and understand vastly more about God than I once did, and have only scratched the service. But, I do so look forward to the rest of the journey."

"One minute!"

"I say these things today, because watching and listening today are untold millions of people. People of all kinds, all origins, all backgrounds, all histories, all beliefs and all personalities. And, one of many Truths about God is that He loves you. No matter who you are or where you are from or what you have done or not done, He loves you, and holds the heavenly door open for you. And, because God loves you, so do I. So does my husband and the people of our church and Christian people and churches and organizations all across this planet. You heard my husband say that if a train is bearing down on someone you love, you need to do whatever it takes to get them off that track! Pull them off, if you have to. I am blessed that God has provided me a few minutes to speak to unprecedented numbers of people whom God loves and I love. If you need it, consider yourself pulled. Amen."

"Time is up! Mr. Stevens of the *Free Us from Religion Coalition*, you have six minutes to offer your closing remarks."

"Thank you," The Tall Man began, "Gloria Jackson, Department head of the Journalism Department at *Western Michigan University*. You have done a fine job moderating what has been a most unusual debate. I am sure it was not an easy thing to do."

Why didn't I remember to thank the moderator!?

"I don't believe I will need anywhere near six minutes. I have only two things to add. First, I must respond to Reverend Martin's cute little story about a frog in a box, and that is only to point out that if there is no frog in the box, no amount of wishing and believing and pretending will magically make a frog appear. The logic runs both ways. Second, I think it is obvious that everything I presented today was factual, logical, measurable and provable. The kind of things intelligent, educated people can believe with confidence. On the other hand, nearly everything presented by the Reverends Martin has been speculative, subjective, fanciful, emotional, illogical, overblown, unmeasurable and impossible to prove. The kind of things intelligent, educated people must dismiss out of hand. Case closed.

"However, I have found the Reverends Nathan and Jennifer Martin to be good, well-intentioned people. Misguided, but nice people all the same. So, I will close by declaring the *mercy rule*. Game over. Game decisively won. No piling on. The end."

"There you have it," Gloria Jackson proclaimed. "This momentous debate—witnessed live by perhaps the largest worldwide audience in the history of broadcasting—has been concluded. What shall be the result, or results? I think it is fair to say we will not know for quite some time. I have received word that both *CNN* and *CBS News*—our broadcast partners here today—will block out all previously scheduled programming—even Sunday sports!—to conduct live panel discussions of the extraordinary events witnessed here today . . . ."

I had no idea there was going to be any sort of *afterward*. Of course, this whole adventure has been one unexpected thing after another.

" . . . and, one can only imagine how the internet will light up in the next hours and days. Extraordinary, indeed. This is Gloria Jackson, with thanks to the *WWW.God Christian Church*, the *Free Us from Religion Coalition*, *CNN*, *CBS News*, our commercial sponsors and the World Wide Web, signing off. Good day!"

With that, the Great Debate was over.

Part 3

Afterward

Chapter 56

Jennifer

I had been so caught up in the debate, I hadn't given a moment's thought about what to do when it ended. A quick look at Nathan told me he hadn't, either. He sat there bug-eyed, seemingly not sure where to go or what to say. Soon, it became clear nobody really had a plan. Chaos ensued.

Our supporters rushed the stage, all babbling one thing or another. The Tall Man's supporters did the same. Before we could even begin to sort out next moves, camera operators and reporters aggressively elbowed their way through the crowd and started firing questions.

"Who do you think won the debate!?!"

"How will we know who won?"

"How did the nasty criticism make you feel?"

"Did you change your mind about anything today?"

"Do you think anyone changed their minds about anything!?!"

"What now!?!"

"Are you worried about going to hell!?!

It was then I realized I was hearing The Tall Man's questions, too. Nathan was responding diplomatically. *It isn't about winning... What happens next is up to God... We are just ordinary people, all the glory goes to God,* and that sort of thing.

Just as I was trying to find my way out of the predicament, I heard Nathan say, "Sorry folks, I have to go now. I have many people waiting for me. Thank you for being here! Good bye!"

Nathan grabbed my arm and pulled me away from the crowd. We escaped into the small back room behind the altar and slammed the door. Alone, at least for the moment.

Nathan kissed me.

Then, he said, "You were great. I am so proud of you! Are you okay? There was a lot of pressure out there. Are you okay?"

"Look who's all wound up," I replied.

"Yeah. Me. How about you?"

"I am excited and tired. I am confused. I feel marvelously well. I am not entirely sure what just happened. I have no idea what comes next, or even what to do this minute."

"Yeah. Me, too," he said, and laughed manically.

"Okay, big guy. We're all over the board, but, seriously, what should we do now?"

I knew he would have a plan.

"I thought I would be anxious to get to a TV and find out what is being said," he began, "but now I realize that I don't care."

"How very Pastor Carl-like of you—leaving the results in God's hands."

"Yeah, I guess so. You okay with holding off on that?"

"I am," I said, even though I was a bit curious.

"What I am thinking is this," Nathan continued. "We have tens of thousands of people outside, doing who knows what. Our people are dealing with huge bathroom lines and the aftermath of all of the food service stuff. Some of them are trying to get to us and others are working."

"Sounds right," I said.

"And, we have no idea what is going on with Stevens and all his people. They might be leaving, they might be gathering for some sort of after-meeting. Who knows?"

"Right," I said, still waiting for the plan.

"So, let's get out there. It is almost 4:00. Spread the word to our members they are free to go home, but some of us will gather in the basement at 5:15—I couldn't decide between 5:00 and 5:30—to debrief and decompress. Maybe we can even rustle up some food. It has been a long day."

"It sure has. Seems like it ought to be pushing midnight," I said. "Let's head out and we'll just take it as it comes," I continued. "Should be a great time to talk about God with lots of people we don't know yet."

"Sounds great!" he responded. "Let's go!" Then he kissed me again and ran out the door.

I followed. I saw him exit the front door and turn left, so I turned right. The first thing I encountered was a *CNN* truck. I stuck my head in the door and saw one of those banks of monitors showing all sorts of different shots. The Tall Man's face was on several of them, interviewing to beat the band. I chose to not care. Other screens showed some sort of panel discussion, but I couldn't hear anything. I chose to not care about that, either, until I realized one of the people on the panel was our own Alicia Skiba. *How did that happen!? Where are they shooting that!?*

"Hey! That's the lady minister!" some guy in the truck shouted.

I took off and didn't look back until I was engulfed in people. They were everywhere. I blended in for maybe a minute, and then I was recognized. The crush and the rolling waves of many voices ruled conversation out of the question. Many were, friendly, excited, and a few even ecstatic. Just as many were cold, accusatory and a few even angry. I kept moving as best I could.

I felt the road under my feet, except, at the moment, it was too filled with people to actually be a road. To my left, the atheist facility came into view. A throng of people milled about, but it didn't look like anything organized was going on. In fact, it appeared the majority of people were trying to move away from the crowd and toward wherever they had found a parking space. I kept my head down and tried to circle back toward the church.

Chapter 56

Nathan

I knew Jennifer could handle herself, but as I waded into the crowd, I wondered if I should have left her on her own. It is one thing to hear the number *thirty-thousand*, but another to stand in the middle of them. I quickly reached the bathroom area, and it was immediately obvious a lot of these folks couldn't wait long enough to get home to their own facilities. The lines were long, but moving.

"Frank!" I hollered.

"Hey, boss!" he responded. "Isn't this somethin'!"

"It sure is," I answered. "I am not sure what, but it sure is somethin'! Tell everybody we are going to meet in the church at about quarter after five. If we can manage it!"

"Will do!" Frank exclaimed and resumed working.

I returned to my quest and shouldered through the crowd. I had all sorts of short responses and pearls of wisdom in my head, ready to go. Turned out I really didn't need them. Nobody demanded answers. People of faith thanked me, or shook my hand, or embraced me. Some did all three. Other people of faith glowered a bit, or shook their heads sadly. Clearly, they were disappointed about some point of disagreement. I was most surprised by those who were clearly not people of faith. There were no red-in-the-face screamers. No attempts to start up renewed debate. Some just shook their heads and moved on. A few even shook my hand and mumbled some form of *thanks for being reasonable.*

One guy said, "I still don't buy any of that, but I think you are the kind of guy I could talk to." Another offered, "I got to give you credit, you don't have any evidence, but you sure hung in there."

With well over a hundred exchanges in an hour, the most common occurrence was that I had no idea what they were talking about, so I simply smiled and kept moving.

The crowd was rapidly thinning, and getting around became easier. I started to feel strongly that I wanted to get back inside the church and be with my people—especially Jennifer, but all the others, too. For months and weeks and days and, especially, the past few hours, we had shared experiences we never saw coming. We had seen and experienced and heard and realized and felt things that, perhaps, no one had ever done before. As I worked my way closer to the beloved little building, I found myself hoping at least some of the congregation had chosen to hang around.

I was glad the outsiders were gone, and immediately chastised myself for considering anyone an outsider. No one is an outsider to God. Still, there was an especially joyous anticipation of reuniting with my friends, my Brothers and Sisters in the faith.

I needn't have worried about seeing enough of them to be satisfying. I stopped short of entering, and peeked around the door jam. They were all there in the basement—our own little Fellowship Hall, the place of gathering. Jennifer was already there, boisterously sharing hugs and high-energy snippets of conversation with several people at once. Condi and Kevin sat soaking it all in. I always thought that Condi's great musical talent was her most distinguishing feature, until her faith grew even more impressive. Kevin had the rational business head that every church needs. Jeremy, our teenaged whiz kid was sitting and talking with his good friend, the aged and wise Edwina Fine. For a woman who only wanted to attend one worship service—just to see the old church that she had almost single-handedly kept alive for many years—she had certainly developed into a huge and important part of our little congregation. And, I could only imagine the kind of future Jeremy had in the church. He would be a powerful leader one day. Janice Pohl was sitting off to the side, making notes on a legal pad. I was so fortunate and grateful that she had voluntarily followed me to the new Triple-W church, where she continued to keep me organized and on course. I also saw several equally important people who helped keep the whole operation afloat, quietly and without receiving much attention or credit. Jane Petra, Art and Leta Walsh, Francine Cook, John and Shelley Drobena, Michelle Garner and Jeff Conway, among others, gave our little God-centered enterprise a solid backbone of support. I also saw Bob—now to be known as Robert—busily laying out a surprisingly lavish spread of food. I made my entrance.

"Robert!" I said, "how did you manage to hold on to all this food after trying to feed thirty thousand hungry souls?"

"I have no idea," he responded. "We brought a boatload of food, but when I saw the crowd, I was sure we were going to run out. We just kept serving and serving and serving until they finally quit coming. When we cleaned up, we still had twelve tubs of food, so I brought it here!"

I heard Jennifer laughing hysterically, and I knew why.

Robert's mother, Martha Williams, had taken a seat off to the side. I was not sure if she wanted to be alone or didn't know if she really belonged. That little conundrum cleared itself up as she was entertaining a constant stream of well-wishers and new friends.

One person present at the semi-spontaneous gathering surprised me. The debate moderator, Gloria Jackson, stood awkwardly against one wall, looking for all the world like she had made a mistake by showing up. As I was deciding on my next move, I saw Jennifer approach Gloria.

"Miss Jackson," she said, "how lovely to see you! Welcome from the Triple-W church family!"

"I am thinking perhaps this was a bad idea," Jackson began. "The other side in this debate has already accused me of taking your side—even though that was certainly not the case—at least in the beginning. If they saw me here, it could cause all sorts of gossip."

"Well," I heard my wife say, "maybe it would help to know why you chose to stay. You are most welcome, but I admit to being interested as to why."

Jackson hesitated. "I have to confess, I am not sure. I have not been a religious person—an academic agnostic and all of that—but things that happened here today intrigued me. I am sorry, Reverend Martin, but perhaps I wanted to see what it was like behind closed doors."

Jennifer smiled and replied, "First, I am Jennifer. We mostly use The Reverend for signing certificates and documents and such. Please call me Jennifer."

"Thank you, Jennifer. I am Gloria."

"Gloria, why don't you simply hang out a while and observe. We are happy to be known, warts and all. And, we would like to know you."

"Thank you. I would like that, but perhaps I should leave before I cause you any trouble."

"Trouble!" came bellowing from halfway across the room. "Makin' a new friend is never trouble! And if it is, well, we aren't afraid of no trouble. We fixed you a plate. Why don't you come right over here and sit with me and my wife Sylvie—best wife in seven counties. We'll tell you anything you want to know!"

Frank strikes again.

Gloria shot a stunned look at Jennifer, with obvious questioning in her eyes.

Jennifer said, "You may as well go eat with Frank and Sylvie. There is really no way out at this point, and you will love them, same as we do."

"Yeah, that's me alright, Lovable Frank!"

"Nice to meet you, Lovable Frank."

Frank nearly bent double with laughter. When he had caught his breath he bellowed again, "Sylvie, come meet our new friend, Gloria. You're gonna like her—she's funny. I think I am going to call her *Glory*."

"Pipe down, Old Man. You're embarrassing the poor woman."

"No, he's not," Gloria said. "My MeMaw called me Glory. It is nice to hear it again. She was the last member of our family to attend church. Maybe she was on to something."

As Glory sat down to share a meal with Frank and Sylvie, the group settled into what might pass for a churchy version of *partying*. Stories and laughter and hugs abounded, as the energy of the day gradually subsided. Jennifer and I sort of worked the room, each member of our church family congratulating us on a job well done. I know they would have congratulated us no matter how badly it went, but I was affirmed by their words, just the same. When the room finally grew quiet, I heard Kevin Cloverton say, "Pastor Nate, what do you think?"

Chapter 57

Jennifer

Just as Kevin invited my husband to speak, Alicia Skiba burst through the door, walking almost as fast as she was talking.

"Can you believe it!" she cried. "Who would've ever thought it could turn into this!?! Did you see any of it? Of course, you would need five TVs and a couple of computers to see all of it! Everybody has it on. I don't even want to know where some of those so-called experts came from. What did you think?"

"Why, hello, Alicia!" I shouted. "Good to see you, too! Hey, everybody, say hi to Alicia!"

She was immediately inundated with shouts of greeting and a dozen hugs.

"Oh, yeah," she giggled. "Hello and all that. Did you see it?"

"Actually, no," Nathan said. "We have been so enmeshed in what was happening here, and then the debriefing with each other, that we have not had any of the media on."

"But, we would sure like to hear about it, now," I added. "Sit down in the front here, and tell us everything."

She sat and Sylvie handed her a glass of water.

Alicia laughed again. "I came in here all full up with the excitement of it all, and now I am at a loss for words. Not really.

A Dragon Outside the Church 287

I am filled with so many words I don't know which ones to use first. It was a most amazing thing. The *CNN* people scooped me up and drove me to a studio in Grand Rapids. It was almost a kidnapping, except I wanted to go. They were already on the air with a panel of I don't know who. Evidently there was supposed to be a couple of religious experts and a scientist and some guy who seemed to be best at complaining. Off to the side was a bank of monitors, showing a bunch of other networks and organizations, all analyzing the Great Debate. Every one of them wanted to get the juiciest scoop, first."

"What were they saying?" Shelley Drobena asked.

"Well, as soon as they added me to the *CNN* group, I only heard that part, but—oh, Ms. Jackson, you're here! I didn't see you. They all thought you were great, except the complainer guy. He thought you were mean to The Tall Man, but the rest of them shouted him down—anyway, so much was said I can hardly do it justice. I will have to rewatch the various shows."

"Any examples?" Janice asked.

"Sure. Sure. I have to admit, most of it sounded like a rehash of the debate, with people stating what they agreed with and what they didn't. Eventually, they got around to the debate itself. They tried to declare a winning side, but they split right down ideological lines on that, too. Then they argued some more. They did find consensus on one thing. They all found this to be a truly historic event. They could hardly believe that—in this day and age—such a huge number of people could be so engaged with religious discussion."

"How many were watching and listening?" Not surprisingly, the question came from Jeremy.

"It is impossible to tell, right away. In fact, we will probably never have an accurate number. However, it went absolutely viral. The two networks have worldwide coverage, and the internet access dwarfed the TV coverage. It was shared and split and posted all over the world with no control at all! Word came in that radio stations all over the world hooked into the internet audio and broadcast it pretty much everywhere. All the experts agree that this was the largest live audience in history . . . by a lot!"

The room went suddenly quiet. I think all of us were thunderstruck to hear we had just spoken to more people at one time than any other event . . . ever. I mean, we kind of knew it already, but it still packed a wallop. Even Alicia seemed a bit shocked, and she was the one who said it.

After a long pause, Frank murmured, "don't that beat all."

"You said it, Frank," Condi said. "And Kevin and I thought we were leaving a big church for a little one."

That raised a chuckle throughout the room.

"Thanks, Alicia, for doing such a great job," I said.

Most everyone affirmed Alicia out loud.

"Now, I am sure we will study this and review the recordings and such," Kevin said, "but I still want to hear what our pastors are thinking."

Nathan started. "Admittedly, my thoughts and feelings are not clear yet. None of us have ever been a part of a thing of this magnitude before. I sure haven't."

Alicia jumped in, "The opening ceremony of the Beijing Olympics was watched by about two billion people. Most of the experts are saying today's debate beat that by quite a bit."

"I'm glad I didn't know that," I said.

"For sure," Nathan said. "The thing is, most of my feelings right now are not about that. My faith in God—and love for God—is at an all-time high. I am about bursting with love and awe for my magnificent wife."

I thought to say something, but couldn't.

Nathan went on, "And, you people. I hardly know what to say. In a relatively short period of time, I have seen you grow and develop into devout, action-taking Christians of amazing power and strength and love. Occasionally every clergy person comes face to face with the realization someone in the congregation is a more mature, devout, fully developed Christian than you are. Now, I face that truth every day. Please, don't say anything in response to that. It is true and a good and wonderful thing."

Nathan started to tear up a bit, so I spoke. "He's right. I feel it, too. I don't want to start naming names, because I would leave somebody out, but look around you. Do you see anyone who has surprised you with moments of great faith, generosity, kindness or insight? Have you shared worship so powerful that you were shocked it could be that way? Have you seen each other take action in ways well beyond what anyone could expect? I know you have."

No one said a thing. In fact, they barely seemed to be breathing.

Nathan said, "I have served churches much larger than this one, with literally twenty or thirty times more members. I am totally sincere when I say I could not choose an all-star team from all of those churches that could exceed the all-in, sold-out, lived-out faith the people in this room have."

Jane Petra spoke. "It is just like what Pastor Carl said. A different kind of church, without a lot of the usual stuff. Odd, maybe. Small. Not suited to everybody. Seemingly irrational, sometimes. But, obedient to God. Powerful. Influential. The day we decided to stick with what Pastor Carl left us, that's when all this really took hold."

There was another long pause, as Jane's words sank in.

"That all goes back to you two," said Leta Walsh. "You have shown us the way, even when we were all getting off track."

"We have tried to do our parts," I said, "but, at times, Nathan and I were just as prone to getting off track as anyone else."

"God does not expect minute by minute perfection from us," Edwina proclaimed. "He knows better. God wants sincerity and fidelity and trust and faith and a willingness to keep trying. You good people gave Him a better dose of that than He gets very often."

"Make sure you include yourself in that, Mrs. Fine," said young Jeremy.

"Thank you, Jeremy. I do. I love God, that's for sure."

"So, Pastors, what about the debate itself?" Kevin persisted.

I picked up the ball this time. "I think we are going to have to figure out how to address that. Maybe we can schedule a discussion event to try to break it down and address all the nuances and ambiguities. I think we will be analyzing this for a long time. Tonight, time and energy are running short."

"I'll say this much," Nathan said. "I felt a great sense of honor and duty. This was about all Christians—and potential Christians—everywhere, but for a little while, God chose Jennifer and I to represent Him. To stand in the breech, so to speak, to weather the onslaught of doubt and unbelief and even hate thrown at God and His people, by those who have not yet encountered Him. Once we got rolling, I never felt alone. Jennifer was there. You were there. Especially, God was there. The Holy Spirit guided us all the way."

"Except when we messed up here and there," I added. "I am more intensely aware than ever of how God uses flawed people to do his work."

"Of course," Nathan said. "And, still, for perhaps the first time in my life, I felt the rush and certainty of doing Godly and righteous battle against the dragon. Please don't ask me what I mean by that. I'm not sure, but you can expect to hear about it in a sermon sometime soon!"

"May I?" asked Michelle Gardner, one of the quiet ones. "What happens now? I mean, we all can see what a huge thing happened here today—a thing of historical and even biblical proportions. What has changed? What happens now?"

"Now isn't that a magnificent question!"

"Pastor Carl," I said.

"Pastor Carl!" my husband shouted.

Chapter 58

Nathan

I immediately forgot everything else and rushed to embrace Carl. All through our incredible journey, I had longed to talk with Carl, to consult with him, ask his advice, to pray with him . . . maybe even to lean on him. And here he was, right in front of me. Pastor Carl was not necessarily a huggy kind of guy, but he embraced me back.

"Carl! I can't tell you how excited I am to see you!" I said.

"Yes," he replied. "It has been hard to stay away."

I almost asked him why he had to stay away, but I caught myself. I didn't really have to ask. Right along, he had been wherever he was supposed to be.

"You and Jennifer have been busy," he continued through a wry smile.

"You think?" I couldn't resist saying.

"Excuse me," Jennifer said as she broke in for a hug of her own. Then she stepped back and looked Carl straight in the eye and said, "You already know every bit of what happened here, don't you."

"Yes. I suppose I do."

"Including things we don't yet know ourselves, right?" I added.

"My dear Jennifer and Nathan, I have no way of knowing exactly what you know, but, yes, probably."

"I don't mean to break up your reunion, but I think it is high time we meet your Pastor Carl," Janice called out. "After all, we are running the church according to his guidelines!"

"Yes, of course," I said. "Everybody, this is Pastor Carl. He has been my—and Jennifer's—friend and mentor and role model and inspiration. Also, Janice is right. Carl gave us the blueprint that has led the *WWW.God Christian Church* to where we are and what we are—whatever that is."

"Welcome, Pastor Carl!"

"Good to meet you, Pastor Carl!"

The greetings were many and heartfelt.

"And, Carl," I continued, "this is everybody."

"It is a real pleasure to finally meet you all, in person," he replied.

"In person, you say," Condi commented. "But, I think you already know us. Am I right?"

"In many ways, yes, I do."

"Okay," Jeff Conway broke in. "Then what is next for us? I think it is obvious we just built up to about as big a climactic event as we could ever imagine, and that climactic event happened today and is now behind us. What now?"

Pastor Carl smiled and said, "I am sure Pastors Nathan and Jennifer have told you how I feel about looking ahead before God speaks. I am not really sure what all is coming, and I have to be content to wait—as do you."

"But it sounds like you know something," Michelle said.

"Okay. That's fair," Carl said.

I don't remember ever seeing him so smiley.

"Please don't try to pin me down to details. Firstly, God is pleased by what has happened here. You have become the small, but powerful church He hoped for. Your obedience and devotion and active faith have had a big influence on the Kingdom. Well done. Your pastors have provided excellent leadership, but not much happens without the lot of you. By the way, what has been done by those anonymous folks out there in that prayer trailer? Wow. Incredible stuff. And, God has really enjoyed the Bathroom Ministry! There has been much laughter and joy in Heaven over that."

"God laughs?" Sylvie declared, more so than asked.

"God finds great joy in what His children do. But, you asked the question of what is next. I don't have much to say, but I would advise Frank and Sylvie to take a break and get some rest. You're going to need it. Condi, I think you might want to rehearse harder than ever in the next month or two. Just sayin'. Glory, you aren't going anywhere. Might as well get used to it. Nathan and Jennifer, keep up the good work, and spend extra time with Alicia. She is going to be a thing now. Martha Williams, your time is growing short. It will take a little while, but you will be remembered as the mother of Robert Williams, who changed the family legacy from owning the town to loving the town. Does that sit well with you?"

"Oh, my, yes. Perfect. But I must say, I was already getting more confident of that."

Robert couldn't speak right then.

"The rest of you, stay on your toes," Carl concluded. "There is much more coming for all of you."

"May I add one more, Pastor Carl?" It was Edwina.

"Of course."

"It is up to this church to provide long-term love and support and mentorship to our good friend Jeremy."

"Indeed," Carl replied. "Your young friend will have a great many opportunities in his future."

"But, you, too, Mrs. Fine," Jeremy burst out. "I need you, too."

The aged saint left her chair and moved over to the young man. "I will always be with you. But, my remaining time in your presence is very short, while your time is long. You will move ahead. You must. And, wherever I am, I will love you and I will be very proud of you. Stick with these people. Most of all, stick with God. You will be more than fine."

Jeremy embraced Edwina and kissed her neck. She cried.

After a long, increasingly awkward pause, Frank said matter-of-factly, "I wish a stranger would burst in here and try to hurt Jeremy, so I could beat him up."

The whole group let out a startled gasp, which lasted only as long as it took for Carl to let out the biggest belly laugh I have ever heard. Permission given, we all laughed heartily with our Frank.

"On that strange note," Jennifer said, "how about we call it a night. It has been an extremely long and draining day, which I think is about to hit us all. I move we stay after church two weeks from now, have a nice meal and have a serious discussion about where we have been, the debate, and where we might heading next. Sound okay?"

"Second," said most of the group.

"All in favor," I said.

"Aye."

"It's unanimous. Let's get cleaned up and head home. I think Jennifer and I are going to hang back and visit with Pastor Carl a little bit."

"I'll bring the food, in two weeks," Robert said. "So far, that's about all I know how to do," he explained.

People moved quickly and it was only a few minutes before the room was clean, the garbage was on the way to the dumpster and the crowd thinned. Even with hugs and more hugs and congratulations all around, the place was soon empty except for Jennifer and I, Edwina, Jeremy and Pastor Carl.

"I will take you home as soon as you're ready," Jeremy said.

Edwina took his hand and led him near the exit. "Jeremy, why don't you go on home. I'll get a ride from here."

"Are you sure?"

"Yes, I think it would be best. And give our love and thanks to that father of yours. He has been a big part of all this." Edwina embraced the young man. "I am so proud of you and thankful that I have had a part in your life."

She didn't let go right away, so Jeremy held on, too.

"I'm not going to see you again, am I," he said in a loud whisper.

"Not anytime soon. No. Probably not."

I thought sure Jeremy would protest or at least ask why, but he did not.

"I love you, you know," is what he said instead.

"I love you more Jeremy. I love you this much," she said and spread her arms out as far as they would go.

Jeremy stepped back and spread his arms, as well. "I win," he said.

"We'll see."

Up the stairs he went and out of sight.

I wanted to ask what had just happened, but I decided to wait.

"Well," Pastor Carl started. "How about this."

"We really missed you," Jennifer said. "We sure could have used some of your wisdom the past few months."

"You didn't need it," he said. "God gave the job to you. I am glad He used me to help get you ready."

I said, "You already know what happened. So, you have been around?"

"In a sense, yes. I must say I could not have envisioned all of the wonderful things that came of this. I had no idea how big it was going to be."

"The more things took off, the more we remembered your advice to not get ahead of ourselves and let God do what God was going to do," Jennifer said. "It worked."

"Carl, I want to go on thanking you. I want to go on thanking God. But, right now, I cannot help but ask what this was all about."

"All right. That's fair, to a point. Mostly, it was about the obedience you two and the others exhibited. At a very particular time and place, you all agreed to stick with the plan to let God be in complete control. Do you remember that?"

"Of course," we both said.

"Did you notice how astounding things, things that could not reasonably happen, began to happen? The numbers of viewers, the money coming in, the response to your many worship times—nice job on that, by the way—marvelous, fantastical things. That was a result of your obedience. And faith. And trust."

"God got highly involved," Jennifer said.

"Indeed."

"I could not be more grateful for that," I said, "but, why?"

"You want to know what has changed since the build-up to the Great Debate, and you want to know what is different now that the Great Debate is over, and you want to know what will happen next."

"No," I said. "At least, not exactly. You taught me better than that. God does not owe me any explanations. Nor does God need to clue me in on what comes next. God owes me nothing. I hope Jennifer and I—and the others—will continue to be used by God, each step as He sees fit. What I am asking—now that this incredible event has happened—is . . . why? What changed? What will be different now?"

"Me, too," Jennifer chimed in. "It is difficult not to wonder what matters about what we just did."

"Of course," Carl said, as Edwina moved closer to him and smiled. "You were used for rare and unusual purposes, beyond any ordinary events. And you responded well. You kept your faith strong when attacked. You stuck up for God and God's word, will and way, even when to do so could cost you dearly. You suffered scorn and insults and hate, in the name of Jesus. You suffered uncertainty. You did not blink. You did not falter."

Neither of us could speak, so we did not.

"Because you did what you were called to do, God used the situation to perform miracles and wonders for the good of the Kingdom. All those people, all that money, all the attention, all the debate, all the learning—God did that. More people reached at one time than Paul, Peter, all the apostles, all the popes and prophets, Billy Graham, Mother Theresa and Dr. King added up together. Relatively speaking, even Jesus appeared to only a few."

"We are not like any of those people," I said.

"That is not for me to say, but I will tell you this. Except for Jesus, those were all regular human beings doing their best to answer God's call to action, and worrying about whether they had done any of it well enough. God put them into the circumstances that made them who they became. Just like you two."

"Did any of them know what they had done?" Jennifer asked quietly.

"Perhaps a better question is the same one you are asking. What changed after the apostles preached and taught and set up churches."

"The Kingdom spread, some people became believers and, in some cases, scripture was written," I said.

"Indeed. Some people believed. Many others did not. Some came to God. Some turned away. The Kingdom grew, but still had a long way to go. What happened after Billy Graham and Dr. King and Mother Theresa answered God's call and did their work?"

"Same answer," Jennifer said. "Some believed, many did not. Some chose for God, some turned away. The Kingdom grew, but had a long way to go."

"Now you see. God was pleased with those people because they obeyed and did what they were called to do. So have you. And, by the way, you are nowhere near finished. Because of recent events, millions of people are aware of the good news of Jesus' gospel, when until now they were not. Millions more will be reinspired to think about faith, maybe return to faith, because they have seen and heard it presented with love and patience and certainty and effectiveness, from two smart and welcoming people."

"Some will believe," I said.

"Some will not," Jennifer responded.

"Some will still turn away from God," I said.

"But some will choose for him," Jennifer said, emotion threatening to overtake her voice.

"The Kingdom will grow," I whispered.

"But it will still have a long way to go," Jennifer said.

Chapter 59

Jennifer

"I believe it is time to go," Pastor Carl said. "I have missed you a great deal and I am so pleased to be given this opportunity to see you again and share in your ministry. You are to press on. I am not sure what happens next, only that God trusts you even more now and will have wondrous things for you to do."

"You can't stay longer?" I asked. I realized I sounded a bit desperate.

"I'm afraid not. The purpose of this visit has been accomplished. You two are the leaders here, now. You don't need me in the way. Maybe we will see each other again one day, but I honestly don't know."

"All right. We understand," Nathan said. "Know that we love you and will always cherish you and what you have done for us."

"We will miss you," I added.

"And I will miss you," Carl said. "I cannot express how special you are to me. Keep doing what you are doing, there are good and wonderful things ahead."

We both hugged Carl and whispered our final goodbyes.

As we finally let go of Carl, Edwina stepped in to hug us both, long and sincerely.

"We love you, too, Edwina," I said. "We'll be happy to get you home."

"Actually, this must be my goodbye as well. This has been the most magnificent time of my life, but it is over now. Please know that I love you, I always will, and I will treasure our time together, in my heart, forever."

"I don't understand," Nathan said. "There is still work to do. You seem fine."

"Yes, I have much work still to do," she said.

"But . . ."

"But," The old woman interrupted, "not here. Are we ready to go, Carl?"

"Yes, it is time."

Up the stairs they went.

About the Author

Michael Riegler resides in Bear Lake, Michigan, with his wife Anne. Both are retired United Methodist pastors. He can be contacted by email at pastormikeriegler@gmail.com or by phone (voice/text) at (231) 631-4712.